O CALEDONIA

and short stories

Elspeth Barker

BLACK DOG
BOOKS

For George
In memoriam

First published in England 2010
Black Dog Books, 104 Trinity Street, Norwich, Norfolk, NR2 2BJ.
www.blackdogbooks.co.uk

Text © Elspeth Barker
Foreword © Shena Mackay
Front cover photograph © Samantha Osborne www.mrspao.com
Rear flap photograph © Jane Bown

All rights reserved. No part of this publication may be reproduced, stored in a retrieval system, or transmitted in any form or by any means, electronic, mechanical, photocopying, recording or otherwise, without the prior permission of the copyright holders.

A CIP record of this book is available from the British Library.

ISBN 978-0-9565672-0-8

Printed in Great Britain by HSW Print, South Wales

CONTENTS

Foreword   5

O CALEDONIA   9

IN VAGLIAGLI   171
DOGS OF ATHENS   181
THE DRESS   188
CARBORUNDUM   193
DOWN BY THE SEA   198
MISSING   203
THE DANCE   212
PACKING FOR INDIA   220
IN THE CAGE   227

FOREWORD

O Caledonia was acclaimed on its publication in 1991. Here was a startlingly original first novel, by a poet and painter in prose, which did not put a foot wrong from its beautiful and heart-rending beginning to its dramatic close. The book is distinguished by its author's erudition and interwoven with poetry and classical references while making its own many of the constituents of popular fiction – a large unconventional family whose home is a decaying battlemented castle with secret rooms and, in Cousin Lila, a marvellous version of 'the mad woman in the attic', and as protagonist, a lonely and misunderstood child who is betrayed by all those who should cherish and protect her.

Since I read *O Caledonia* almost twenty years ago it has glowed in my memory like the jewelled light falling through the emblematic stained glass of Auchnasaugh, the castle at the story's heart. 'Auchnasaugh, the field of sighing, took its name from the winds which lamented around it almost all the year . . . .' I had forgotten, though, how very funny it is, the twists of the plot, the details of its wincing depictions of social agonies at, for example, a hunt ball or boarding school (the delightfully named St Encumba's), the horrible sexual encounters, the depth of its psychological perceptions, its engagement with the natural world and botanical expertise. In short, the treasures found on every page. A new edition of *O Caledonia* is long overdue, and Black Dog's timely reissue comes with the bonus of nine short stories which proves that Elspeth Barker's range extends far beyond childhood and her native Scotland.

Moriens sed Invictus. This legend, running round the circumference of the glass panel depicting a white cockatoo with its breast pierced by an arrow, which is set in a gothic arch in the great hall of Auchnasaugh, provides a fitting epitaph for the heroine of *O Caledonia*. Yet Janet, whose fate is as bloody as any in the Scottish ballads she loves, is despised in death, as she was in her short life. A murder most foul, of a sixteen-year-old girl 'oddly attired in her mother's black lace evening dress', heaps opprobrium not on the perpetrator of the crime but on the victim herself. Vera, her mother, who smoked cigarettes and wore slacks and gave the girl books to read is said to be at fault, as is her father Hector, with his ideas about education, but the final verdict delivered by the local people, the Calvinistic and malign Greek chorus of speywives, fishwives, midwives and ill wishers, is that 'The lass had only herself to blame.'

Janet is consigned to a shameful and bathetic grave, mourned only, heartbreakingly, by her pet jackdaw and, belatedly, her sisters. But what a death she had. What an operatic, supernatural, whisky-and-Chanel-scented denouement awaits the reader. However, such is the enchantment of the narrative, the engagement with Janet's progress through childhood to the fatal night that, although hindsight illuminates clues along the way, the ending comes as a shock.

Janet's story begins during the Second World War when, born to disappoint, she is placed in the blue crib intended for a son and heir. Perhaps the die was cast when her parents named her Janet – a good Scots name but lacking any of the romance and poetry which will imbue her soul. Her younger sisters are given fancier names and turn out conventionally prettier and fit in as Janet never can. Some time after the death of her grandmother, the one person who loved Janet unconditionally,

FOREWORD

her grandfather 'looked at Lulu, four years old, angelically blonde, weaving a little posy of ivy tangled snowdrops and he had said to Janet, "You were like that once, a beautiful wee thing. But now you're plain, my dear, very plain". He had not meant to hurt her, she was certain of that . . .' Francis, her adored brother, ally in some of the misdeeds which land Janet in such dreadful trouble and set seal on her reputation for wickedness, defects to one of the other girls. As he grows older, Francis develops a male arrogance, a camp superiority towards Janet, and is guilty of a sustained act of spite, for his own amusement, to undermine her relationship with the jackdaw, who has become her dearest friend.

More often than not Janet's misdemeanours are the unintentional results of her inability to see things as others do. Passionate about words, although her brilliance at Greek and Latin go largely unappreciated, and animals, she is appalled by the casual cruelty she witnesses, to deer and rabbits, and in the castle kitchens where lobsters 'would scream a high thin scream and wave their inky antennae and scrabble at the steep sides of the great black cauldron.' She feels revulsion for the servant Jim 'with his bloodstained trousers and his hands ingrained with soil and blood and death and his hinged knife with fur and entrail fragments stuck to its blade.' Increasingly isolated and thwarting her mother's hopes of a more feminine daughter with whom she could bond, Janet reflects that 'she had the dogs, the cats, her pony and all the woods and hills and waters and winds of Auchnasaugh. And she had books.'

It is an incident concerning animals which gives Janet the following insight as, not for the first time, an act of kindness ends in disaster. She comes across a squirrel hit by a car and, while burying it she accidentally impales a frog on the tines of her fork. In 'a confusion of anger and grief', she considers Divine and human pity and 'It seemed to her then that the nature of Caledonia was a pitiless nature and her own was no better. What use was it to be racked with pain for animals and the general woes of the world when she was unmoved by the sorrows of the people she knew?'

Tragically, it is Janet's falling in love for the first time which leads to her death. We will never know if time would have turned her into 'crazy' Cousin Lila or if her gifts would vindicate her and bring eventual happiness. *Moriens sed Invictus* – dying but unconquered. When Janet's spirit flies away we are left lamenting the person she might have become, and celebrating the wild, courageous girl she was.

Shena Mackay

O CALEDONIA

O Caledonia! stern and wild
Meet nurse for a poetic child!

Sir Walter Scott

JANET

Halfway up the great stone staircase which rises from the dim and vaulting hall of Auchnasaugh, there is a tall stained glass window. In the height of its Gothic arch is sheltered a circular panel, where a white cockatoo, his breast transfixed by an arrow, is swooning in death. Around the circumference, threaded through sharp green leaves and twisted branches, runs the legend: 'Moriens sed Invictus', dying but unconquered. By day little light penetrates this window, but in early winter evenings, when the sun emerges from the backs of the looming hills, only to set immediately in the dying distance far down the glen, it sheds an unearthly glory; shafting drifts of crimson, green and blue, alive with whirling atoms of dust, spill translucent petals of colour down the cold grey steps. At night, when the moon is high, it beams through the dying cockatoo and casts his blood drops in a chain of rubies on to the flagstones of the hall. Here it was that Janet was found, oddly attired in her mother's black lace evening dress, twisted and slumped in bloody, murderous death.

  She was buried in the village churchyard, next to a tombstone which read:

> *Chewing gum, chewing gum sent me to my grave.*
> *My mother told me not to, but I disobeyed.*

Janet's parents would have preferred a more rarefied situation, but the graveyard was getting full and, as the minister emphasised, no booking had been made. They had long before reserved a plot for their own ultimate use at a tiny church far off on the high moors; there was scarcely room for Janet there either, and under the circumstances they could not feel they wanted her with them. Her restless spirit might wish to engage with theirs in eternal self justifying conversation or, worse still, accusation. She had blighted their lives; let her not also blight their deaths. And so, after her murderer had been consigned to a place of safety for the rest of his days, and grass had grown over the grave, Janet's name was no longer mentioned by those who had known her best. She was to be forgotten.

For a while her jackdaw remembered her and he searched for her unceasingly. High above the glen he floated, peering down into the woods where she used to ride. He swooped to the sunken garden below the terrace; there, in the rare warmth of summer, the air perfumed by azaleas, she had fed him with wild strawberries which grew among the ivy at the base of the wall, leaving none for her family. Down the back drive to the derelict stables he flew, then up to the castle again, hurling himself against windows, hopping about the high, hidden chimney pots, bobbing his inquiring head into one after another and provoking furious flusters and punitive forays from the jackdaw colonies within. Each night he returned to her barren room to roost. His house was the only thing in it now. Before, he had always perched on the end of Janet's bed, but now he crept under cover and slept in loneliness. He lost interest in food and no longer joined the family at the dining table, jabbing his beak in the mustard, rearranging the spoons, guilelessly hopping through mounds of mince and cabbage. At last, in desolation, like a tiny kamikaze pilot, he flew straight into the massive walls of Auchnasaugh and killed himself. Janet's sisters found him, a bunch of waterlogged feathers in a puddle, and they buried him. They shed bitter tears for him and for Janet too, then, but they knew better than to mention it.

After that, only the speywives, the fishwives, the midwives, the ill wishers spoke of her, endlessly rehearsing a litany of blame;

for blame there must be, and no one could blame the murderer. Their voices whined and droned, spiteful as the sleety wind which slashed their headscarves across their faces as they huddled by the village bus stop, dreary as the wind which spat hail down the chimney as they took Sunday afternoon tea in the cold parlours of outlying crofts, where the Bible was open beside a ticking clock and rock buns were assembled on snowy doilies, malignly aglitter with the menace of carbonised currants. So they blamed the mother for giving the child all those books to read: 'It's not natural for a bairn'; they blamed the father for his ideas about education; they blamed everyone and everything they could think of, but in the end there was grim assent: 'The lass had only herself to blame.' The subject lost its appeal and was closed in favour of the living, who offer continuous material for persecution.

CHAPTER ONE

The sixteen years of Janet's life began in wartime on a fogbound winter night in Edinburgh. Her father came home on leave and looked into the blue wicker basket. He strode to the window and stared out at the discreet square of Georgian houses and the snow dripping from the bare trees. 'It's about the size of a cat,' he said.

He returned to the war and Janet and her mother went to live with his parents by the sea. The house was a square Edwardian manse, damp, dark and uncomfortable as Scottish houses are, but set solid against the sea winds, facing inland into a beautiful garden and affording a warren-like sense of safety in its winding, stone-flagged passages, baize doors, and lamplit rooms where Grandpa wrote his sermons, his parrot made proclamations and the blackout nightly excluded the warring world. The nursery in the attic overlooked the sea and Janet slept to the sound of foghorns booming out in icy waters; the lighthouse swept its beam over her ceiling, a powerful guardian. She woke to the cries of gulls. Someone gave her a purple silk flower, and she watched it growing towards her through the bars of her cot, as it came out of dimness, its petals lapped in all shades of mauve, violet, heliotrope. She did not know then that it was a flower but, as she lay gazing at it and as the days went by, she loved purple with an intensity that remained always. In that first memory she had found entrancement.

And so the babe grew, among her adoring grandparents, her anxious mother, and Nanny, in her blue print uniform, Nanny who knew best and could control the ceaseless battle for possession which raged between Ningning the grandmother and

Vera the mother. When Janet was fourteen months old, her brother Francis was born, and this brought about a change in the balance of power, for now Ningning could have Janet and Vera could have Francis, a baby each and a most satisfactory arrangement. Grandpa emerged beaming from his study, the blue wicker basket contained its rightful occupant. Vera's pedantic friend Constance wrote to congratulate her: 'In the manufacture of human pride, there is no ingredient so potent as the production of a son.' Ningning said it all sounded like something from the grocer's. Nanny, always ready with a grim *bon mot*, said that pride came before a fall. None the less, christening photographs show a happy family group, marred only a trifle by Janet's gaping black mouth; she was yelling because the photographer had plucked her thumb from its comfortable residence in her palate. Nanny's face lowered in the background.

At this time there were many Polish officers in the village. The Marine Hotel had been requisitioned for them. They were popular with the lonely girls and the more flighty wives, so that after the war some stayed on and married, while others left behind girls who were even lonelier now, alone with tiny children in the unrelenting chill of a Calvinist world. A home for these Unmarried Mothers was opened; it was named after Janet's grandfather, a tribute which the family felt he should have declined. He silenced them with talk of Mary Magdalene.

The manse was always full of people coming to talk to Grandpa in his study, and on Friday evenings Ningning often gave modest dinner parties, modest because of wartime restrictions but merry in spirit. Nanny disapproved fiercely of these occasions, retiring to bed even earlier than usual with her stone hot water bottle. She was a fearsome figure at retirement time, stomping about the kitchen in her huge white flannel nightie; her hair, which by day was scraped back into a tight bun bristling with pins, at night swung about her back in a wiry grey pigtail. 'Tears before bedtime,' she would mutter as she banged the kettle about, obliterating sounds of laughter and, worse, the clinking of glasses, 'There's some should know better,' as she flapped and thumped up the stairs to the nursery and settled creaking into bed with *The People's Friend*; the cold air was suffused with peppermint as she sucked a vengeful Pandrop.

On one such evening Grandpa was off at a conference, and Vera was away, bicycling around Scotland in search of somewhere else to live, far from her mother-in-law. Ningning had invited some Polish officers to dinner. Polish officers were the guests Nanny hated most, apart from merry widows. That evening she lay awake for a long time, listening to distant laughter and imagining the ingestion of the evil water-coloured spirits which Poles always had about them, even bulging in their uniform pockets. They were singing too, 'And not hymns either', as she said later. At last she heard Ningning go into the kitchen and fill the kettle. She heard her put it on the stove. They must be going soon. She was almost asleep when the smell of burning roused her. Down the stairs she billowed, and there in the steam filled kitchen was the kettle, boiled dry on the stove, and Ningning dead on the floor: a heart attack. From the far side of the hall, behind the dining room door, the sounds of revelry continued.

Janet knew nothing of Ningning's death, for she continued to see her, holding her hand as she climbed the stairs, walking beside her in the sunlit garden up the long path between low, fragrant box hedges to the raspberry thicket, hurrying past the droning beehives. Once they stood together in the greenhouse under the rampant tomato vines. Ningning picked a tiny scarlet tomato and rolled it carefully over her palm, weighing it, treasuring it; then she gave it to Janet to hold. The leaves engulfed them in warm underwater light, smothering and pungent. At midday when Janet and Francis were playing in the garden, someone would beat a gong to call them in for their rest, and just before they heard the gong, Ningning would wave to them from her bedroom window. One day Vera came out to fetch them because the gong was broken. She saw Janet waving and asked what she was doing. It was then that Janet was told that Ningning had gone and would not come back; she did not see her again.

She became devoted to Francis; she loved the way his beret sat on his round head, over his round face. She loved his stout form, snugly buttoned for winter, in coat and leggings and gaiters. She loved the way she could make him laugh, and the shining of his eyes in conspiratorial merriment. In the garden stood an old laburnum tree with rippling satin bark. There, in a fissure of the trunk, Janet found some handsome, striped shells and brought them in to give to Francis after their rest. Carefully she arranged them by her pillow. When she awoke, she put her hand out to find them; they had gone. Instead, dreadful horned creatures were contracting and elongating with silent purpose across her sheet, clambering over the peaks and troughs of the blankets, silhouetted monstrously against the curtained light. In terror she screamed and screamed for Ningning, who did not come. Nanny came and was angry; 'You're a dirty girl, Janet, bringing in the likes of thon.' She threw them out of the window.

And now there was a new baby, scarlet-faced, black-haired Rhona. Nanny and Vera were preoccupied. Francis and Janet spent their mornings banished to the garden and the wet fallen leaves; they stumped about, endlessly filling and emptying a small wooden wheelbarrow. When the sun shone they stared at the rents in the clouds, searching for glimpses of God. Nanny had told them about God's watchful and punitive presence and his place of residence. Janet dreamed about going to heaven, up a ladder from the beach, into the blue sky; God greeted her at the top, clad in a butcher's striped apron. In the afternoons Nanny put on her coat and her felt hat, skewered to her head with an abundance of jewel-bright hatpins, and they went out walking, one on each side of the pram, the baby prone within. When Francis was tired, he was allowed to sit in the end of the pram, but Janet must walk.

'You're a big girl now.' She didn't want to be a big girl. It seemed she was punished for something which happened without her choice or knowledge. Her dismal feet discerned miles of walking, interminable pavements, a vista of life-long streets. In the draper's shop there were consolations. The oily smell of the paraffin heater and the clean smell of piles of linen and furled spools of cloth offered a warm, ordered atmosphere. In tall, glass-fronted cupboards behind the long dark counter were gleaming reels of thread in every colour. Janet was mesmerised by the rusts which shaded to orange, to coral, almost imperceptibly to pinks; the deep glory of crimson, and the holy splendour of all the purples. Which purple did she like best? She could have dedicated all her day to resolving this question.

It was then that she saw the grey, knitted donkey; it was standing on the counter. Her heart lurched. Its packed, cubic body reminded her of Francis; she wanted to hug it so tightly it might be squashed, she wanted to keep it for ever. Its gentle, dreamy face and drooping ears indicated that, like herself, it preferred standing about to brisk exercise. Her knees were weak with longing. Each night before she went to sleep she thought about the donkey and added a silent coda to her spoken prayers, begging God to send it to her. She mentioned her great desire to the grown ups, but was told that it was not her birthday, and it would not be her birthday for a long time. A long time. What if someone bought it first? But each time they visited the draper's shop the donkey was there, and Janet began to think that God was keeping it for her. One afternoon the garden gate opened and a woman came in. She was carrying the grey, knitted donkey. Janet's heart stopped for a moment and then a great flood of happiness, gratitude, religious fervour, swept through her. She seemed to float towards the visitor, smiling and stretching out her hands. She could not speak, but she could hear, 'How's your mother, Janet? I've brought a present for your darling baby. I saw it in the shop as I went by; I couldn't resist it.'

Later that day, when Rhona was sleeping in her pram in the garden, Janet and Francis carted barrowload after barrowload of sodden leaves and laboriously piled them over her. Then they brought earth from the chilly flower beds with their stands of rustling sepia stalks, and scattered it in clods and handfuls over the leaves. Puffing and panting, they toiled back and forth all afternoon. At last Rhona was out of sight, even the outline of her was obliterated. She was silent, she was effaced. Janet would have liked to put the pram out of sight too, at the bottom of the garden, for now no one needed it, but she couldn't undo the brake. She went in to tell her mother the important news:

'A nasty rat has buried your baby. She's gone now.'

Later at the nursery tea table the baby, who had emerged unscathed from her tumulus, beamed adoringly and impartially at Nanny, Vera, Grandpa and her assassins. The grey donkey, infinitely unattainable, stood on the high cupboard. Janet and Francis had been spanked. They were in deep disgrace, and they could not be trusted. Janet did not care. A splinter, a tiny shard of ice crystal, had entered her heart and lodged there.

In the evenings now, when Janet and Francis were tucked in their white iron beds in the nursery, with the sea wind clamouring against the windows, Vera would come in and read to them. She read from Hans Andersen and from the Brothers Grimm, looking herself like some gold-haired and icy princess who might dwell in the depths of aquamarine waters. In the basket chair she sat reading, impersonal and feline, and then she would hear their prayers, 'Gentle Jesus, meek and mild, look upon a little child, Pity my simplicity, suffer me to come to thee, God bless Mummy and Daddy and Grandpa and Francis and Rhona and Nanny and all the animals and the birds and Mr Churchill.' In a perfumed drift she would vanish from the room, leaving cold and darkness behind her.

Francis fell asleep quickly, making little chewing noises to himself, but Janet lay awake and thought of the great black forests and the lone knight swinging his horse through their pathways, the poisons and perils and the witches. When she thought of the witches she was very frightened. She saw them floating upon the night wind off the sea, hovering in flapping black outside the window, clawing at the panes, clambering and clinging on the house walls. She sucked her thumb so hard that her jaws ached. But then the lighthouse beam came in mercy, revolving its reassurance over the ceiling and down the walls, round and out again, and she was safe enough to return to the forest, the knights and the princesses and maidens and their bleeding hearts. When she was older she intended to be a princess. Almost as much as its image she loved the word, with its tight beginning and its rustling, cascading end, like the gown a princess would wear, with a tiny waist and ruffles and trains of swirling silken skirts. Purple of course. On such thoughts she slept.

One Saturday afternoon in waning November light Nanny took Francis and Janet to the village hall; they were going to a party, a party for everyone, to celebrate Saint Andrew's Day. Down the lane from the manse they went and into the street, past the draper's shop, the grocer's, the butcher's, the greengrocer's, all with their blinds down to prevent the sin of weekend covetousness. Then round the corner to fearful Institution Row, where the war-wounded lived in grim pebbledashed houses with big square windows. If you looked in, you could see them, sitting mournfully by small electric fires or limping on crutches about the room. One lay propped upon a great heap of pillows staring unforgivingly at those who could pass by. Janet used to duck down and run past his window in case he saw her; she was afraid of his hard angry face and the shapeless shrouded rest of him. It was worse in summer when they would sit outside in the mean front garden, a strip communal to all the houses, a length of gravel punctuated by wooden benches constructed from the timber of sunken enemy ships. Some were crazed from shell shock and nodded and muttered to themselves, others displayed the magenta stumps of amputated arms and legs. One sat in a wheelchair and the bright sea breeze whisked about his empty trouser legs. But this November afternoon their windows were dark; there was not one to be seen. Janet's spirits rose; she looked forward to the party. Nanny and Vera had made carrot cakes and jellies and little pies and they carried these in wide wicker baskets covered with white cloths. Janet saw herself, a good kind little girl, bringing her provisions through cold and darkness to the needy, very like Little Red Riding Hood. She banished the thought of the wolf.

The village hall was an ugly desolate building, surrounded by high iron railings; it was the source of the disgusting wartime orange juice that children were forced to take from sticky urine coloured bottles. But today all was changed. In they went to a glowing haven of Tilley lamps and magical candles. Tables of glamorous food stood all along one wall; chairs were arranged round the other three sides. There were bunches of balloons and there were jam tarts and Mr McKechnie was playing his accordion and Mr Wright the blacksmith accompanied him on the fiddle. The children played games, Ring-a-Ring-o'-Roses and Blind Man's Buff, then In and Out the Bluebells and Who's Afraid of Black Peter? Janet became wildly excited and hurtled back and forth. Her hair had been allowed loose from its usual pigtails and was crowned by a blue satin Glamour Girl bow, firmly attached to an elastic string; in her stiff blue organdie dress she felt almost like a princess. Even the sight of the war wounded, gathered with their helpers in a cheerless group at the far end of the hall, did not check her glee. Other children joined her, skidding and shrieking, 'Who's Afraid of Black Peter?' 'NOT I. NOT I,' they yelled, colliding, tumbling, fleeing the length of the room, too far, too near the grown ups. Nannies and mothers sprang to their feet. 'You'll all sit down and have your tea.' A solemn silence came, suited to the serious ingestion of food.

Janet finished first. Watching Francis, with bulging eyes and bulging cheeks spooning quivering green jelly into his gap-toothed mouth, she felt the fatal tide of merriment rise again. Up on to her chair she leapt. 'Francis!' she cried, 'Tins of jam! Tins of jam! TINS, TINS, TINS of jam!' Francis choked; shards and globules of glancing emerald shot across the table. Janet ran. Beside herself, with flying skirts and hair, she careered down the hall; she was chanting her favourite nursery rhyme, 'Hink, minx, the old witch winks, The fat begins to fry; There's no one at home But jumping Joan, Father, Mother and I.' As she neared the war-wounded she saw that they were laughing; they were laughing at her. She had made them laugh. Aglow with power she postured in front of an amputated arm, 'Hink, MINX,' she began again, 'The old witch WINKS.' The man was mouthing at her; fearless she stepped up to him and curtseyed deeply. 'You're a braw wee lassie,' he said. 'What's your name?' 'Janet.' 'That's no name for you. I'll call you Beth.' Beth. A beautiful name, a velvet name, brownish mauve.

Nanny was bearing down with a face like the North Sea. Janet had one thing to do before doom cracked above her. 'Please may I touch your arm?' she asked. The man stared at her, still smiling. Her knees were shaking but she stretched her fingers up and gently she stroked his puckered stump; it was like paper, dry and smooth, even where the violent scar lines twisted and rippled and enlaced it was smooth like the bark on branches. Nanny seized her and dealt her a resounding swipe on the backs of her calves. 'Your father will hear of this when he's home. You'll sit with me now.' She dragged her up the hall again. 'Showing off. Talking to men. I never saw the like. Your poor grandfather.' Janet's eyes stung and her legs burned and stung, but she was filled with happiness. She had rid her life of one haunting fear. And she had known the toxic joy of power.

Now she sat, thumb in mouth, eyes glazed, quiet and good. The other children were dancing to Oranges and Lemons and The Grand Old Duke of York but she might not join them. Nanny was talking to Miss Pettigrew, one of two ancient sisters. The other sister was having tea in the first sitting of grown ups, the very old, the war wounded and the men. Nanny and the younger Miss Pettigrew would have their turn in a more refined company. The men ate with intense absorption; some of them had tucked handkerchiefs into their collars for bibs. They were like the little children at tea, even the ones whom Janet had seen come lurching and ranting out of the Ship Inn on a blast so pungent with smoke and whisky that for a moment she could not smell the sea; even those wild tattooed men were as homely and douce with their scones and jam as the fat-bellied tea cosies clothing the brown teapots. O Caledonia.

Very old Miss Pettigrew came trembling up, leaning on her stick. 'Here you are then, Annie', she said to her sister. Her jaw dropped loose, her mouth hung limp and open; in went her black-veined claw; out came a set of pinkly glistening false teeth. Her sister grabbed them; with no ado she popped them into her own mouth. She paused for a moment, sucking noisily. 'Macaroons!' she cried, 'Och, that's braw!' She and Nanny headed briskly for the tea table. Janet and the ancient sat silent together, both dribbling a little.

Now that Janet and Francis were older, Grandpa would let them visit him in his study, where the parrot lived. Grandpa came from a long line of parrot-keeping men, and Polly's predecessor, a white cockatoo, had fought with Wellington's armies in the Napoleonic Wars. Janet's father's earliest memories were of the astonishing oaths known to this bird, who was then a hundred and two years old and spoke in ripe gamey accents long since gone from the world of men. Grandpa believed there must be a fair number of such long-lived birds in Scotland – even perhaps in England – and it would be a fine thing to have them all gathered in a great dining hall, invoking ghostly midshipmen and dragoons, violent drinkers and merry rhymesters, perhaps even occasionally an elderly lady of refinement. This, he said, would afford an historical experience of rare value; indeed, ancient parrots should be fêted and cultivated as true archivists.

The current parrot was unfriendly but interesting, with his black tongue like a neat sea-smoothed stone and his sarcastic sideways stare. If they sang 'Away in a Manger' to him he would dance, swaying from side to side, lifting his feet high and raising his wings. Janet tried chanting 'Hink, minx' but it was too fast and drove Polly into such a frenzy of action that he collapsed palpitating on the floor. Francis laughed a lot, but Janet was appalled. She fed him toast in placation and he bit her finger. Blood spurted disgustingly on to his gravel floor, but Janet was glad. Justice had been done. This Polly, too, had lived for a long time and much of his enigmatic utterance was addressed to a host of invisible dogs, cats and visitors. 'Go to your basket, Donald', he would yell, and 'Wipe your feet', 'Goodnight, Miss McPhail', 'Wet dog'. His two favourite sentences were, 'Would you care for a dram?' and 'Mr Baird has a short beard', both compellingly effective. He could also reproduce the sound of whisky being poured into tumblers and one day Janet discovered a great secret, to be known only to herself and Grandpa. He could imitate Grandpa's typewriter in busy action, so that people knocking on the study door would steal away again, finger to lip, 'We mustn't disturb him; he's writing his sermon.'

Grandpa and Janet would sit by the fire and he would tell her stories of the Seven Champions of Christendom, and the Angel of Mons. On his wall were huge steel engravings of soldiers dying on far battlefields among charging, rearing horses and smoking cannon, consoled by the visionary cross which hung in the sky, or the benediction of a brooding angel. Grandpa's God, like Nanny's, was all-seeing, all-powerful, but, unlike Nanny's, He was protective and compassionate, not vengeful. In His dealings was great glory and nobility. Janet tried to imagine one of His angels visiting the war-wounded in their desolate concrete dwellings, softening their hard, hurt faces, wrapping them in loving warmth, bestowing that nobility on their mutilated limbs and lives, so that they, too, shone in glory. It was impossible. She wanted to ask Grandpa about this, but she could not find the words. She was left with a sense of agonised pity, a powerless pity which made her cry sometimes when she was alone and looking out of the nursery window at the unforgiving sea and the seagulls, who lived nowhere but on air and water, floating free and comfortless above it.

But within the warmth of Grandpa's study such thoughts could be banished as she twirled round and round, faster and faster on his magic revolving chair, reaching giddy heights where the angels in the pictures and the parrot's beady eye and the shine of firelight on Grandpa's spectacles all swam in dizzy, whirling confusion, then the abrupt jolt of stop and round the other way, down, down, down to the safe plateau of ordinary life, her feet planted firm on the faded hearthrug with its two worn patches, one on each side of the fire, where generations of men had stood, partaking of their evening dram. In this room was a genial liberality absent from the outer household with its routine, its timetable of rests and walks and meals, its grim insistence on self-control and cleanliness, scratchy vests and liberty bodices, tweed coats buttoned tight around the neck, hair brushed until the scalp stung, then dragged back into pigtails.

CHAPTER TWO

That summer the war ended and suddenly there were men everywhere in the village and the children's father Hector was home for good. There were flags strung across the village street and a great procession with bagpipes and drums and all the children following in fancy dress. Janet was in a dream of happiness for she was dressed as Snow White, the person she most wanted to be, in a tight-waisted blue and yellow gown which almost came down to her laced-up shoes. Her hair was released from its pigtails and sprang, in a wild and electric fuzz, about her shoulders; it stuck out in stiff points like a Christmas tree. Francis went as a gypsy with a scarlet waistcoat and bandanna, and to their mutual pleasure Rhona went as Rhona, being too young for it to matter. Best of all, Janet and Francis rode in the greengrocer's pony trap and took turns in holding the long slippery reins. From her station above the pony Sheila's gaunt hip bones, Janet mused on the new word which everyone kept saying, 'Victory, victory', and she felt a great personal triumph as they passed through the flag-waving, cheering crowds. But when they reached the war memorial there was sudden silence and stillness.

Grandpa stood facing them in his purple vestment and the men gathered before him, with the wounded at the front. He spoke a prayer for the dead, the hurt, the bereaved, and the sun squinted through Janet's tight-shut eyes, making dazzles of orange and blue. For a moment she opened them and through the blur of brightness saw two old men standing stiff and straight, with tears shining on their faces. Then the sound of the pipes spiralled upwards in inconsolable lament and the great drums beat in their midst and she saw the sombre clouds piled like monuments over chasms of sunlight, with the phalanxes of the dead gazing down. Somewhere among them must be Ningning. She felt cold and longed with a yearning as strong and tearing as the plangent music for that time when they stood together in the greenhouse, lapped in warm, subaqueous light, a time before needs and sorrows of men and beasts, when the world held only two people, Janet and Ningning, whom she loved, who loved her.

That summer the sun shone through long days and it was safe to go to the beach. The great concrete blocks and rolls of barbed wire were wrenched away in carts and in lorries and the children wore bathing suits and sandals and in the late afternoon the warm, prickling comfort of a jersey. There was the delight of powdery sand on the soles of their feet, then, as they ran to the sea, a sudden cool firmness, then the mirror-bright sand filmed in water and the thrill and chill of the first sparkling waves which snatched breath away into the breeze so that for a moment they were nothing but a part of air and light and water, abandoned to the elements. On colder days when the tide was out they walked across the long shore to the harbour and saw the fishermen digging for bait and the fearful blanched and bristling worms that emerged from the depths of the clean sand. In the rock pools were jewel studs of anemones and transparent shrimps like water fairies, and sometimes the black questing pincers and antennae of a lobster lurking in myopic retreat beneath the weedy ledges.

Janet built castles for princesses with strandy green lawns and walls hung in pink shells and cowrie shells, pillared gateways of razor shells, roof-tops of mussels and limpet battlements. She ran in and out of the curving waves or sat among them, feeling the sands pull and sink away from under her and then come billowing back with a rush and a splash. Francis stood still for hours spinning flat stones across the shining water and Rhona dug holes in tireless absorption. The dogs dug holes too, flinging up showers of sand into the wind; or they rushed after storms of seagulls barking hysterically.

The beach spread in a great curve, fringed by mournful dunes. At one end was the harbour with its high grey pier and the fishermen's boats pulled up on the shingle; far off at the other end crags and cliffs loomed, with the scar of a lofty boulder-strewn cave where once Macduff had hidden for his life from murderous, mad Macbeth. Above, on the short turf scattered with pink thrift, stood the ruins of a tower and there in happier times Lady Macduff and her women had gone to bathe, clambering down the secret stairway hewn in the cliff face into a glass green cove where the wind could not reach the water for the surrounding basalt walls. In the summer you could hear the ladies' laughter, for the sound of the sea then was an echo, a soft sighing, the hushed murmur in a shell; but in the storms of winter the air swirled and boomed with the howling of the damned, the outrage of the murdered innocents. Janet was afraid of this place and did not like its sinister jutting outline, even against the blue and sunny skies. She also knew that one must be brave and so she would walk carefully, accompanied by Rab, the heroic lion dog, each day a little further, but never very far, along the shore towards it. When she had felt brave enough, her hand plunged in the dense gold fur of Rab's neck, she would turn around and look back at her family, diminished and vulnerable under the great sky, before the great sea – Francis still as a cormorant at the water's edge, Rhona squat by her mound of sand, Hector and Vera laughing, smoking and flicking ash on to the lesser dog's wiry coat. Then she would run as fast as she could, feet slapping through the wet, and hurl herself down beside them in the warm soft sand, sending it flying into Rhona's eyes, into sandwiches, into the precious thermos of tea.

Retribution and exile immediately followed, but not for long, for those days were a breathing space between the war and the rest of life and they were days of a rare happiness, goodwill and forgiveness. When the chill of evening came on the sands although the sun still shone, they carried their baskets back up the path through the dunes, across the lane and into the manse garden. Dazed with the long hours of bright sea air, the children trailed rugs behind them through the lingering perfume of phloxes, past the clump of golden rod where Dandelion the cat was curled in his den, glaring out at the dogs with unflinching malevolence. Nanny issued from behind the white rose hedge wielding a rough towel; now came the ritual of rubbing off sand and emptying sandals and shaking out jerseys. Then, at the exact moment when they began to feel cold, it was through the house, up the stairs and into the blissful hot waters of the bath big enough to take all three of them. After the bath came Nanny's dreadful question, 'Have you done what you should do today?' If the answer was wrong they were briskly purged with Gregory's bitter brown powders. Janet and Francis became accomplished liars on this score and acquired a lasting hatred of the word 'should' which developed in time into a hatred of the notion of duty. Indeed, they met other children whose nannies actually asked them whether they had done their duty; never could any of those principled women have dreamt of the horde of artful dodgers they were unleashing on the world.

   Vera would come and read to them when they were in bed or Hector would tell them marvellous and terrifying tales of the wartime exploits of Strongbill, a parrot secret agent. All these stories gave Janet nightmares, but she had learnt to tell herself these were only dreams and then she would wake up. They were worth it, and now she had the solace not only of the lighthouse beam and her thumb, but of a black bear dressed in a purple velvet coat. She had removed this coat from an unpleasant doll which Vera had given her at Christmas. Janet did not like dolls; they were too like babies and entirely without the charm of animals, real or toy. Once, to please Vera, she took the pink blob-like creature with its mad stare and flickering eyelids on her afternoon walk with Nanny. Halfway along the village street Nanny noticed its nude presence. 'It's home we're going right now, and you'll dress that doll before you take it out again. I never saw the like.' Janet stuffed the doll in the very back of the nursery cupboard and took her bear instead. She had also been given a doll's pram which she knew she was expected to trundle about like a little mother. She had seen the grown ups smiling in approving complicity at other small girls as they tucked up their celluloid infants or rocked them to sleep. Her bear could not be demeaned in this manner, but she found that the pram made an acceptable chariot for Dandelion so long as in transit he could gnaw at a sparrow's wing or other pungent trophy from his lair. Eventually Dandelion moved all his treasures into the pram and each day it provided Francis and Janet with a vicarious excitement of the chase; he was a prodigious hunter. By the time that Nanny and Vera decided that since Janet never played with the pram properly it should be given to Rhona, it had become a stinking ossuary of parched bones mingled with fur, feather and the sullen reptilian sheen of rats' tails.

Grandpa taught Janet to read, accompanied by wild alphabetical shrieks from Polly. On the great afternoon when she found that she could master a whole page fluently Hector went out and returned with a tissue-wrapped bundle. It was a china parrot, a wild green parrot rampant on a blossoming bough. Francis wept, claiming that he could read too, and indeed on the very next afternoon this was accomplished, and Hector was off to find another prize. Janet watched with anxiety as Francis tore the paper open, but all was well; this bird was no rival to her parrot; in fact it appeared to her to be a penguin, although the grown-ups maintained that it was a Burmese parrot. Francis was delighted. On the nursery mantelpiece their birds sat in beady-eyed accolade and Janet and Francis lay on their stomachs by the crinkled red bar of the electric fire and read to themselves at first in loud, jarring discord, but soon in a deep and satisfying silence.

*

Now they started to go to a little school. They walked there each morning with Nanny, over a track which crossed the fields, into the grounds of a huge house. Here, in what had once been a summer house, a tiny Hansel and Gretel cottage, ten small children learnt reading, writing, spelling and arithmetic. Janet loved it all, apart from arithmetic. At eleven o'clock they each had a short, squat bottle of milk, its cardboard lid's inner concentric circle pierced precisely by a straw, and a dark crimson apple, polished to gleaming ruby on cardigan sleeves. Wide lawns surrounded the little house and nearby stood a ruinous hayloft with a stone staircase to a black gap high on its outer wall. It was clear that a banished witch might live up there, using the platform at the top of the stairs as a useful take-off point. Janet imagined her triangular black form sweeping across the windy sky, blotting out the sun, descending to the house in which by rights she should dwell. But inside the school such fears evaporated. Reading, writing, spelling and arithmetic were soon supplemented by Nature and stories from Scottish history, and the French verbs *être* and *avoir*, in the present tense only. At midday Miss Mackie, rosy and rounded as a robin, would cry, 'Let's flit', and they would push the tables and chairs to the side of the room and hurtle into singing and dancing games. Sometimes these were of a cautionary nature; there was one about brushing the Germs away, requiring vigorous elbow work, stooping, twisting and shaking of imaginary brooms. All the children assumed that Germs was short for Germans and performed with patriotic fervour.

In spring a dazzle of crocuses, gold and white and deepest purple, gleamed in the grass. Janet stood staring at them, breathing the sudden soft air, spellbound. Her favourite boy, James, told her that he too liked purple best and asked her to marry him when they were grown up. Janet consented. Another boy, Bobby, also asked her to marry him; again she consented. She had no intention of marrying either as she still wished to be a princess, but she liked the idea of their hopeless dedication and she devised quests in which they might prove their devotion. At first these were modest: James was to find a ladybird, or Bobby was to bring a pink shell from the beach; but even in the brilliant light of those May mornings the black gap of the witch's loft stared fearfully down and soon she knew that the boys must go together up the staircase and find out whether or not the hag was there. Tle children were forbidden to go anywhere near the barn and so some strategy was needed.

At noon, when they were putting on their coats to go home for lunch, Janet offered to take the apple cores from the wastebin to the pig Beatrice who lived in a pen behind the school. The children often visited Beatrice; she was a friendly black pig, a white stripe encompassed her stout middle and her eye was bright and roguish. She would come hustling out of her shed with gleeful snorts, stand motionless with a meaningful twinkle, then pick up her bucket on one deft twist of her wrinkled snout and hurl it over her shoulders to clatter down upright on her other side, and repeat the performance. Today Miss Mackie was pleased to let Janet feed her, and to let Bobby and James go with her. Janet had not told the boys about her plan; she did not want them to know about her fear of the witch in case they said they didn't believe in witches. So when they reached Beatrice's pen, she grabbed the bucket and flung the cores straight in. Beatrice, about to perform her trick, stared in disappointment; the twinkle faded from her eye; grumpily she rootled after the cores and subsided back into her house.

'Quick!' said Janet, 'Quick! There's a wee lost kitten crying up in the loft. It will die up there. We've got to get it before Miss Mackie sees.' The boys were off in a flash, racing up the path and across the grass. Janet followed more slowly, feeling a tiny twinge of compunction at their trusting rush into danger. She stationed herself behind a flowering currant bush, redolent of tomcats, and watched. Up the steps they sprang, two at a time, James just in the lead; for a second they paused at the top and looked round to wave to her; then they were gone into the black gulf. Immediately there was a rending crash and a dreadful scream, a moment's silence and then howls and shrieks. Janet flung herself face down on the grass; she dug her nails into the earth and, holding on to the slippery grass, shut her eyes while the world spun and rocked about her and the screaming went on. She heard Miss Mackie hurtle past her making gasping noises; the yelling stopped, there was only Miss Mackie's voice. She raised her head a fraction of an inch and saw them coming out of a door at the side of the barn; Miss Mackie led them by the hand. James was limping and Bobby's face was covered in blood, blood which poured from his nose, saturating his Fair Isle jersey, splattering the white crocuses. Janet started to scream. 'Come out of there at once, Janet,' yelled Miss Mackie. 'I'll deal with you later. And stop that ridiculous noise.' Janet stayed where she was, screaming and hanging on to the ground. Nanny came and walloped her and marched her into the school. Miss Mackie was sliding a great black iron key down the back of Bobby's shirt to stop his nosebleed. Mothers and nannies stood by in pregnant silence. His nose stopped bleeding. His bloodstained jersey was removed and replaced by a spare and girlish cardigan. His face was washed. James's knee was bandaged. Only the crocuses bore witness to the horror that had been.

'Now,' announced Miss Mackie, 'it's time to ask some questions. And about time too.' Janet found a voice, unusually high and staccato, 'Where's the witch gone?' 'That's quite enough, Janet. We'll hear from the boys first. Come along, James, tell us the truth.' The moon face of James's large and masterful mother hung above him. 'We were only trying to fetch the wee cat for Janet.' 'What wee cat?' 'She said there was a wee lost cat there,' James sobbed anew. 'She said it was going to die,' Bobby mumbled, clutching his mother's hand, tears pumping down his cheeks. 'So what's this cat, Janet?' Janet wept silently; she shook her head about and wept. 'You've just been up to your tricks, haven't you? There was never a cat up there; you were teasing the boys. And now look what's happened. It's a lucky thing they fell on the straw. It's a lucky thing for you there's not a broken leg. All those rotten floorboards. You know fine none of you can go up there. I'm ashamed of you, Janet, you're the oldest in the school. I thought I could trust you.' Janet had a dim memory of hearing these words before, then she remembered; it was after Rhona had risen from her tomb. Anger and outrage welled within her: she would speak the truth. 'It was because of the witch. I wanted them to see if the witch was there,' she wailed. 'Don't talk such nonsense; you know as well as I do that witches are only in fairy stories; and you read far too many of those, if you'd like my opinion.' The mothers exchanged satisfied glances: they all thought Vera went too far in her choice of children's reading; and she smoked cigarettes and wore slacks. 'So if you sent them to look for a witch, why did you say it was a wee lost cat?' demanded manly Mrs Marriot, her faint but dark moustache moistly atremble, her eyes beadily accusing. Janet put her thumb in her mouth; she saw the mothers in their circle around her and each face was stiff with distaste, anger, scorn. They were like a whole coven of witches, but she did not feel afraid of them, only cold and angry; there was no point in telling them the truth. She had tried; a waste of time.

Home she went in mutinous silence, with Nanny and a chastened Francis, to face the wrath of Vera and Hector. In the late afternoon she sat sullen and alone in the chill damp of the spring garden; she watched the pale bright sky dim and deepen to luminous blue while the birds' jostling voices faded into sudden single notes of sweetness. In the air was sadness and excitement. After a little Rab came and sat beside her and she wrapped herself about his golden shoulders and felt warm. Dandelion's form looped through the dusk, back arched, tail aloft, uttering his monotone triumph call. He settled before her to devour his sparrow and she heard the brittle crunch of splintering beak and bone. It was time to go in. And to her surprise the indoor house was warm and bright with forgiveness. Nanny and Vera were clanking about in the kitchen; they smiled when they saw her and Francis and Rhona treated her with special politeness, as though she had returned from a long journey. There were tomatoes for tea, their tops sliced off and sprinkled with sugar so that they could be eaten with a teaspoon. Vera shook green crystals into the bath and the water changed to dazzling emerald and the steaming air was sweet with lily of the valley.

Janet almost abandoned the vengeful plan she had made earlier, which was to read illicitly under the bedclothes with the big black bicycle lamp she had removed from the garden shed. But in the end this pleasure was too great to be forgone, with its added comfort of prolonging the day and creating a cavern of light in the windy darkness. However, it proved extremely difficult to focus the light on the large thick pages of Arthur Rackham's Grimm's, to cope with the tissue covering each illustration and to stop the sheet sagging down – all in silence under the blankets. Soon the lamp crashed to the floor and went out. Another crime, another strategy for the next day. Meshed in guilt Janet lay awake for a long time; she worried about the lamp and she worried about the forgiveness in which she had basked all evening; in the dark she knew that it had been offered because they thought she was sorry for what she had done, and she wasn't sorry at all. In fact, she was angry with the boys for falling through the rotten floor and failing to clear up the matter of the witch and for telling their mothers about the lost cat. Her power had been broken; she would not be wanting them as suitors any more. She shut her eyes and prayed for help with the bicycle lamp. In the morning it was clear that God had answered her prayer, for Hector and Vera were away and Nanny was busy ironing baby clothes.

Later in the day, Hector reappeared and told the children that they had a new little sister, Louisa, born early, before they had expected her. He took them to the nursing home and Janet was moved by the baby's tiny crimson feet, delicate and soft as silk or rose petals. None the less she would have preferred a new little dog or cat, but at least she had been able to replace the lamp in the shed and no one would be likely to care about it with this new confusion in their lives. Vera and the baby came home. The scent of baby powder pervaded the house, visitors came with flowers, tender little white garments were constantly airing over the nursery fireguard and an exuberance of nappies billowed in the sea breeze. Vera's room was in contrast to the bustle everywhere else; it was the baby's sanctuary, profoundly still and warm. The dogs, the cat, Francis, Rhona and Janet were all drawn to it, edging the door open, tiptoeing in, only to be seized and expelled by the sentinel form of Nanny. Once a day was the decree, and once a day only did they gain admission to its mysteries. Then they could watch the baby being fed, or bathed, or even hold her. Janet found this boring; it was the sacred atmosphere of the room itself which she enjoyed.

She and Francis were usually sent out quite soon because they were fidgeting but Rhona loved helping with the baby and was allowed to stay. She was a peaceful, self-contained child; her black hair was smooth and shiny and it hung in a neat curve about her pointed face. Vera took great pleasure in her 'piquant little features' and her neat, nimble ways. Francis, like Janet, was naturally untidy, but then as Nanny would say to Vera, 'He's a real boy.' Janet had no hope of ever being tidy: her hair grew wilder and frizzier, escaping from its pigtails, tangling in everything it touched; her hair ribbons fell off, her buttons pinged to the floor, she tripped over and collided with objects so often that she had to have a special eyesight test. There was nothing wrong with her eyes. Soon after this she had a hearing test too, occasioned by her habit of not answering because she was reading or day-dreaming. People didn't mind the reading so much, but the day-dreaming really annoyed them. 'Wake up! For goodness' sake wake up!' they would suddenly yell in her ear, causing her heart to lurch, almost to stop, and thrusting their cross faces into hers; and always for some meagre purpose: the setting of a table or the grim afternoon walk.

One afternoon she was told to bring the baby in from the garden. Reluctantly she trailed out into the still early autumn air. The pram was on the lawn some way from the house. With clumsy fingers Janet undid the stiff navy cover, pulled back innumerable blankets and scrabbled under the hood for the swaddled occupant, who began to roar, fixing Janet with an unblinking glare. It was difficult to pull her from under the hood; Janet tried to lower it and cut her finger in its joint so that blood dripped on to the baby's shawls. Louder came the roars. It began to rain. The shawls were unravelling and catching on the metal parts of the hood; she pulled at them and tore a great hole in the lacy cobweb. In desperation Janet seized the infant by her head and dragged her out, clutching at corners of shawl and looping them over the flailing torso. The whole bundle slithered through her hands and lay shrieking frantically on the dank grass. Janet could not lift it up; it was far heavier than she would ever have guessed; when she had held the baby before, she had simply been deposited on her lap; she had never carried her. So she grabbed such projections as she could find, a shoulder and a fiercely resisting arm and dragged the whole mass, shawls trailing, through mud and snagging on leaves, over the grass and across the gravel and at last to the kitchen door where Vera and Nanny greeted her, first with horror and then with fury.

'What in the world have you been doing? What have you

done? Where's the pram? You were told to bring the baby in, in the *pram* of course. You've no business to try to carry her. How dare you?' Not one word of Janet's explanations did they hear. Once again it was spanking and disgrace and a distant overheard muttering of '. . . simply can't be trusted', 'We should have known better', 'After what she did before', 'Keep her away from the little ones'. Good. But then, 'Best not to tell her grandfather, it'll break his heart.' A BROKEN HEART. Nanny's sister had died of a broken heart. She crept away to the glory hole under the stairs and sat howling in an abyss of guilt among the boxes of candles and dusty jars of lentils and syrupy bottled gooseberries and raspberries, until she could howl no more. Then she went to the nursery and lay on the floor and read stories of princesses with broken hearts. She was bad and she knew she was bad and she could see no end to it.

September was a beautiful month in Scotland, even by the sea. The air was soft and delicate, the headlands shadowed in mild green and violet, the sea calm, an aftermath of limpid azure in the fading days of warmth. Hector and Vera took the children for a last picnic. Soon they were to move to a place far to the north, a huge place with an unpronounceable name which Hector had been left by an uncle on condition that he allowed his cousin Lila to continue to live there. Vera, at first overjoyed at the prospect of a house of their own at last, had been angry about Cousin Lila, whom she had met once – 'And once was enough. She's very peculiar, even you must admit that, and she reeks of whisky.' 'Poor woman,' said Grandpa, 'she's had her sorrows. A wee dram never hurt anyone.' 'That's as may be, but it's not a case of a wee dram with her. You can always tell.' '*Tant pis!*' yelled Hector, who relished the occasional French phrase, *'je m'en fous*. There's room enough for the whole clan. She'll have her own little place at the back and you'll never need to see her. Anyway, look at your family. Particularly look at your Aunt Maisie.' At this point

Vera became aware of Janet's interested face hovering about the doorway, seized her and bundled her off to find bathing things for the picnic.

At last they were all sitting in the dunes, much farther along the bay than usual, for it was the Glasgow holiday and the nearer beach contained roistering Glaswegian families. Hector and Francis and Janet collected driftwood and made a fire and the smoke for once went straight up into the still air and blinded no one. Rhona helped Vera amuse baby Lulu while they bathed, then she and Vera ran down into the sea while Hector tried to hold Lulu who squirmed and rolled and finally yelled. Janet and Francis skulked off behind the dunes but Rhona was back in a moment, hugging her, soothing her. It was time for tea. Vera handed round special bags, one for each child. Janet grabbed hers and retreated to a sand throne she had made high above them, near the spikes of marram grass and pink thrift. Vera called her back. 'Come on, Janet, Rhona's been helping all afternoon. It's time you did something. Let Lulu sit beside you; just hold on to her and don't let her tip over.' Lulu couldn't sit at all and she flopped all over Janet and pulled her hair and put sand in her sandwiches and dribbled on her knee. 'Stupid baby,' hissed Janet. 'Why did they have to bring you?' Lulu stared at her doubtfully, put a sandy fist in her mouth, choked on the sand and began to yell again. Vera snatched her away. 'For goodness' sake, you could make just a little effort sometimes for other people. Look how thoughtful Rhona is, and she's much younger.' Janet flicked sand into Rhona's gentle, beaming face. 'That's it. Off you go, take your picnic right down the beach and don't come back until you can say sorry.'

Glowering, Janet shambled to her feet and tramped off, gripping her paper bag. She would go as far as possible, so they could hardly see her and so she couldn't hear them. She went towards the sea, where the receding tide had left great shining rocks. She cast a scornful glance back at her family but they were not watching her. They had their backs turned, gathered about the small fire. Janet turned west towards the looming black headland where the cave was. Today she did not fear it. She was powerful with a cold anger; she was an outcast, a tragic dwindling figure soon to be seen no more. When she reached the basalt cliffs and the cave, the darkness would take her. This would be her revenge. Her paper bag began to tear where she clutched it. She decided to sit down and eat her picnic first. She found a long low grey rock, pleasingly warm and dry, and clambered on to it. She ripped open her paper bag and began to eat in a savage, vulpine manner, tearing the rolls apart, chewing with her mouth open, staring grimly out at the hazed blue sea and the great sinking sun. Gradually her anger left her; she breathed the soft air of early evening, heard the gulls cry, watched them swoop and skim over the tiny waves at the water's edge, over the track of radiance which led to the horizon. She thought of Orion, the blinded giant who had to wade through the farthest depths of ocean, following the setting sun to the limit of the world, and her heart stirred with pity for his lonely fate. She would forgive her family and go back to them. She would even say sorry although she would not mean it.

The headland seemed menacing now and she felt cold. She scrambled to her feet and as she did so she was aware of a strange and dreadful stench all about her. It seemed to come from the rock. She jumped off it and stared at it. Then she screamed loud and long and again and again. She had been sitting on a huge dead bull seal.

CHAPTER THREE

Auchnasaugh, the field of sighing, took its name from the winds which lamented around it almost all the year, sometimes moaning softly, filtered through swathes of pine groves, more often malign, shrieking over the battlements and booming down the chimneys, so that the furnace which fed the ancient central heating system roared up and the pipes shuddered and the Aga top glowed infernal red. Then the jackdaws would explode in a dense cloud from their hiding places on the roof and float on the high wild air crying warning and woe to the winter world. 'A gaunt place,' said the village people, and they seldom passed that way. Besides, the narrow road which ran along the floor of the glen, far below the castle on its hillside, was crossed by two fords, swollen brown and turbulent through the winter months, treacherous and glinting in the brief summer; either way your bicycle would rust up, your car would almost certainly break down in them, you would be soaked through and you could depend on no one helping you. People kept themselves to themselves in those hills and in the village too.

'Do as you would be done by' went the credo and it meant 'Ask for nothing and you will be given nothing and no one will ask you for anything either.' On Sundays those of the devout who had transport joined the small congregation in the village church and there Mr McConochie the minister addressed them on the wrath of God. 'Be ye ashamed,' he thundered, leaning forth from the pulpit propped on his arms like Mr Punch, 'for ye were born in sin.' Forgiveness there might be in the next world, but not in this, and there would be the Day of Judgement and the separation of sheep from goats to get through first. 'And ye'll no pull the wool over God's eyes.' The damned sat bleakly upright on the hard bare pews, unflinchingly accepting his verdicts. There was no colour in that church, no flowers, no stained glass, only plain white walls and small windows into the shifting clouds. It was a far cry from Grandpa's church where high cheekboned knights of Christendom leant on their swords in noble contemplation and the damsels they had rescued rolled ecstatic eyes heavenwards and the waning sealight beyond them changed violet to mauve, azure to viridian, while the air was sweet with lilies and roses and Grandpa spoke of love and peace and rejoicing. However, this hill church suited Nanny, whose hat, Janet noticed, bristled with more hatpins than any other of the fierce felt hats in the assembly. Every Sunday Hector would drive them down, explaining how much he wished he could join them, and then, regardless of the weather, they would walk back.

The joy of release from Mr McConochie's angry glare and booming voice made all consideration of climate irrelevant. Janet and Rhona frisked ahead, Rhona skipping, Janet pretending to be a horse, cantering and bucking, while Francis, Nanny's favourite, walked beside her carrying their hymn books and regaling her with imitations of the cooking and cleaning staff at Auchnasaugh. Up the windswept road they went, through bare moorland where sheep rose suddenly from the heather and scudded off and only a few stunted rowan trees clung to the steep slope. The mist left cobwebs clinging moist and delicate on the heather, and strands of wool flickered about the thistles. If they looked back they could see the village, unfriendly with its low grey houses, one shop, the church and the Thistle Inn, packed in a graceless huddle down the hill; beyond it the land rose again in barren pastures outlined by drystone walls, until pasture gave way to empty moors. But for Janet it was the view ahead which held all the enchantment she had ever yearned for; in the distance the hills lapped against each other to the far limits of the visible world; nearer the great forest climbed to meet the moor, ancient rust-trunked pine and delicate silver birch, swaying and tossing over grass so green and fine that only harebell and wood anemone could grow there without seeming crude, even blasphemous.

Once this forest had been the hunting ground of a Scottish king, in the days when Scotland was divided into several kingdoms. A lord called the Mormaer and his family lived then at Auchnasaugh and their son had joined in a plot against the king; for this he was executed, but his parents were exonerated and the king continued to come to Auchnasaugh to hunt the deer. The Mormaer's lady concealed her bitter grief, but from the day of her son's death she wore only the colour green, a colour which the king and his courtiers associated with wanton merriment but which was for her, as for the Greeks and Egyptians, the colour of life and of death, of youth, of love and victory. And so one day, as the king called his hounds aside and plunged his dagger into the quivering throat of a young stag, grounded and bleeding among the moss and the harebells, the Mormaer's lady, hidden in a larch tree in her larch green dress, hurled her son's hunting spear and transfixed him. Then she was off, leaping and swinging through the high tree branches, on through the forest for a day and a night until she reached the coast and the cliffs and flung herself a hundred feet down into the boulder-strewn breakers. The hounds, who hunted by sight, not scent, saw nothing but their master lying dead beside their quarry and returned to mauling the stag. Over the years occasional travellers claimed to have seen this lady as a flicker of green, gone as the sun passed behind cloud, high in the forest, and she was sometimes invoked by workmen called to deal with the manifold woes of Auchnasaugh – the boiler and its pipes, the crumbling battlements, the damp and the roof. They did not enjoy working in this cold and lonely place and would leave abruptly after one of them had met her vengeful figure stalking the stairs. Janet would have liked to have met her too, but as the ancient Auchnasaugh had long since been burnt to the ground and buried and the current one stood two miles away from its site she felt there was no chance. Indeed, for her Auchnasaugh was a place of delight and absolute beauty, so although she could understand that many a spirit might wish to return to it, and she hoped that in time she too might do so, she felt the circumstances and mood of such visitations could only be joyous. She had no fear of its lofty shadowed rooms, its dim stone passages, its turrets and towers and dank subterranean chambers, dripping with verdigris and haven to rats. So running now down the narrow twisting road through the forest, she looked forward to the moment when it dropped to the dark, secret glen, where the great hills rose steeply on each side and halfway up one of them, hidden by its trees, stood the castle.

Hector and Cousin Lila were in the drawing room. Hector had a glass of sherry in hand and Lila was refilling a tumbler from the whisky decanter. Vera peered in through the tall window making gestures at the decanter and the cupboard. She had been cutting the pink roses, which clambered up the front of the central tower and clawed at the windows on wild nights. Roses, azaleas and rhododendrons all grew well at Auchnasaugh, but nothing else did. Vera had planted an orchard at the back, next to the washing green, when they first came there five years ago, and soon all but one of the trees were dead, scorched and blasted by the winds and frozen by the five months of winter snow. The survivor stood, twisted and tortured, producing a few black-spotted leaves each year, a maimed reminder of that pretty dream of apple blossom, a girlish aspiration, an echo of the *douceur de vie* of the southern regions of Vera's upbringing. ('Edinburgh suburbs', said Hector when in a bad mood.)

'Come in for a moment, Janet, and play the lyre,' invited her father. Lila beamed uncertainly, her ragged black locks hanging over her dark and bloodshot eyes, her tumbler tremulous in her hand. Janet stood by Lila's chair in her social position, one foot firmly planted on the carpet, the other entwining the opposite leg and moving up and down while she slipped the end of a pigtail into her mouth. 'Well,' demanded Vera, stepping over the low windowsill, 'What did Mr McConochie have to say this morning?' 'It was the wrath of God again,' mumbled Janet, chewing vigorously at her green hair ribbon. 'Take that out of your mouth. Were there any good hymns?' 'We had "Work, for the night is coming" and "There is a fountain filled with blood" and "Who would true valour see".' She liked 'Who would true valour see', especially she liked the bit about 'Hobgoblin nor foul fiend', it reminded her of Jim the gardener and Miss Wales, the choleric cook. However, it wouldn't do to say this. Instead she adopted a solemn downward stare and withdrew into a pleasant dream in which hunchbacked Jim and Miss Wales were crouched in deadly combat on a steaming marshland and she was riding by, casting an unruffled glance their way, above and apart from their feud, one of nature's elect. A gleam from the occluded sky illumined the fearful pink knob which rose through Miss Wales' grizzled hair. Jim's face was darkly murderous. Janet had seen this look when he was clubbing the myxomatosis rabbits and stuffing them into a sack. When he had filled enough sacks he would stow them in the tractor trailer and roar up the back drive and hurl the lot into the gaping maw of the furnace which throbbed and quivered in the boiler room, ineffectually labouring to feed the central heating system.

The horror of this was comparable only to the times when Miss Wales boiled lobsters and they would scream a high thin scream and wave their inky antennae and scrabble at the steep sides of the great black cauldron. None of the grown-ups paid any attention to Janet's desperate pleas for intervention, for mercy for these creatures; in fact, they became angry; 'Don't interfere Janet. It's none of your business, you don't know what you're talking about. And don't answer back.' She could not bear it. The kitchen was the one part of Auchnasaugh which she avoided. Besides Miss Wales' resentful presence and distressing scalp, besides Jim with his bloodstained trousers and his hands ingrained with soil and blood and death and his hinged knife with fur and entrail fragments stuck to its blade, there was almost always a wide enamel bowl containing salted water tinging to rose pink. In this water lay two skinned and headless rabbits, pale and foetal, slaughtered innocents for all to see. The next day, when they were being forced to eat their rabbit stew, outside the french windows on the lawn and up the steep bank where a thousand merry daffodils blew in the spring breezes, rabbits would be scampering unaware.

'You will finish it up. You will not leave the table until you have finished.' This was the rule for all meals, for all courses, and many were Janet's counter stratagems, some more disgusting than others. While patting her lips daintily with her voluminous table napkin she could systematically disgorge her mouth's contents and enfold them in the snowy linen. At the end of the meal napkins were rolled, ringed and placed tidily in a drawer. Janet would return in stealth and shake the grisly wreckage out of the window; the feral cats who lived in the rhododendron thickets would streak out and crouch greedily over it. Near the dining table stood an old harmonium, long disused and silent. Behind its pedals a substantial cavity offered a refuge for food too repulsive even to enter her mouth, chiefly herrings and kippers. It was quite easy to drop her napkin, bend down to retrieve it and, with a deft flick of the wrist, lob the fish into the dark recess. Vera's dog Clover could be relied upon to clear it out later.

Once, when chewing lettuce leaves (thirty times for every mouthful), she discovered a slug in her mouth. It felt enormous and thrashed about. She was afraid that if she screamed they would tell her to stop making a scene and swallow it. She managed to spit it out unseen. It was vast; ribbed, grey and viscous. She put her plate on top of it. The plate danced. In desperation she seized it by the rim on each side and with all her strength pressed it downwards. There was a squelching sensation; the plate was still. A thin trickle of frothy liquid seeped on to the table's gleaming chestnut surface. Janet sat rigid, praying so hard that the words seemed to mass visible and solid in the air before her, 'Forgive me, forgive me, forgive me'; but it was not God's forgiveness she craved, it was the slug's; and never could this be given, so she must carry her guilt with her for ever. 'Come on, Janet, wake up, it's lunchtime, go and wash your hands,' they were shouting. She shambled gloomily out of the drawing room.

The dining room at Auchnasaugh had once been the ballroom, lofty, corniced and swagged with fruits and flowers; chandeliers still glimmered through layers of dust, swaying in the draughts. Now, at the end of the summer holidays, in late September, one massive table spanned its far end, overlooked by a great mirror. The grown-ups sat with their backs to the mirror and the children faced it, so that they might see what they looked like if they chewed with their mouths open or dropped food down their chins. In the mornings only Nanny joined them and they swallowed down their porridge in silence, desperate to escape to the wild outside world of the rhododendron thickets, stables and animals. Sometimes tinker children would emerge from the bushes, noiseless and scrawny as the feral cats, and make munching faces at them through the windows; they vanished into shadow the moment Nanny turned her stare.

Pudding today was pink junket, the delicacy so relished by Miss Muffet; it reminded Janet of the blanching rabbits in the kitchen bowl, but she had perfected a way of ingesting it with almost no physical contact by tipping tiny fragments into the very back of her mouth and swallowing quickly. Soon the ordeal was over. She looked at her family. Hector was flushed and jovial from his sherry, looking forward to an afternoon when he and the dogs would disappear in his car for a run in the hills. Vera as usual was dreamy and detached, her eye occasionally lighting lovingly on the newest baby, Caro, harnessed in her high chair and opening and closing her mouth like a goldfish as Nanny's pinkly laden spoon advanced and retreated. Janet had heard Vera telling her friend Constance that she only really liked babies and found children annoying. In fact, she had said, it was possible for a mother to dislike her own child. Constance, who was childless and a psychologist, had much enjoyed this confidence and embarked on a lengthy interpretation. Janet had tiptoed away from the nursery door where she had been listening in the hope that the newly arrived Constance would be commenting on her intelligence and beauty. Her suspicions about Vera were now confirmed. Anyhow she had no need for a mother. She had the dogs, the cats, her pony and all the woods and hills and waters and winds of Auchnasaugh. And she had books.

She looked in the mirror at the assembled faces of her siblings. Francis the freckled and green eyed was sitting far away from her. He was no longer her closest friend; he had defected to Rhona. Rhona was good at tennis, she loved swimming, her neat little fingers could tie an exquisite trout fly in no time at all. Her bicycle worked because she looked after it. Besides all this, she was pretty and kind and loving. 'You've done well with that one, Vera,' remarked Constance, leaving unspoken the corollary of how badly Vera had done with Janet. 'Be good, sweet maid, and let who will be clever,' Grandpa had said, defecting too, on one of his last visits. He had been very ill and when he came in Rhona had run forward to help him sit down by the fire; she set his stick beside him and brought his tea. Janet had clambered on to the arm of his chair, knocking over his stick and joggling his tea into the saucer, so that she could show off about having learnt the Greek alphabet. It was on that same visit that Grandpa had looked at Lulu, four years old, angelically blonde, weaving a little posy of ivy tangled snowdrops and he had said to Janet, 'You were like that once, a beautiful wee thing. But now you're plain, my dear, very plain.' He had not meant to hurt her, she was certain of that; he was not a worldly man. But hurt her it did, like a punch in the solar plexus. Now, looking at her sisters' faces, blonde and cherubic or dark and flowerlike, and looking at her own pallid frizzy-haired reflection, she was overwhelmed by prickling tears. Her name was dreadful too; all the others had names with some romance about them; even Rhona had a suggestion of inappropriate turbulence, a tawny river in flood rushing and foaming about its boulders. But Janet had nothing; its only possible association was with junket.

Grandpa was dead now and she could never regain her place in his affections. His church was gone too, pulled down to make way for a car park for the gin drinking patrons of the Golf Hotel and Club House. Francis and Janet had been taken to his funeral. It had been terrible standing in the great Victorian cemetery in Glasgow, while a violent rainstorm beat about them, darkening the grief-stricken faces of the monumental angels, smashing the petals of the funeral flowers, whisking hats into the long wet grass. An umbrella rocking in the wind poked Janet's eye and allowed her at last to weep. Afterwards she and Francis had been sent to walk through the streets of Pollokshields, while the grown-ups drank tea and ate fruit cake and had things to discuss. She remembered the clanging of trains passing by on the suburban network, and saturated posters peeling off the advertising hoardings. The air reeked of petrol and made her feel sick. All the others had gone to see Grandpa in hospital before he died. Janet had not gone; she had forced two fingers down her throat and made herself vomit because she was afraid of what she would see there. Hector and Vera had left her behind with surprising alacrity. And now that was that, and there she was in the dining room mirror – plain, treacherous and guilty. Outside, sombre clouds were massing and a squall of rain splattered the windows. 'Never, never, never,' she said to herself. The bright day had gone.

Lila had not been present at lunch. She rarely attended meals, nor did Vera encourage her to do so. Sometimes Hector, flushed with preprandial bonhomie, would urge her to join them, but she would give her vague, sweet smile, shake her head and move off in her strange gliding manner into the dark winding passages, pungent with Jeyes fluid, which led to the back quarters where she had her demesne.

Lila's two rooms overlooked a small and ancient lawn whose turf was underwater green even in winter. Beyond was the washing line and the blighted apple tree, and then the giant hogweed grove, forbidden in the summer months when its great heads of flowers swayed in menace against the windy sky and its serpentine stems reared triumphant and rutilant. 'An army terrible with banners,' Janet thought, and those banners bore their dread device. '*Noli me tangere*' and '*Nemo me impune lacessit*', they hissed as their huge leaves scarcely lifted in breezes which scattered the petals from the roses and made the rhododendrons roar like the sea. Now in early autumn they stood withdrawn and spectral, parched skeletons drained of their venom, and occasionally, without warning, one would crack, rend and plunge in airy slow motion to the ground, there to lie in majesty like the great Lord of Luna. It had pained and angered Janet that they should be called hogweed, uncouth in sound, doubly insulting in intention, and she was overjoyed to find that their real name was indeed heroic: *Heracleum giganteum*. In her thoughts they were still Lords of Luna, but she now referred to them as Heraclea and tried to persuade others to do so too. No one would, not even Lila, who at this time of year would bring these broken ghosts into her room and sit in the afternoon dusk gazing at the shadows they cast on the white walls as her fire smouldered and her seven branched candelabrum flickered and glowed.

About the room were many other desiccated trophies: bracket fungi like Neanderthal livers, long-dead roses in jam-jars green with algae, bracken and rowan berries hung in shrivelled swags round the mirror frames, straw hats pinned to the walls, dust lying heavy on the brims, turning their wreathed flowers a uniform grey. The crumpled rugs bore a patina of cigarette ash, the ashtrays brimmed, books lay open on the floor and tables, stained with coffee, dog-eared and annotated. These books were in Russian, for Lila, like the Heraclea, originated there. In one corner of the room a low archway led into a turret and here Lila's cat Mouflon slept on a pile of old fur coats draped ineffectually over a mighty stack of empty whisky bottles. The aromas of ancient tom and evaporating spirits combined with Schiaparelli's Shocking and Craven A tobacco to create an aura of risqué clubland. On the mantelpiece, just visible behind a watercolour of the cat and a spilling powder compact, was the curled corner of a photograph of Lila's deceased husband, cousin to Hector. Lila had met him long ago in Russia, where he had been employed as a naval adviser to the Tsar's fleet, and when he had asked her to marry him she had been unable to think of any polite way of saying no. So he had brought his silent black-eyed bride to Scotland, and the Revolution had happened and she had never returned; all her past was gone.

At Auchnasaugh she had been neither happy nor unhappy, passing her days in reading, dreaming, painting watercolours of animals, landscape, mushrooms, and politely refusing all contact with the world beyond the glen. She collected wild flowers and pressed them in albums, she brought in baskets of fungi and identified them from their spore prints, covering any empty floor space in great sheets of paper dotted and oozy with deliquescent fruit bodies. For thirty-five years she had kept a record of mysterious botanical presences and absences. Sometimes people saw her sitting on a moorland boulder, staring into space, or scrabbling with a trowel at its mosses and lichens, or gliding through the woods with the curious veering gait, the bowed head and solitary absorption of the mushroom seeker. It was generally supposed that she was mad and a sorceress as well. Her rare visits to the village did nothing to help her reputation; she would sit bolt upright in the back of Vera's car, shawls wound about her head and across her face, looking neither to right nor left, a widowed queen. Vera would take her list into the shop, the shopkeeper would bring her box out and pack it into the boot, she would hand the money through the car window, and not one word would she say. As the car drove off the village children would appear, pointing and jeering, but they were also afraid of her.

Lila's husband, Fergus, had been dead for many years now, gone into the silent past with Lila's Russia. Janet asked her if she wished she were back in Russia, if she missed her life there. 'It's over,' she said, 'It's the past. It doesn't matter now.' And as to Fergus: 'It's a long time since I last saw him. I don't remember him very well. There's nothing much to be said.' Much, however, was said in various places about the manner of Fergus's death. Hector and Vera said that he had collapsed and died from a stroke, precipitated by an old war wound. Nanny said that Lila had poisoned him with her nasty toadstools and he had died in convulsions of agony, his screams echoing down the glen, unheard by his deaf old father, and unheard or unheeded by Lila who had retired with a nightcap. This story was popular in the village. In fact, said Lila, it had been the doing of her cat Mouflon, whom Fergus had hated. Mouflon had been young and playful then, and during dinner he had skittishly made off with Fergus's trout. Fergus had leapt up and hurled his plate at him. He missed the cat but broke the plate. Mouflon fled with the trout to a high shelf and crouched there, snarling and devouring. Fergus was puce with rage; he began to rant about Lila's devotion to her cat and her mushrooms, her failure to make friends of his friends, her refusal even to acknowledge acquaintances. 'You may pass through life without friends, but you can't manage without acquaintances.' Lila could, and did, but this she did not say. Instead she diverted him, spoke admiringly of his prowess at the wheel of his Lagonda, his joy, his ink-blue close-couple coupé, swan-curved of running board. She pretended that she would like to go for a drive with him the next day. Fergus was mollified. He told Lila about his dentist's admiration for his teeth and how the dentist had said that as teeth went these were Rolls Royces and he had riposted that they should be Lagondas. To prove his point he would now bisect a Fox's Glacier Mint with one snap of his front teeth. He set the small gleaming iceberg in position; Lila watched, dreamy in the candlelight; down came his teeth like the blade of a guillotine, down hurtled Mouflon, a ginger streak from the high shelf, embedding his claws in Fergus's neck. Fergus gasped, jerked backwards, inhaled the half glacier mint and choked to death. Lila thumped him and shook him to no avail. It was over very quickly. Beneath the table the cat Mouflon licked the other half of the mint, twitched his whiskers in distaste and sauntered off to Lila's mushroom chamber. Presently she joined him there. After all, nothing could be done until the morning.

Her life was little changed by Fergus's permanent absence. He had always passed long periods away, in Glasgow or overseas on his mysterious naval business, and when he was at home he spent most of his time fishing for trout in the burn which ran along the floor of the glen, or for salmon in the brawling whisky-coloured river which cascaded from the hills, leaping impatiently past its boulders, raucous and jostling until it reached the long tranquil stretch of water which brought it to Loch Saugh, the sorrowing pine trees and the solitary swan. In the evenings they met with Fergus's aged father in the drawing room; there they drank whisky, played cards and listened to John McCormack in plangent lamentation for lost faces, lost loves, the past for ever eddying away. The servants had long since gone, pedalling through the dusk to the village, all except Jim the hunchbacked gardener who tramped off up the hill to his mother's lonely croft on the edge of the moor. Night enclosed the glen and roofed it with stars. Wind stirred the great trees; owls hooted. At ten o'clock Fergus went out to the dynamo shed where their erratic electricity supply was produced by a sullen generator and switched it off. Up the stairs they went, their Tilley lamps fitfully reflected in the great stained-glass window; a drift of cats followed them; the dogs ran ahead. At dawn Lila would come down again, escorted by the cats, and repair to her mushroom room, or, in the autumn, to the woods in search of specimens. After Fergus's death she moved a bed down to the tiny room next to the mushroom chamber and slept there instead, still spending the evenings with her father-in-law, until he too died. Now she sat alone in her room and played John McCormack on a more modern gramophone and drank her whisky as she read or painted. And now she drank whisky in the afternoons, staring balefully at the foggy windows.

Vera had hoped, when they first came to Auchnasaugh, that Lila might wish to help with the children; she visualised her as a cross between a doting and quaintly dotty aunt and an eccentric family retainer, who would know her place but find fulfilment in a modest share of their family life. She would be grateful to Vera for brightening her drab existence. Lila had countered by dropping cigarette ash in the baby's cot and providing a steaming bowl of daffodil bulbs cooked in parsley sauce for the children's lunch, claiming that they were onions. Nanny said she would be obliged to leave if that woman was allowed in the nursery again and so contact with Lila was limited to downstairs. At first the children would shriek with terror as she materialised soundlessly behind them in the corridors or out of the dripping winter afternoon, but soon they grew used to her and as time passed Janet, who had taken to reading Edwardian books about isolated, misunderstood young girls whose intelligence and courage were noticed only by one adult friend, decided that Lila was fitted for this part. Her only regret was that neither of them was crippled.

Lila, although not effusively welcoming, did not appear to mind Janet's visits to her room; she continued to do whatever she was doing and Janet moved about fidgeting with things and asking questions about mushrooms and Russia. Lila would not talk about Russia but was happy to show her her beautiful old botanical volumes. Janet had begun to learn Latin and was intoxicated by the plant names: *Clitocybe nebularis, Asterophora, Flammulina,* or *Rosa gallica, Rosa mundi, Rosa versicolor, Potentilla fruticosa.* She set these names to hymn tunes and wandered about chanting them. Vera forbade her to pick or handle mushrooms. Janet had no intention of obeying. One day, Lila had promised, they would go together on an early morning fungus foray. Janet was aware of the hostility which hung between Vera and Lila and she wished to be on Lila's side. So, on this rainswept Sunday afternoon, the last weekend of the summer holidays, Janet made her way, by a devious route in case her mother was watching, to Lila's murky chamber and sat reading *Lorna Doone* while the wind boomed down the chimney and lashed the chestnuts from their leafy branches and whirled the jackdaws and rooks into a wild confusion beneath the racing clouds.

CHAPTER FOUR

It was Hector's belief that a girl was an inferior form of boy; this regrettable condition could be remedied, or improved upon, by education. For this reason he had started a boys' school for his daughters to attend. And so in term time Auchnasaugh was transformed, full of boys and benches and clattering boots. Another of his beliefs, and one which he shared with Vera, was that children should study languages from an early age and learn poetry by heart. Miss Christie read them 'Hiawatha' and even her bleak Aberdonian tones could not dispel its glories: 'Minnehaha, laughing water!' (*Potentilla fruticosa*!) Rhythms and rhymes galloped through Janet's head. For this reason too she loved learning Latin, the pleasing oddity of declensions, the greater eccentricity of principal parts – *tango, tangere, TETIGI, tactum.* She had been learning French since she was four and when she was ten she started Greek, whose words were even more astounding than Latin. But best of all was the poetry. *Smith's Book of Verse for Boys and Girls* began with narrative poems. 'It was the schooner Hesperus that sailed the wintry sea.' Janet enjoyed these, as usual visualising herself as the heroine bound to the mast or drifting in elegant death along the shoreline: 'O is it weed or floating hair?' But then she discovered the ballads, Sir Patrick Spens, Otterburn, True Thomas, The Unquiet Grave. The wind and snow and waters of the world she knew were there, inhabited not by her family or Miss Wales the cook or the chilled and prosaic churchgoers, but by fiercer lonely figures driven by passion and savagery, love for ever lost and yet for ever held, old feuds, undying jealousies, a moral code of pagan nobility without pity.

I leant my back unto an aik
I thought it was a trusty tree,
But first it bowed and then it brake . . .

Ye'll set upon his white hausbane
And I'll peck out his bonny blue e'en

I hacked him in pieces sma'

It was mirk mirk night
There was nae starlight
We waded through red blood to the knee
For all the blood that's shed on earth
Runs through the springs of that country.

Last night I dreamed a dreary dream
Beyond the Isle of Skye
I saw a dead man win a fight
And I think that man was I . . .

The sound of the wind, the dawn wind, and the sound of the sea, eternally mournful, cruel, tender, were in those pages, were in Janet's head and heart and blood.

On summer afternoons, when Hector and Vera thought that she was on the cricket pitch, a place she feared, she slipped away through the rhododendron jungle to the mossy silent path which led to the old hen house. The hens had all escaped long ago. Rab the hero dog had slaughtered most of them. He was condemned to wear a bloody corpse slung round his neck – primitive aversion therapy. Now and then a solitary Rhode Island or a snowy Leghorn would emerge from the bushes, peer about, squawk in horror and retreat. No one cared. The flock of hens had been another of Vera's attempts to introduce some element of gentle domesticity to the unyielding landscape of the glen, and like her orchard it had not prospered. However, the dank shadows of the hen house, its rotten lichened timbers and shafts of sunlight, received Janet's taciturn presence and gave her sanctuary. Here she spent the long afternoons reading, and copying her favourite poems into an exercise book. Sometimes she would go farther up the path and come to the wide grassy clearing where the two gaunt old swings, tall and angular as guillotines or gallows, dominated the slope; there, with minimal effort, it was possible to soar to great heights, the steep bank falling away beneath, the black pine branches against the blue sky rushing outstretched to embrace her. The scent of the pines, the throb of wood pigeons, the shearing glissade of the circular saw at the distant wood mill and the perfect arc of the swing, as it rose and sank and rose again, lulled her into a trance of happiness. One day, as she swung, she watched a pheasant lead her brood of chicks through the long fine grass. Suddenly the mother bird sank low to the ground, the little ones ran straggling and cheeping towards her, and a great shadow fell across them, across Janet too, as she whirled round and round, unwinding from the twisted chains of the swing. A huge eagle was passing slowly above her, impervious and purposeful, its wings scarcely beating. It drifted on up the glen until in the distance it spanned the rift between the hills, a creature greater than its landscape.

Not all afternoons passed so happily, however. Janet was expected to benefit from the masculine activities available, to puff and pant her way down the drive on early morning runs, to play cricket in the summer and rugby in the winter. She loathed games and was notably bad at them, cringing as the cricket ball hurtled towards her skull, dropping the bat and jumping out of the way. Nor could she catch balls, nor could she throw them. It was even worse in winter on the rugby pitch, in the scrum where boys would seize her plaits and wrench them; she would overbalance and fall flat on her face in the squelching mud while their great boots trampled over her. Mercifully, fog descended on the glen in late afternoon and she could ebb backwards into it, unnoticed, unmissed, until the straining, baying packs of players were scarcely visible. Then she ran for the shelter of the trees and fled up the hill to Auchnasaugh, sliding in through the back doors and vanishing into its dark passages until it was safe to be seen, when the lights glowed warm in the old ballroom and eighty boys were clamorous over tea, and beyond the tall uncurtained windows trees and hills withdrew into lonely self absorption in the wet dusk.

It was a rigorous life, but for Janet it was softened by the landscape, by reading, and by animals whom she found it possible to love without qualification. People seemed to her flawed and cruel. She saw Vera's small unkindnesses to Lila, Lila's lack of feeling for anyone save her balding cat, the boys' savagery. Everywhere there was hideous cruelty to animals. Once as she rode past the sawmill she saw a deer hanging in an open-sided lean-to. They had chopped off its head and its legs to the knee. Then there was the frightening and constant seethe and surge of eruptive anger in Nanny, in Mr McConochie who grew more and more like horrible murderous Mr Punch or like the passage he himself had read them, describing John Knox in infirmity and old age, leaning weakly on the edge of the pulpit, but by mid-sermon 'like to ding that pulpit in blads and fly out of it', his eyes fixed and sparkling with menace, his complexion choleric. She recognized in herself a distaste for people, which was both physical and intellectual; and yet she nurtured a shameful, secret desire for popularity, or at least for acceptance, neither of which came her way.

The boys regarded her as an unwelcome intruder into their masculine world and a potential spy. Girls were sissy. She tried to prove her worth: she climbed the great chestnut tree which hung above the woodshed. The next task was to wriggle on your stomach to the end of a branch and then swing from it and leap across the void on to the steep corrugated-iron roof, skid to its edge and land on your feet on the ground. Janet stood helplessly high among the yellow leaves clutching the trunk, feeling her feet slithering on the damp bark, watching the conkers tumble past her to the ground. Dizzy and dappled lay the sunlit grass below. She could not move. She looked at the sky. The sun was watching her, the clouds hung motionless. The boys were watching her too, silent but mirthful. Soon the familiar chant began: 'Sissy, sissy. Cowardy cowardy custard, dipped in the mustard. Sissy, sissy, girly, girly, girly.' 'I can see your knickers. We can see your knickers.' In desperation she let go with one hand and tried to jam her kilt between her legs. She slipped and hurtled head first to the ground, a sharp scent of earth and leaves, an agonising jolt, a flash of lightning, darkness. The darkness did not last long; she opened her eyes; the boys had melted away and Vera was standing above her, her face contorted with fury. 'What in the world are you doing, Janet? Have you no sense at all? If you can't get up a tree without falling out just don't climb trees.' Janet got cautiously to her feet; her head ached and she felt sick. 'Are you all right now?' added Vera as a sort of bitter afterthought. Janet nodded dumbly. 'Good. Well, off you go and play with the others. And take more care in future.'

Janet stumbled over the gaping shards of fallen chestnuts and made her way painfully down the path through the beech trees to her pony Rosie's field. Rosie was grazing but when she saw Janet she lifted her head and whickered and trotted to the gate. Janet sat on the gate and buried her face in Rosie's mane and breathed in her warm tarry smell; Rosie nuzzled her jersey, champing over her last few blades of grass, leaving a trail of green slobber across the Fair Isle pattern. Janet hugged her tightly. Here was comfort, here was communion. A great peace descended on her, bestowed by the still autumn air, the sweet perfume of the pines, dark on the hillside before her, the great love she felt flow from her into Rosie, flow back from Rosie to her. Calm and tranced she walked up through the beeches again and saw two red squirrels leaping along their sinuous branches; they leapt and curvetted, stopped dead, flourished their tails and were off again, swift and smooth, fleeting like light up the trunks, so bright and merry and joyous that she wanted to shriek with delight. Thus armoured, it mattered nothing to her that the boys were sulking because Hector had forbidden them to swing from the chestnut tree. 'The boys must not bounce on the corrugated-iron roof' he had pronounced, giving every vowel its maximum resonance and rolling the r's into a thunderous finale.

CHAPTER FIVE

Winter descended on the glen; in mid-October came the first thin fall of snow, gone an hour later in the wet wind. The deer ventured down from the hills at dusk, tawny owls shrieked as they hunted through the darkness and shooting stars fled across the night sky. Leafless, the beeches and ashes shivered; the grass was parched with cold; pine and monkey-puzzle stood black and dominant. Only the red earth of the hill tracks retained its colour; the puddles looked like pools of blood.

Of all the seasons this was the one Janet loved most. In the afternoons she would ride up through the forest on to the lonely moors; she felt then, looking into the unending distance of hills ranged beyond hills, that if only she had the courage to go on she, like True Thomas, might reach a fairyland, another element, the place of the ballads, of 'La Belle Dame Sans Merci'. But as the light ebbed away to a pang of sullen gold on the horizon she would turn back. Often it was too dark for her to see the way down through the forest, but Rosie stepped briskly onwards, never faltering, never stumbling, until they reached the eerie cobbled stable yard. The stables were almost derelict. The roof of the central tower had fallen in and willow herb grew in profusion from the coach house. Once there had been stalls and loose boxes for twenty horses; now only one small part was safe to use, but it offered snug winter quarters for Rosie. Janet lingered, listening to the steady munch of hay, the rustle as the pony turned in her deep straw bed; through the cobwebbed window she watched the moon rise, the stars come out. The air grew warm. It was the most peaceful place she knew; she would have liked to stay there all night. At last she made her way up the back drive through the looming trees to the great glowing windows of Auchnasaugh; she walked slowly then, for she loved this moment. No matter how many times she did it, it always filled her with a strange and intense excitement, the traveller coming home through cold and darkness, returned from a great distance and after many days, moving silent and unseen towards the lighted windows.

One November afternoon Vera and Nanny took Lulu and Janet to the dentist. The dentist was in Aberdeen, forty miles away, an unending journey by car. Before they left they had to clean their shoes, brown StartRite walking shoes, taking the laces out and laboriously rethreading them when Nanny had approved the gleaming leather. By this point Janet was already feeling sick. Whenever they went anywhere by car they had to clean their shoes; as Janet was sick every eight miles, sometimes sooner, the merest whiff of shoe polish, the sight of a polish brush, the texture of a yellow duster sent her stomach into churning mutiny. After the shoe ritual they were clamped into their good tweed coats with velvet collars, berets were jammed on their heads, gloves found and they were off.

Lulu looked charming, her blonde hair waving prettily beneath the navy blue beret; Janet's beret was dark green and did nothing to enhance her complexion. It kept slipping sideways; she pulled it firmly on to her forehead where it made a tight welt and pushed her eyebrows downwards, giving her a fierce Neanderthal look. Vera wore her driving headscarf, printed with the flags of the allied nations and bearing the slogan 'Into Battle', many times repeated. She drove with verve, anxious to minimise the number of times they would have to stop for Janet to be sick. They had tried travel pills, they had tried dragging a degrading chain behind the car, leaving all the windows open, putting Janet in the front, all to no avail. Nanny had banned her from eating anything red or orange for twenty-four hours before any journey on the grisly premise that this was the cause. 'I've aye noticed it when the bairn spews up.' No good. Now a new theory was abroad. Constance had said that Janet must stop thinking about herself, must concentrate on others or at least on other things. 'You've no difficulty the rest of the time in concentrating; you can learn your Latin and your poetry, so really, speaking candidly, I think you've just got to get out of yourself; take an interest in the landscape, talk to the family, play spelling games.' The crime of self-centredness had been added to the miseries of her condition. She always looked at the landscape anyhow; she was far better at spelling than her brother and sisters, so games with them were boringly limited. And she didn't want to talk to her family; she couldn't think of anything to say to them. Instead she silently rehearsed a poem which had made her laugh so much that tears came out of her eyes when she discovered it the previous evening.

> *It was a summer evening,*
>   *Old Caspar's work was done,*
> *And he before his cottage door*
>   *Was sitting in the sun.*
> *Before him sported on the green*
>   *His little grandchild Wilhelmine . . .*

It occurred to her now that Lulu looked pretty much like Old Caspar's awful little grandchild. Lulu turned, caught Janet's broadly grinning and sarcastic stare and pinched her sharply on the calf. Janet pinched her back, harder. A silent struggle ensued; then, 'Mummy, Mummy, Janet's pinching me.' 'Miserable little clipe,' muttered Janet, subsiding to the far end of the seat. She stared out of the rain-dashed window, where the light was already fading. They were passing out of the hills, over the crossroads, towards the bare stone-walled pasturelands where the few trees hunched and bent inland, straining away from the bitter blast of the sea wind, their branches clawing vainly for the shelter of the glens. The hills stood enigmatic and shadowy, guarding their own.

> *Lady, weeping at the crossroads*
> *Would you meet your love*
> *In the twilight with his greyhounds*
> *And his hawk on his glove?*

thought Janet, looking back at them with a strange yearning. She felt that she was being borne away from the lands of high romance and magic towards a bleak world of making do and commerce and department stores and petrol fumes; headscarves and gabardines. Looking at that grim and vengeful sea she could imagine the satisfaction with which it had disposed of Sir Patrick Spens' lords and their plumy hats and their corkheeled shoon.

> *Then up rose the mermaiden*
> *Wi' a comb and glass in her hand*
> *Here's a health to you my merrie young men*
> *For you never will see dry land.*

Was the mermaiden drinking the blood red wine or was she somehow holding a mirror and looking in it amid the green billows?

There was a clicking noise beside her and a rush of cold air. The far door was swinging open. Lulu was gone. Silently Janet leaned across and closed the door. She sat rigid, her mind spinning. 'Oh God,' she prayed, 'bring her back, let no one notice, let them not blame me.' How long would they not notice? Could she jump out? They were driving along the stretch of cliff road above the dreadful caves once inhabited by Sawney Bean and his descendants. Sawney Bean had run away with a maid from the great house where they both worked; they were wanted for theft; they would be hanged. They hid in these caves and kept themselves diverted and alive by making man-traps on the high road to Aberdeen and consuming their prey. When the law finally tracked them down they found a pullulating tribe of Beans, mainly the issue of incestuous unions, but still guided by the patriarchal Sawney. Smoked black flitches and plump haunches of human flesh were suspended from the cavern walls drying in the salt breeze; the babies cut their teeth on finger bones. They were all burned in Aberdeen market square, the last cannibals in Europe. Or so it was said. Janet wished that one of Sawney's man-traps would gape open in the road and the car plummet into it. Anything rather than the doom which waited for her.

Rise again Sawney Bean, Sawney Bean, Sawney Bean,
Rise again Sawney Bean, come from your cave and eat me

squeaked a mad voice in the back of her brain. The car slowed for the first traffic lights of Aberdeen. Vera glanced back, grimly helmeted by the 'Into Battle' scarf. 'Lulu, sit up!' she commanded. 'Lulu, what are you doing? Are you down on the floor? Get up at once. Janet, *where is* LULU?' 'She got out,' said Janet. Her gorge rose. 'A while ago,' she said and vomited mightily.

In the event things were not so bad as she had feared. They found Lulu, muddy and grazed, soaked through and without her beret, sitting on a roadside bank surrounded by a comforting group of farm workers and their bicycles. She was holding court and showed no particular pleasure in Vera's fervent embrace or Nanny's insistence that she travel home in the front, on her knee. In fact, she said: she wanted to go on to the dentist so that they could have tea at Fuller's in Union Street afterwards. For a moment Janet was roused from her sombre apprehensions by this redeeming notion. Fuller's was the good thing about trips to the dentist. With faces frozen by the sleety wind and the jawscrunching needle they would step from the granite street and the granite sky into a warm lamplit haven. The carpets were pink and dense so that you moved soundlessly; there were no windows; you could forget the outer world. Teaspoons clinked on porcelain saucers, tiered stands shone, laden with the snowy glory of Fuller's walnut cake. Reverently the waitress raised the silver dome from a fragrant mound of buttered toast, flaccid and dribbling with amber rivulets. 'Jerusalem the golden, with milk and honey blest,' thought Janet. And, like that heavenly vision, unattainable. For the numb jaw and tongue, the rubbery lip, flawed and mortal, could not cope. But it was enough to sit in that rosy hush and feel its benediction, watch the hard faces of the women in their hats grow gentle and animated. Fox tippets were discarded, carelessly slung on chair backs so that their glassy eyes and snappy jaws were invisible. There was twinkling, there were indiscreet confidences and girlish laughter. Extravagant quantities of tea were drunk, lavish tips lurked coyly beneath emptied salvers. Men did not come here. Once Vera had lured Hector in on the grounds that it was his duty to help her cope with five children. As they emerged from the Ladies' Room they saw Hector staring moodily at a light fitting while baby Caro, beside him in a high-chair, poured scalding tea in an unsteady stream on to the pink carpet. Later he had removed the largest chip from Rhona's plate and placed it on his shoulder; then he waited through the rest of the sacred hour for someone to ask him why he had a chip on his shoulder. No one tried to get him into Fuller's again.

But today it was back to Auchnasaugh in the deepening murk. The appointment would have to be rearranged, the car must be swilled out before Hector saw it. If they were quick they might catch Jim the hunchbacked gardener before he went home. Jim would not mind; after all he spent most of his life involved in blood, guts, dung and effluvia. Janet could run in the back way and see if he was in the kitchen having his tea; she would have to explain the situation; it was her fault anyhow.

To Janet's relief Miss Wales was not in the kitchen but to her chagrin Jim was. He was huddled over the little side table gazing intently at a magazine. In one hand he held his Jammy Piece; the other hand was scratching his stomach. When Janet spoke he gave an almighty start and shoved the magazine behind the teapot. 'Ech,' he observed, shambling to his feet, buttoning his clothes. '*Ech*,' he spat in the sink and went out into the darkness, leaving behind a gamey whiff of sweat and dried blood and stale tobacco. Janet tiptoed over to the teapot and extracted the magazine. She was horrified; it was full of disgusting pictures of women with no clothes on. To think anyone could want to look at things like that. She was overwhelmed with shame. She lifted up the Aga lid and stuffed it into the glowing depths, prodding and pushing with the poker until at last the pages caught, blazed up, turned to grey powder. She fled from the kitchen.

It was time for prep. Arithmetic prep. What a dreadful day. She hated arithmetic and was spectacularly bad at it. Year in, year out, new maths masters spoke kindly to her about her special difficulties. Each assured her that with his guidance she would understand; she must not worry any more. She didn't worry; she just went on hating it, went on failing to grasp any concept more advanced than simple fractions and percentages. Geometry was also boring, abstract and incomprehensible but at least she could learn the theorems by heart and have the tiny pleasure of writing QED and being done with them. Algebra was less awful because there were letters mingled with the numbers and there was even something satisfying about tracking down the identity of the mysterious *x*. But tonight, after half an hour of futile conjecture about how long various baths would take to empty or fill, her head had become a bombinating vacuum. With relief she turned to English. They had been reading 'Sohrab and Rustum' and now they were to learn the closing passage. This was wonderful, so wonderful that later, when Hector and Vera were giving her a serious talk about responsibility, duty and caring for others, she heard their voices only as 'the mist and hum of that low land', while she floated with the majestic river 'into the frosty starlight And there moved rejoicing, through the hush'd Chorasmian waste.' The hush'd Chorasmian waste!

CHAPTER SIX

During the next few months a dreadful thing happened. Knobby protrusions appeared on Janet's chest. They hurt. The boys noticed them through her jersey and liked to punch them. Then they hurt seriously. 'Show us your tits, Janet,' became their new taunt. These bumps felt like the tender horn buds on calves' foreheads. If only they would produce horns, short, spiky stabbing ones. What a surprise that would be for the boys. She prayed for this without much hope. It was not to be. She went about with her arms permanently folded across her chest. Vera, exasperated by her new stooping posture, explained to her that there was nothing to be embarrassed about: 'It's just part of growing up. A bosom is a beautiful and natural thing.'

Hector and Vera went away on a spring holiday, leaving Janet a small book to read. It was an account of more of the beautiful and natural things which lay in store for her. Janet was appalled. This meant that all the peculiar jokes the boys told – jokes she had thought were just part of the whole oddity of being male, like obsessions with war and Meccano and cars and tearing wings off insects – were based on truth. She had known how animals procreated of course. The feral cats coupled all over the washing green and she had often seen the dogs locked together, straining in a union which seemed painful and protracted; only buckets of water could separate them. But she had assumed that people were different, metaphysical. After all there had been the Angel Gabriel. No wonder God had driven Adam and Eve out of Paradise. What a disgrace. It was lucky that she had never had any intention of having babies; now she would certainly never marry either. She would live out her days at Auchnasaugh, a bookish spinster attended by cats and parrots, until that time when she might become ethereal, pure spirit untainted by the woes of flesh, a phantom drifting with the winds. What fun she would have as a ghost. She could hardly wait.

But then it was summer and a rare, most exquisite summer. The honeysuckle which drooped down the terrace wall scented the air all day and all evening, the azaleas lingered on and on, wood pigeons throbbed and cooed, and only the softest of breezes stirred the pines. Janet forgot her earthly doom and rose before light to ride bareback up the grassy tracks through the woods to the moors. She watched the sun rise over the far hills, the mist float in steamy filaments off the glen and the silent golden day bring glory to the sombre pines. She was the first person in the world; only she disturbed the dew. Riding back she saw secret wonders: three baby hedgehogs feasted on a rotten chestnut husk; a doe and her fawn moved across her path, unafraid, absorbed in their separate world. Once she came upon an avenue of *Phallus impudicus*, gleaming white and joyous in the fresh grass, an elfin priapic festival or a tribute to a fairy queen. She thought of True Thomas' faery queen, with her grass-green dress and the silver bells on her horse's mane; fifty silver bells and nine. She would be her for a while. When she reached the glen she galloped the length of the meadows by the burn, wild with glee, the pony wild too, until they skidded to a panting stop at the gate to the stable drive.

She stood on the terrace shaking the wet honeysuckle over her face, breathing its perfume, a creature momently compounded of dew and air and fragrance. There was still not a soul about. The great windows shone and flashed in the rising sun but the curtains hung black and motionless behind them. All this early morning belonged to her alone; she need share it with no one. She thought of Christmas and the thrilling parcels addressed to her which turned out to contain board games or jigsaws or boxes of crystallised fruits to be shared with her siblings. 'Mine, mine,

mine,' she said to herself. Twice only was her solitary triumph marred by the sight of Jim moving furtively about on the small lawn near Lila's room, apparently uprooting daisies. She pretended not to see him and when she turned again he had vanished.

The pleasures of the day continued. Lessons were conducted outside. They were reading *Macbeth* and it was clearly set at Auchnasaugh. Lying on the warm grass, Janet watched the house martins skim and hover about the battlements.

>*Where they most breed and haunt I have observed*
>*The air is delicate*

She was usually given the part of Lady Macbeth to read and this was deeply satisfying. There were also some lines of Macbeth's which she coveted, especially

>*The multitudinous seas incarnadine*
>*Making the green one red*

but these she swiftly learnt by heart. The dark night of the Macbeths' souls was the dark night of Auchnasaugh in winter. She felt that Shakespeare couldn't have liked babies either. Later they read *The Tempest* and Janet was Miranda. She imagined Lila as the witch Sycorax and Jim as Caliban, but Caliban was too robust and talkative. Hector could be Prospero and Auchnasaugh could be adapted to island form.

In the afternoons they took a great picnic into the hills, where there was a brimming deep brown pool and dam; the burn cascaded down a steep fall into a dark mossy ravine and wound its way past rocks towards the glen. High grassy banks and groves of pine surrounded the pool and beyond in all directions massed the hills; the shadows of clouds moved over them, their colours changed from minute to minute, now crowding near, now withdrawn and remote. This was Janet's favourite place on earth, the place where she wished to be buried. She would ride up there and set the pony loose to graze the delicate forest grass. In a glade nearby she could change unseen and slip through the trees into the icy waters of the pool. When the shock had gone she swam lazily about, watching the sunlight probe the pebbles on the muddy floor, the trout flicker under the banks, listening to the boys splashing and shouting far on the other side. When she came out she would creep through the bushes to the place where the capercailzies had their nest and watch the astonishing huge green and black male bird stamping about his little clearing while his dim wife crouched in admiration. The cock was less impressive when he tried to fly, veering and tilting from side to side, brushing branches, narrowly missing tree-trunks. His wings droned as he went.

When the sun sank behind the hills they returned to Auchnasaugh down paths fringed with campion and foxgloves and fresh bracken. Once Janet came upon Lila in the midst of a thicket of wild raspberries. She was wearing her wide brimmed straw hat with its faded wreath of flowers and her bare arms glimmered through the green gloom of the flickering leaves and the pendant fruits. When she saw Janet, she smiled her rare sweet smile and Janet knew that she too was happy and recognised for the first time that Lila had been beautiful, at this moment was beautiful. She felt deep shame at having imagined her as Sycorax. The scent of raspberries was poignant as the sound of pipe music, the scent of romance, of loss.

Late into the evening they lingered out on the terrace. So rare a summer must not be wasted. The boys vanished into the rhododendrons or down to the burn. Francis and Rhona went fishing, Janet sat on a rug reading Tennyson. They had given up trying to make her go and build a dam or play tennis. The grown-ups wandered back and forth with glasses in their hands. Even Lila was there, mothlike in her long old-fashioned white dress, with its flounces around the hem. The drawingroom windows were wide open and the plangent tones of the Papal Count drifted out into the tranced dusk. He was singing 'The Last Rose of Summer'.

> *So soon may I follow, when friendships decay*
> *And from Love's shining circle, the gems drop away*
> *When true hearts lie withered . . .*

Looking back on this summer in later years, Janet saw it as the happiest time of her life, its intensity deepened by an elegiac quality. For who knew if ever such a season would come again to that northern land, and for Janet it could not. In the autumn she was to go away, to a girls' boarding school.

In August the weather broke. Thunder rumbled through a leaden sky, sheets of rain obliterated the hills, the burn burst its banks and flooded the meadows. When the sun shone it shone weakly, the ground steamed and the air was dense with swarms of midges. Vera's friends the Dibdins came to stay. Hector was annoyed. 'You know I can't be doing with them. They never stop talking, especially Melanie. Typical English.' Like Hector and Vera, the Dibdins had been blessed with several daughters and only one son. The youngest girl was about Janet's age, the others older. They had jolly English names – Jill, Raymond, Gail, Hilary – and they were very good at sports. 'And not only are they good at sports,' said Vera, looking hard at Janet, 'but they are also something more important. They are good sports.' Francis sided with Hector, 'They needn't think I'm going to help entertain them. You'll have to do it, Janet. Anyhow Hilary will be a nice friend for you. After all she's going to be in your form at school. I bet they love Enid Blyton books.' Francis and Janet had only one bond these days: it was their scorn for Enid Blyton, and particularly for the Famous Five. They would stagger about convulsed with mirth, clutching each other, vying in quotations, ' "On the rocks," said Bill grimly', ' "Food always tastes so much better out of doors," said Dinah' and best of all, 'Julian was pulling on his bathing drawers'. 'What a pity Master Dibdin isn't called Julian,' mused Francis. 'And do you know where they live? A place called Dymchurch. Can't you just imagine it? Thatched cottages and crematorium-style rose beds, I bet. And what a surname. The Dibdins of Dymchurch. *Mon Dieu!*'

While Janet agreed that the Dibdins had a ridiculous surname she had nothing against the English *per se*. After all, most of her favourite poets were English. And she thought that she might like people who talked a lot. No one talked much at Auchnasaugh, except about dogs, cats and cars. She often felt that they all led such separate lives that any one of them could have been a murderer or a god come down to earth and not one of the others would have known. Besides, it would be interesting to meet some girls; she didn't know any, apart from her sisters, who didn't count. She had secretly started reading girls' school stories, including (too shameful to admit to anyone) *In the Fifth at Malory Towers* and *Summer Term at St Clare's*, and she had hopes of being the madcap of the Fourth, or at least of having a friend or two. No one there would call her 'Sissy', or lie in wait for her in dusky corners, intent on rape or at any rate carnal knowledge. Janet had dealt with this new hazard in her life: she had perfected a technique of simultaneously seizing the assailant's hair, walloping him on the nose and kneeing him between the legs. Her virtue had remained intact.

The Dibdins duly arrived. Francis and Rhona vanished up a tree. The grown ups and Jill drank sherry in the drawing room, while Janet was left to show Raymond, Gail and Hilary around. It had stopped raining, so they braved the midges and she took them to the Heracleum grove. 'This is *Heracleum giganteum*,' she said proudly. 'But I call them the Lords of Luna. You mustn't touch them, they are poisonous.' There was an uneasy silence.

They all stared at her with their identical frank blue eyes. Then Raymond laughed. 'It's giant hogweed, isn't it? My word, your father ought to get rid of them. They spread like nobody's business. They're a really pernicious weed.' Janet began to hate him. 'Let's have a look at the tennis court,' suggested cheerful Hilary, pushing her smooth blonde hair off her smooth pale brow. 'There's enough of us here to have some really good doubles tournaments.' Oh God, thought Janet, I should have known. It hadn't occurred to her that they would wish to be sporty even in this rain-sodden weather. Besides, the tennis court at Auchnasaugh was a parody of a tennis court. Its aged surface was pitted and cracked and willow herb and nettles grew out of the cracks. The net sagged and had holes in it. When you hit a ball out, as most people did most of the time, it sped off for ever into the encroaching jungle of rhododendrons. It was the worst place for midges and Janet had rarely played more than a couple of games before she was forced to withdraw by a hideously swelling eyelid. Again there was a silence as they looked at it. Again there was a spurt of boyish laughter. 'Well, it will certainly give a new meaning to the word "challenge",' said loathsome Raymond, tossing his head back and exposing his sharp, wolfish teeth. 'Gosh, it'll be really good fun,' said Gail. 'Anyone can play on a slick modern court. This will sort us all out.' The rain began again. Janet saw no end to the tedium of this visit. If the sun shone there would be sporting activities. If it rained she would not be allowed to read because of Hilary. What on earth would they all do?

In the event it went on raining. Everyone except Janet went for a drive up the glens in the afternoon. Janet was excused because she would only be sick. Blissfully, she retired to her room and copied David's Lament for Jonathan into her special book. In the evening the Dibdins announced that they always enjoyed a good sing-song around the piano. Hector choked and went out of the room, muttering something about checking a gasket. Francis rushed after him. Mr Dibdin sat at the grand piano in the drawing room, his family gathered about him in a statuesque group. He played 'Sweet Lass of Richmond Hill', nodding his head from side to side and casting roguish glances over at Janet's family who were gathered in an implacable huddle by the fire. His children sang the song in parts, proflouncing the 'i' of 'hill' as if it were a double 'e' and beaming and nodding and twinkling like their father. Encouraged by fervent applause they went on to perform madrigals and then a couple of German *Lieder*. Worse was to come. The following evening they pushed the furniture back and gave an exhibition of morris dancing. 'You're all so brainy you should be interested,' fluted Melanie Dibdin. 'They're based on ancient fertility rituals. You know, earth mothers, the king must die, stag dances, all that sort of thing.' Janet thought they looked more like Little Noddy or Andy Pandy. It was shocking to see grown people behave in this ludicrous way. Only Lulu and Caro joined them; it seemed a suitable activity for the very young.

Then the sun came out and shone quite strongly and the sporting activities began. There was cricket, there was tennis, there was swimming. Luckily none of them rode. 'We aren't really keen on animals in our family. We're more people people.' The Dibdin girls called their mother Mumsy and their father Poppa. Raymond called them Ma and Pa. The girls embraced both parents constantly; Raymond put his arm round his mother as though she might fall over at any moment, but managed to keep his hands off his father apart from the occasional virile slap on the back. The girls were kind to Janet but they did not understand one another. 'Gosh, what fun it must have been for you, being the only girl among eighty boys,' said Hilary, eyeing Janet in a suggestive manner. 'Not really,' said Janet. 'Oh, why ever not?' 'It just wasn't.' 'Oh.' But they assured Janet that she would simply love St Uncumba's. 'We adore it. Such a funny name for a school. The dear old thing who founded it was really keen on education for women and votes for women and things; she was absolutely anti-marriage, so she called it after this weird mediaeval woman who grew a beard so that she couldn't be forced to marry anyone. But it's not a bit like that now, is it Hilary, is it Jill?' Tides of tinkling laughter. Raymond was at a boys' public school in England. Then he would go on to Sandhurst, he was to be a soldier. 'I hate war. I'm against war and I'm against armies. I'm a pacifist,' announced Janet, suddenly furious. She had never used this word before, but now she believed in it with passion. 'What, you mean like those awful conshies? Traitors, they should all have been shot. My dear Janet,' said Raymond, turning red in the face, 'I don't actually think that at your age you know what you're talking about. Things aren't as simple as that.' 'Yes they are,' yelled Janet. 'Killing is wrong and you're wrong. You have no right, you make me sick.' She rushed out of the room, panting and shaking with rage.

Gail sprained her ankle, tripping over a crack in the tennis court while leaping winsomely up to a volley. They were all covered in midge bites; the drawing room reeked of DDT. Everyone was glad when the last full day of the visit dawned. The sun shone brilliantly from a cloudless sky. 'Typical, isn't it?' said Vera. 'Never mind, let's make the most of it while it lasts – and while we last!' beamed John Dibdin. 'Outdoors, everybody!' Rosie was lame; Janet went down to the stables to bathe her swollen fetlock. She loitered about, putting off the time of return. She went for a wander upstairs through the forbidden and dangerous empty rooms and corridors which ran over all three wings of the building. They were lovely rooms with cornices and mouldings of grapes and flowers, the walls still washed in pink or blue, but the floors were decayed and the ceilings had gaping holes where rotten lathes sagged through. Fungi grew on the windowsills and swathes of cobweb hung about the corners. There was one little room, like a dressing room, off a larger chamber, which she had never been able to explore. The door was either locked or jammed. Today she thought she would try it. She pushed and pulled and shook at the door. Plaster fell on her head from the decaying frame. She kicked it hard. Suddenly it gave.

The tiny room was windowless and smelt of mushrooms and ammonia. Sunlight streamed in from the other room and in a moment Janet's eyes adapted to the dimness. It was entirely lined by shelves full of ancient-looking leather-bound books. Her heart thumping with excitement, she carefully lifted one out and opened it. *Aubrey Beardsley. Erotica* was the title. It meant nothing to her. She turned the pages, stared, dropped it as if it had burnt her. Plate after plate, shielded by tissue, of the most unspeakable male and female goings on, far worse than Jim's magazine had been. She pulled out more books; different titles, different authors but all the same theme as far as the lavish illustrations went. She pushed some back, dropped others. Surely there must be some sort of normal book here. Her eye lighted on a name she knew, P. Ovidius Naso; she had not yet read any Ovid, but she felt a Latin poet must be safe. In fact this was just as bad as the rest, and worse than some. It was called *Ars Amatoria*. Suddenly the hated voice of Raymond Dibdin was calling her from the courtyard. 'Janet, Janet, where are you? Your ma wants you.' 'All right, I'm up here, I'm just coming,' she shouted.

'I say, can you get up there? What fun, I must just have a look.' Before she could move he was galloping up the stairs and into the little room. 'It's hellish hot out there,' he said, wiping sweat off his forehead. He was wearing nothing but a pair of soldierly khaki shorts. 'Good God, whatever are all these books?' 'Nothing, come on, let's go,' said Janet, putting the Ovid behind her back. He picked up the Beardsley and stood with his back to her to catch the light. 'Well well,' he said, his voice changing, 'Janet, you naughty little thing. I'd never have guessed it of you.

Do you come here often, as they say?' 'I've never ever been in here before, I was just exploring,' squeaked Janet, her throat going dry. He wasn't listening; he was engrossed in the Beardsley.

Janet decided to sidle past him and run for it. She was afraid. He shot out an arm and grabbed her. 'Have a look at this then, Janet, since you're so bloody interested.' He was panting; he brandished and twirled a dreadful dark pink baton out of the front of his shorts. A dictum from Kennedy's Latin grammar flashed crazily through Janet's mind, 'Masculine will always be / Things that you can touch and see. (Example: curculio – weevil.)' He pushed his face against hers. 'Come on then, give me a kiss.' His clammy mouth moved across her cheek. With all her strength Janet jerked her head back and smashed the corner of the *Ars Amatoria* into his eye; at the same time she kneed him. He gave a retching gasp. 'You bitch, you dirty little bitch,' he hissed. She ran, down the rotten stairs, across the cobbles, up the steep back drive. She heard him pounding after her as she reached the top. She grabbed a sharp chunk of quartz from the bank and spun round, at bay, ready to scream. His face was still red but it was rearranged into a mask of boyish contrition. 'Janet, I'm most dreadfully sorry. Please, please forgive me. I can't imagine what came over me. Put it down to the heat and those weird books. Now do please say you'll accept my apology. Please.' He put his head on one side and looked down at her with a mock woebegone expression. Janet didn't answer. She dropped the quartz and walked on. He walked beside her. 'Look, do you want me to go down on bended knee? What can I do to atone?' Then as they turned down the path by the Heracleum grove, he suddenly changed his tack; he looked her straight in the eyes: 'I beg and implore you not to tell anyone about this. May I have your word?' Janet stopped dead. 'Bugger off' she said. He looked astonished, but he turned away. She was astonished too; she did not remember ever seeing or hearing this expression. A great tide of anger rose within her, overwhelmed her. How dared he, how dared he! All her dreams and yearnings for high romance, all her love for Auchnasaugh were pitted against his miserable filthy mind, his disgusting cowardice. He had paused, he was looking at bald, crippled Mouflon as he edged painfully out of Lila's window. 'That thing should be put down,' he was saying. 'I'd be glad to . . .' With a wild shriek Janet charged forward, arms and legs flailing and shoved him headlong into the giant hogweed patch. Down he crashed, clutching frantically at the great Lords of Luna. Down they crashed about him, under him and over him. The sun blazed on the sap as it trickled freely over his bare skin. Janet slipped into the dark haven of Auchnasaugh, seen only by Lila, who kept her counsel.

That evening Janet's family gathered in the drawing room. The Dibdins had gone, Raymond preceding them by ambulance to a burns unit. Their farewells had been of necessity a trifle brisk; they had made it clear that they would not be returning while the Heracleum grove stood: 'I must say, it's a tiny bit irresponsible, don't you think?'

'What was the young idiot doing in the hogweed anyhow?' demanded Hector irritably. 'Chasing a cat, I expect,' said Rhona. 'I warned him about the poison, the day he came,' said virtuous Janet. '*And* he wanted to kill Mouflon.' 'How could he?' With the enemy driven from their gates, they spent an evening of unusual gaiety and kinship before resuming their separate lives.

CHAPTER SEVEN

Janet stood at the nursery window, high in the central tower. It was a golden, hazy morning in mid-September. She gazed down the glen at the autumnal trees and the scarlet rowanberries which scarcely trembled in the mild air. She was trying to learn this view by heart, for today she was to be driven away, far south to St Uncumba's. She wore her new school uniform with pride and excitement. In her brown felt hat and oatmeal tweed coat she felt that she was refashioned, a different person, vibrant with possibilities. Behind her on the big green chest of drawers Polly leant from his cage, intent on his woodwork, skilfully prising splinters from the top surface, shredding them and flinging them to the floor. The dogs shifted and groaned in their derelict armchairs. A striped cat was coiled like an ammonite on the sunlit window ledge. The boys were at morning prayers. They were singing 'By cool Siloam's shady rill'. Their voices floated up to her, pure as holy water. Down in the terrace there was a flicker of movement. She saw a weasel glide through the fallen leaves, almost on its belly, slower, slower. It was motionless. In the shadow crouched a rabbit, palpitating. It stared at the weasel, the weasel stared back.

> *O thou whose infant feet were found*
> *Within thy father's shrine*

sang the boys. The weasel leapt, a chestnut streak in the sunlight. The rabbit screamed, threshed violently, was still. Limp and open-eyed, it lay on the green grass; the weasel was curved lovingly at its throat. Janet shivered.

Thine be the glory, forever and ever,
Forever and ever amen

sang the boys. It was time to go.

Janet's boarding house at St Uncumba's stood above the cliffs on a rocky peninsula. It overlooked another heaving expanse of the North Sea. The main school buildings were a short walk away, sequestered by high walls from the grey town. Once there had been a great cathedral here, and a mighty fortress had reared up from the edge of the sea bed, higher than the cliff, its outer defences running along the shore and curving inland to encircle the town. Now only shattered towers and the ribs of arches loomed against the starry sky, faintly phosphorescent. In their memory, it seemed to Janet, bells tolled almost continuously – sometimes faint, tossed back and forth by the wind; sometimes heavy with portent. The air was wet with the haar. From her dormitory window Janet could see the grey sea imperceptibly merging into the grey sky; nothing else at all. It was like living at the end of the world.

The excitement and pride of being a real schoolgirl with a real uniform had rapidly given way to bewilderment, and bewilderment to a numb desolation. She did not know how to talk to the other girls. At Auchnasaugh the boys had taken great pleasure in words, rehearsing new discoveries, competing to find the most resonant, succinct or bizarre. They had also, she realised now, been interested in so many things, applying themselves with the same unquestioning absorption to making balsa wood aeroplanes, building dams, composing sonnets, developing photographs, stalking Janet. The girls were interested in clothes and their families and games. A few were interested in boys. When Janet used words which had delighted or amused her they fell silent and stared and moved away muttering to each other. First they thought she was showing off, then they thought she was mad. She became silent, lost in dreams at meal times, so that on the few occasions when anyone did speak to her she did not hear them. They put pepper in her tea to see if she would notice, and for a while she didn't. They hid her hockey boots so that she would be late for the game, a cardinal sin. Janet assumed that she had lost them; she lost things all the time. She hid in the back of the music practice room and read all afternoon. The housemistress summoned an emergency meeting of all girls before supper. 'Someone, who is in this room, *cut the game* today. There can be no excuse for letting sides down. In this school and in this life we work together, no matter how small our contribution. This is the first rule of social behaviour, and you are here at St Uncumba's to learn it. All for one, one for all. If you think you know the identity of this girl I trust you will make your feelings clear to her. I shall say only this. *Be ashamed.*'

Janet was sent to Coventry. For three days no girl spoke to her, no one answered when she tried to find her way to classrooms or games pitches; she was late for everything. It became clear to her that she would have to pretend to like hockey and she would have to try to talk in simple language, if she could think of anything at all to say. Also she needed someone to plait her hair. Nanny had always done this; Janet was hopeless at it; it unwound in maddening wisps and frizzy scrolls, as fast as she twisted it back. By surrendering her weekly chocolate bar, the sole pleasure of a Sunday, she obtained a helper. Hilary Dibdin was not friendly. Apart from a curt 'Hallo Janet' on the first day, she ignored her. Janet overheard her telling a group of girls that if they thought Janet was peculiar they should see the rest of her family. 'And the place they live in. Enormous and freezing cold. They've hardly any carpets and they let the animals climb all over everything and lick the butter. In the garden – well you could hardly call it a garden, it's all overgrown and wild – there are a whole lot of really poisonous plants. My poor brother got stung by them and he was in hospital for *weeks*. There's a disgusting bald cat too, who goes around being sick everywhere.' Janet fled to her icy cubicle and sat clutching her photograph of the dogs on the back drive, looking around at her, smiling in the sunlight under the great trees. Soon a monitor came and dispatched her to the study room to get on with Knitting for Charity. Every moment of the day was timetabled. At night she lay in her cold white bed listening to the bitter sea wind; the lights were still on and for twenty minutes you could read a book of your own choice. Next term she would bring back a torch. But now she was too forlorn even to read; the print was a long grey wet blur, like her life. At the far end of the dormitory the bath taps were running. Someone was singing:

> *Seven lonely days make one lonely week*
> *Seven lonely nights I cried, cried for you.*
> *Oh my darling, I'm crying, boo-hoo hoo hoo . . .*

She was drowned in desolation.

She wrote a letter to Hector and Vera every Sunday morning before church; she told them what a wonderful time she was having, what a lot of new friends she had made; she described a game in which she had shot the winning goal. She made it all sound as like Malory Towers as she could. Hector was unimpressed; to her surprise he wrote back saying that she hadn't been sent to St Uncumba's to be like Hilary Dibdin; he would like to hear about her work. Apart from maths, work was easy, so easy that it bored her. She had done it all before, years before and in the case of Latin and French, many years before. No one else did Greek; she had her lessons alone and these were a pleasure. They also enabled her to miss needlework. She could hardly believe that people could spend eighty minutes hemming what she called dishcloths and they called tea towels, when they might be roistering and revelling through the Attic world. Soon she was to start reading Euripides' *Medea*; soon they were to start making cotton knickers.

At half-term Janet was moved up a year and lessons became more interesting. Now she had an excuse for her friendless state: you made a best friend from your own house and your own year during your first term and you stayed together for the rest of your schooldays, a married couple. Naturally everyone in her new form had already paired off. Her status was altered too. Instead of being mad, as in mentally disabled, she became mad, as in mad professor. Girls began to ask her for help with their prep. They were obliged to smile when they did this. She no longer had to give up her chocolate bar; her neat pigtails were earned by a few adroit French sentences. Her feeling of numbness receded. One day as she sat alone on her side of the tea-table and looked at the row of complacent unfriendly faces opposite her, framed by the window and the billowing sea beyond, she imagined a great octopus emerging from the waters and floundering up the cliff. In through the window it would burst, fling its tentacles round their necks and tow them all off, wiping the sly grins off their faces, back to the depths whence it came. She began to laugh. 'So what's the joke, Janet?' 'Nothing,' she said, and then, with a new daring, 'Nothing you would understand.'

She became aware that there were one or two other girls who were nearly as unpopular as herself. There was Ellen, a tiny, stunted creature who suffered from severe eczema and had to wear bandages which covered her arms and legs and neck. She scratched constantly and gave off a faint odour of putrefaction. Her life was a misery. Janet reflected that Raymond Dibdin would doubtless have wanted to shoot her. She thought of him with hatred; besides everything else, he had ruined Hallowe'en for her. Rhona had seen him being taken to the ambulance. 'His head was all swollen up; he looked like a whopping great turnip lantern,' she told Janet. Fortunately, at St Uncumba's Hallowe'en was not celebrated, for it was an evil, pagan ritual. Instead they lit an enormous bonfire on Guy Fawkes night and burned a human effigy. How they cheered and clapped as the guy smouldered, blazed up and sagged forward, collapsing inwards, horribly real. 'It's always an anxious moment, waiting for him to catch,' confided the housemistress. Janet watched the figures round the fire. Squat in their winter boots and heavy coats and scarves they looked like peasants from a Breughel painting; they were intent, mesmerised by the flames, by the pitiful burning figure. A mob, she thought, mob violence. She remembered the organ stop which was called Vox Populi. She wanted none of it.

She saw Ellen's glimmering, bandaged form away in the outer darkness; she was coughing and wheezing in the smoke, for she also suffered from asthma. 'Ellen doesn't seem well,' she said in responsible tones to Miss Smith. 'May I take her indoors?' 'Of course, Janet,' beamed the housemistress. 'What a thoughtful girl you are.' Janet could scarcely believe it was so easy to escape. Ellen could scarcely believe that someone had bothered about her plight. Clutching Janet's sleeve, she spluttered her way to the study room. Janet sat down firmly and opened her book. Ellen crouched over her inhaler in front of the gas fire. Every now and then Janet looked up and found Ellen gazing at her, eyes moist with gratitude. Oh God, she thought, I hope she doesn't want me to be her friend. Ellen had an official friend, a brutal hockey fanatic named Cynthia, the only other left-over new girl. Cynthia called Ellen 'Smellen'. Janet felt a monstrous urge to be unkind to Ellen, to obliterate that gratitude and establish her aloofness; but she knew that this would bring her to the level of the other girls; she would be one of the mob. Twitching with irritation, she bestowed a vague, non-committal smile on Ellen and plunged back into her book. A few days after

Ellen's parents removed her from the school; it was too much for her frail constitution.

This meant a worse fate for Janet. She and Cynthia were now forced into unholy union, a union which was to last for four more years. Cynthia was very good at games and very bad at lessons; Janet was the opposite. Each despised the other's abilities and let her know it. They had nothing in common save their mutual scorn. In grim silence they walked to school together through the windy streets, Janet panting to keep up. On the way back Cynthia would sing at the top of her voice and spin about like a dervish, squealing, her cloak whirling round her, to attract the attention of the grammar school boys as they meandered homewards; she was happy because the day's work was over. Janet scuttled along, with downcast eyes; her pigtails slapped her about the face. She dreaded the long cold evening, prep, charity knitting, the gleaming white walls of the dormitory where other girls huddled companionably together in their cubicles, giggling over their diaries. She tried to read, tried to sleep and yearned for Auchnasaugh.

At last the Christmas holidays came. Very early in the morning they were on the station platform. The air was vaporous, the sky mother of pearl. Circlets of ice crunched and melted under their feet. Then there was the anxious thrill of climbing on to the train – was it the right one? would it stop at the right place? had she lost her suitcases? would it ever start? – and the great surge of relief as it jolted into motion, the gathering speed, the landmarks, at last the great rusty dinosaur of the Forth Bridge. Janet remembered the old railway poster 'Over the Forth, To the North' and excitement rose in her, so that she could hardly breathe. On and on and over the Tay, and the first sight of the hills; tears welled in her eyes. The other girls had all gone now, some even wishing her 'Super hols, Janet'. No one lived so far north as she. Hector was there to meet her at Aberdeen station.

There was a sparsely decorated Christmas tree at the end of the platform. Looking at it, Hector observed, 'This will mean death to thousands of innocent birds.' Through falling snow they drove west into a hushed landscape. It was dark when they reached Auchnasaugh. The snow had stopped and the stars glittered in myriads. She had forgotten that the heavens held so many. She stood for a moment on the drive, straining after the intense silence of the hills, the damp pine scented air. She thought, 'I am alive again.'

When she went to see Lila she found the room in darkness; the fire spluttered low and fitful, illuminating only the inert shape of Mouflon. She shuffled cautiously across the room, sliding her feet as though walking through deep sand, lest she kick over any of the books, cups, glasses or ashtrays which she knew would be littered there. She reached the long table where the lamp stood. Blindly she stretched out her hands, feeling only empty air. Someone knocked on the window. Three times the knock came. 'Who's that?" she shouted. 'Wait a minute, I can't find the lamp' No one answered. Janet stood motionless, suddenly afraid. She heard footsteps retreating, crunching across the frozen grass. Her shaking hands found an object. Slowly she moved her fingers over it. The texture was delicate, soft like vellum or the skin on a baby's head. Her heart began to thump. She felt a broad plane like a brow, now cheeks, smooth as her own, but cold, cold. It was a head. It was a severed head. She lurched back from it, screeching.

Lila came gliding through the door and switched on the lamp: 'Janet, my dear, whatever is the matter?' On the table was that prize of prizes, a giant puffball. 'I kept it specially to show you. It's so rare to find one at this time of year.' Janet sat down abruptly; she was still shaking. 'Someone was knocking on the window. They ran away when they heard my voice.' 'Don't be absurd; it would just be a branch in the wind.' 'There isn't a wind. It's really still tonight.' 'Well, I shouldn't worry. If it doesn't worry me, it shouldn't worry you. Tell me about school.' Janet started to tell her. Lila poured herself a tumbler of whisky. Soon it was clear to Janet that Lila wasn't listening; she was gazing at Mouflon and her eyes were glassy. Everyone that evening had asked her what school was like, and Janet had willingly begun on either the official Enid Blyton version (for adults) or the dismal truth (for Francis, Rhona and Lila). In each case there was a brief show of keen interest from grown-ups, 'Oh, what fun it sounds! Of course, we were sure you would love it! Things have certainly changed since my day!' (Vera); 'An excellent opportunity' (Hector); 'Aye, it was fair time you were awa' frae those great gowking lads' (Nanny). There was no interest at all from her siblings, 'How dreary. Tell me no more. If I were you I'd jump over the cliff' (Francis); 'Oh yes, good. Have you heard about my stick insect?' (Rhona). She heard Vera telling Constance, who was staying for Christmas, how pleased she was that Janet had made friends with Cynthia: 'She sounds such a sensible, wholesome sort of girl, a good influence.' 'Yes,' said Constance, assuming her didactic manner, 'it's so interesting that even quite young children will choose a friend who is entirely different.' 'Attraction of opposites, I believe it's called,' said Hector helpfully. 'No, Hector, that's really rather crude. It's something infinitely more profound, that yearning for completion which we find in Plato. The desire and pursuit of the whole.' Then, as usual, they drifted off into their own compelling lives, Constance and Vera to the nursery where Constance liked to observe Caro ('The infant is primitive'), Hector to his motoring magazine, Rhona and Francis to their vivarium, and now Lila into her whisky and her vague, unfocused sorrow.

Janet now realised that, inconceivable as it seemed to her, life at Auchnasaugh had moved on without her. Her absence had made no difference. But without Auchnasaugh she had been maimed, deprived of her identity, living in two dimensions only.

At Christmas Janet read, as she always did, in the village

church. She read from Isaiah, 'The wilderness and the solitary place shall be glad for them . . .' and Francis sang 'O for the wings of a dove'. Every year this miracle occurred; cynical, unkind, freckled Francis stood there, his eyes piously raised to the ceiling and, by the beauty of his voice, transported her to that shadowed chasm where the restless dove fluttered and soared, searching, driven by its tragic quest for something it would never find, something which perhaps did not exist. Even the village women were moved; with brightening eyes they leant forward for a moment, their chapped hands gripping the pew front. This year, however, as he sang 'In the wilderness, build me a nest', his voice suddenly swooped downwards as though a gramophone needle had stuck and skidded. 'And remain there, forever at rest' emerged in a jolting, husky baritone. With icy self-control he sang on, and God rewarded him by restoring his soprano until the end of the service.

'Never again,' he boomed in his new voice as he and Janet trudged homeward through the snow. The others had gone ahead in the car; Rhona was excused from walking because she would be so helpful with preparations for the festive meal. 'Never again. This, Janet, is the onset of manhood. I shall grow a beard and keep birds in it, like Edward Lear.' For a moment Janet felt sorry for him. But only for a moment. At the top of the drive his labrador came to meet them. She wallowed joyously in the deep drifts, tunnelled out, flicking the powdery white off her muzzle, then swaggered up, ducking and bowing. 'O Celia,' said Francis. 'What a seal you are!' He hugged her. Watching him, Janet felt again that odd flicker of pity. How he loved his dog! How he loved his cacti and his slow-worm! Did he love anything else? She thought not.

After Twelfth Night they took down the Christmas tree which had stood so proudly in the hall, by the foot of the stairs, its gold and blue and crimson lights vying with the great stained-glass window; the dying white cockatoo in his luminous circle of leaves seemed to hover above it like the paraclete and at times the blood drops from his breast were scattered over the piled and gaudy presents. A bonfire was built and Nanny seized her chance to rid the nursery of the dogs' armchairs. A couple of days later Hector and Francis had replaced them with others of almost equal dereliction; there was no shortage of such furniture at Auchnasaugh.

One afternoon Janet was returning from the stables through the trodden snow; it was twilight and the sky was the soft intense blue which occurs at the close of sunny days in the cold of winter. The stars and crescent of moon were already brilliant and in the air was a haunting sweetness, no sooner sensed than gone, a harbinger of spring, no matter how long yet the days of darkness. She saw that Lila was sitting in one of the chairs on top of the bonfire, staring at the black humps of the hills. Janet climbed up and sat beside her in the other chair. Lila did not speak; suddenly Janet realised that she was weeping. Great tears rolled down her cheeks, followed by a sooty wake of mascara. 'Sorry,' she said, 'Pay no attention. It's nothing.' She took a quarter-bottle of whisky from her pocket and drank straight out of it. 'Well, it's almost nothing.' Her voice became steadier. 'It's only money. I have no money left and I need some.' Janet was astonished. Money was never mentioned; she had never thought about it. She never had any herself; Hector and Vera sometimes said mysteriously that they were going to give the older children pocket money because it would teach them about the world, but they never seemed to have any loose change on the appointed day and no one really cared. You would have had to go to the village to spend it and the only things they ever wanted from the village were bottles of Barr's Iron Brew and long black straps of liquorice. These were provided anyhow, in an erratic way, but often on Saturdays. Now, looking at Lila's woebegone face and the bottle gripped in her shaking hand, she could, as so often, think of nothing to say. 'Oh dear,' she mumbled, wishing that she hadn't climbed on to the bonfire. 'Oh gosh!'

'How now, thou secret, black and midnight hag!' came Francis' voice. They both jumped. There was a small bright explosion in the shadow beneath them. 'Thank you, *mesdames*, and God bless you,' he said, winding on the film of his new Christmas camera and sauntering off. In time to come he was to make a brief reputation for himself with this photograph, and an accompanying article in which he claimed that he had discovered a place in the hinterlands of the Rhine valley where witches were still burnt. 'After all, we know now that we can believe anything of the Germans.' The thin moon was lucent in the background, curving beyond the filigree of the giant hogweed grove; the two white frightened faces stared out from the pyre, with gaping mouths and glittering eyes.

Lila said that she was hungry. They went to her room and Janet watched her prepare her frugal meal. First she chopped a wizened tomato on the cover of a handy book; then she removed a grimy tub of cottage cheese from the mantelpiece. She put a blob of this on the palm of her hand and added the tomato; then she wandered about the room, daintily eating it with her fingers and dripping tomato pips and squelching globules on to the floor. She never sat down to eat. She said that she found it boring, a waste of time. Vera had remarked, not only once, that Lila dwelt in a waste of time. 'And spirits,' she sometimes added. But Lila had told Janet that meals at tables reminded her of Fergus, and especially of Fergus's last supper. Janet had found this a moving and noble confidence, had felt honoured to receive it.

At dinner that evening, with great boldness, she addressed Hector and Vera. 'Lila seems to be very worried. She says she hasn't any money. Couldn't you maybe give her some?' Vera's features tightened into icy fury. 'Good heavens, that woman has squandered a fortune, and on what, one may wonder. Well of course, it's the whisky. She's better off just living here and doing without it. She has everything she wants here, all provided. She should count herself lucky; not many people would put up with her. How dare she go complaining to you. I shall speak to her about this.' Hector supported Vera, 'You shouldn't meddle in grown-up people's affairs, Janet. Lila has made her bed and now she must lie on it.' Vera stalked off to Lila's room. In a little while she returned, her face slightly flushed, her eyes gleaming with vindictive satisfaction. No more was said.

Janet felt sick and treacherous. She decided that she must apologise to Lila. As she went down the dark stone corridor she heard the door from the boiler room creak open. Someone was moving stealthily along the unlit passage towards her. 'Lila?' she called; there was no answer. 'Francis?' No answer. Then she heard the footsteps retreat softly, the boiler room door swing to, silence. She panted into Lila's room. 'There was someone out there, they wouldn't answer, and now they've gone! It was horrible. Do you think we should get the policeman?' Lila was standing at the window, clasping Mouflon. She turned and stared at Janet; her eyes were black and opaque. 'I've told you before; it's only the wind. I expect the outside door wasn't shut properly. Do please stop fussing. I have things to do now, and it's time you were in bed. You've made enough trouble today. Goodnight.' Janet withdrew. She was shocked; Lila had never before spoken to her like that. It was clear that there was as little point in trying to help people as there was in telling them the truth. You would be misunderstood or disbelieved and it would all be worse than ever.

One icy January afternoon, under a baleful sky, Lila left Auchnasaugh. All morning, unwilling kitchen staff had been trudging in and out bearing sagging cardboard boxes of books, mildewed hat boxes, brass-bound trunks, the leather frayed and peeling off in strips which flapped in the wind. Then came Mouflon's great pile of fur coats; only Jim could be persuaded to carry these out; he laid them on the back seat of the car, creating an instant and intolerable miasma, whose separate elements could not be defined, but which breathed unspeakable corruption and the mortification of feline skin and bone. Vera, briskly supervisory, shook a whole tin of Elizabeth Arden Apple Blossom talcum powder over them. Francis said that he now knew the perfume of post lapsarian paradise. 'Oh do be quiet, Francis. And stop being so affected. Go and see if Lila's ready; your father will be impatient.'

Vera had arranged a kind of job for Lila. She was to go to Vera's unmarried Aunt Maisie as a lady companion and occasional cook; for this she would receive a handsome salary; Maisie's family had had enough of her and wished to lead lives of their own. 'So really we're killing two birds with one stone,' Vera announced in chilling triumph. Maisie lived in a small modern house on the outskirts of Edinburgh. 'So convenient and cosy, which frankly is a consideration, Lila, when you're not quite so young as you were. And you can always go and look at *things* in the Botanical Gardens. And there's the theatre, and the Festival! Really I quite envy you.' Lila had shown no feeling of any kind, had barely spoken; passively she had stowed away her possessions. Now she emerged, tenderly cradling her cat, who was swaddled in more furs. She had made herself look startlingly different for her new rôle. Instead of her habitual trailing, flapping garments, black for most of the year, white for summer sunshine, she was attired in twinset, pearls and a lovat-green Hebe Sports suit; its box-pleated skirt swung crisply over her tattered black stockings and stained velvet slippers. She had forgotten to provide for her lower extremities. Her ragged dark locks were confined by a Jacqmar silk headscarf, firmly knotted under the chin. Peering myopically in the mirror, in the dimness of her room, with shaking hand she had applied liberal quantities of mascara, rouge, powder and lipstick, for a healthy competent glow. Her cheeks flamed as though she had just been slapped. Then she had sneezed, so that the mascara made streaks all around her eyes like clown makeup. She looked like a murderous parody of a lady companion.

Vera's cheek hovered a glacial fraction off Lila's. 'You must come back, of course, whenever you want to, though I'm sure you'll be far too comfortable there to stir! Your rooms will always be here for you.' The car moved off, the children waved; Lila ignored them, staring bleakly ahead. Janet went to look at the strange, denuded mushroom chamber, now flooded with harsh winter light. The men were dragging out crates of empty bottles and Vera was telling them that the curtains and carpets were to be put straight on the bonfire. 'Everything out. And then we'll have it painted; a pretty shell pink, would you say, Janet?' Janet had nothing to say, nothing at all. And indeed she could not speak.

Janet returned to school on the train, relishing the first two hours of the journey, when she was alone. She could still see the hills massed and remote to the west, to the north, guarding her dream kingdom. But already, even before they rattled over the Tay and into the flat coastlands, she was aware that she was slipping into that sense of half life, of a two-dimensional existence. Troops of girls got on at Edinburgh. To her surprise they greeted her and some came and sat in her compartment. They chattered among themselves and Janet stared out of the window, thinking of what she had left, trying not to think of what lay ahead, trying not to think of Lila. She concentrated on Rhona, who had been forced to practise the piano for forty minutes every day during the holidays, including Christmas and New Year's Day. Vera was determined that she was musical. Francis was musical, Rhona and Francis had so much in common, therefore Rhona must be musical. The fact that Janet was not musical didn't count. Janet took pleasure in the memory of Rhona grimly thumping out a lugubrious melody whose title was 'Myrtle the Turtle'. You moved on to 'Myrtle the Turtle' after you had mastered 'Rabbits in the Corn'. 'Rhona tries hard but makes little progress' had been the piano teacher's verdict at the end of the autumn term. It had been worse for Janet, who had not tried at all and had made no progress. 'Myrtle the Turtle' had been her musical débâcle.

> *Myrtle the Turtle is just a slow poke,*
> *Myrtle the Turtle thinks life is a joke.*

She would not, could not get it right. It made her feel ill. Finally she had knocked the sheet of music over and the piano lid had slammed down on her knuckles and she had burst into tears. The music teacher had also burst into tears and that very afternoon had persuaded Hector and Vera that Janet should give up piano lessons. Janet urged Rhona to do the same, but Rhona was not like that. 'She's a sticker,' said Constance. Janet laughed aloud now, thinking of nimble-fingered Rhona's dismal fate. The other girls glanced uneasily at her, saw that she was not laughing at them, exchanged winks, rolled their eyes, and resumed their chatter.

But nothing could assuage the cold, familiar dereliction of night in the dormitory, with the sea booming below the cliff and the sea wind whipping the sleet against the windows. Then she could not ward off thoughts of Lila, the enormity of her exile and her own part in it, her treachery, her guilt.

The days passed, merging without colour, as the melancholy sea merged into the melancholy sky. She was finding ways of coping with life in the boarding house; not only was she in demand over matters of prep but she had discovered that she could make people laugh by telling them exaggerated stories of her incompetence in every aspect of the day's routine, and the dire consequences it provoked. Work remained an exception to all this. It was her pride and joy, of necessity secret, for no one cared to hear about it. Lessons were regarded as the tedious, time wasting price you had to pay for the thrills of sport, the pleasures of gossip and girlish society. Janet learnt never to mention the intense excitement which she found in Dido's doomed love or Medea's implacable heart. She took a perverse delight in caring for anything the others found especially wearisome. Sometimes she still went too far, as when she had listened vaguely to endless moaning about the subjunctive, its futility, its stupidity, the drab impossibility of learning it; unable to contain herself she announced in patronising tones, 'I *love* the subjunctive. You just don't understand what it's for. It's subtle, it makes the meaning different, or it gives you a clue to the rest of the sentence. And it's perfectly easy to learn.' They were silent, staring at her with loathing. 'I call my cats subjunctives,' she finished. This was true; she felt the word had a wonderfully feline shape and sound. But even as she spoke she knew that she should never have said this. 'And I suppose you call your parents past participles?' 'Or ablative absolutes?' 'Bet her brother's called Gerry, short for Gerund.' 'God, how pukey can you get?' 'Show-off, show-off, pukey little show-off.' Soon it was round the whole school. 'Janet's family all talk Latin to each other and wear togas.' Girls lay in wait for her. 'Miaow, miaow subjunctive,' they squealed, leaping out of the shrubbery. The queenly head of house drew her aside: 'You will get nowhere at St Uncumba's by that sort of behaviour. We are simply not impressed. Life here is about give and take, caring and contributing. That's why games are so important; you learn the rules, you obey them and you move in harmony with your team. If you make your own rules you let the whole side down. Contrary to what you clearly believe, you are not superior to the rest of us. In fact, you are a rather silly, very conceited little girl and if you don't make a huge effort now you will never fit in, here or anywhere else. I shall be watching you.'

For a week or two Janet crept about looking humble. She

complimented Cynthia on her tackling, she stood in the front line of the yelling crowd at hockey, matches; she listened admiringly when girls boasted of their boyfriends or described the excitement of the Boxing Day meet. The phrase from Oscar Wilde 'The unspeakable in pursuit of the uneatable', which she had gleefully copied down for use at such a time, remained silent in her notebook. She even pretended that she wished she was a member of the Pony Club. Gradually her crime was forgotten, if not forgiven. It was Janet's view that forgetting was the only possible way of forgiving. She did not believe in forgiveness; the word had no meaning. At last she was reinstated in her rôles of idiot jester and brainbox (pronounced as though it meant leper). Only at night under the bedclothes did she allow herself the tiny luxury of muttering two expressions favoured by characters in Greek tragedy: 'Woe for me in my misery' and 'My woe is their laughter'.

To placate Cynthia further she took up riding at school. Red-faced, shrill-voiced Mrs Jarvis led them out at great speed, trotting, trotting, trotting along the slippery roads, regardless of weather. Sometimes they performed exercises in her field instead. Cynthia excelled at these and was much admired by Mrs Jarvis. Janet hated them; it was just like Pony Club, which she had attended once, as a spectator only. The riding out was not much better; Mrs Jarvis harangued her pupils, sometimes reducing them to tears, and effectively destroying the little pleasure such outings on a February afternoon might provide. One day as they clattered and slithered down the steep road to the stables, they met an old woman and her obese spaniel. The aged, puffing dog shrank back against its mistress's legs; it cringed and shuddered. Its mournful eyes rolled in mute terror and yet there was about it a passivity, as if it accepted that it might be crushed and trampled by those flailing hooves; this would be its lot, and it would not resist. Janet was overwhelmed by pity; something was stirring in her memory. Then it came to her; It was Lila's face. This was how she looked after Vera had been talking to her. She remembered Vera's special satisfied look.

Back at the stables, as she made her way out into the yard, Mrs Jarvis suddenly called to her, 'Watch that horse'. Obediently Janet stood and gazed at the rounded chestnut hindquarters and the swishing chestnut tail. Nothing happened; it was boring; her feet were very cold. She became aware that Cynthia and the others were giggling at the doorway. 'Come on, Janet, whatever are you doing? We'll be late for tea' 'Mrs Jarvis said I was to watch this horse.' 'She meant keep away from it, not stand staring at it, you idiot.' 'What did I tell you?' Cynthia added, to the faces by the door. 'Gormless. Completely gormless.'

Janet began to hate the sea. There was so much of it, flowing, counter flowing, entering other seas, slyly furthering its interests beyond the mind's reckoning; no wonder it could pass itself off as sky; it was infinite, a voracious marine confederacy. She saw how it diminished people as they walked along the shore; they lost their identity, were no more than pebbles, part of the sea's scheme. Once there had been a great forest below the cliffs; there the hairy mammoth had browsed and raised his trunk and trumpeted. There had been mountain crags and deep, sweet valleys of gentle herbivores. The sea had come and taken them. Later it had taken churches too, and on wild nights you could listen for their bells. The air was loud enough with bells already; Janet preferred to listen for the hairy mammoth.

On Sunday in church she sang with fervour

> *O hear us when we cry to thee*
> *For those in peril on the sea*

The minister often chose a maritime text: 'Out of the depths have I cried unto thee, O Lord', or 'Many waters cannot quench love'. The wonderful words were almost enough to make Janet believe in God. At Christmas too, the starry sky and the beauty of language and music caused a great surge of mystic yearning in her; then Mr McConochie would harangue them, remind them of their unworthiness and guilt, the innocent babe born to die on their behalf. 'Sighing, crying, Bleeding, dying, Shut in the stone cold tomb' they sang and the glory faded to heartbreak and desolation, the bleak light of afternoon.

She thought now of something which had happened the previous summer. Early one morning four students from Edinburgh University had stolen a fishing boat from the harbour and merrily set course for deep waters. The sun, an enormous orange disc, cleared the misty horizon, the air was still, the sea sparkled. They dived from the high bows and swam and frolicked. Then they realized that they had forgotten to put a ladder down; there was nothing, no rope, no lifebelt, only the steep black sides of the boat, slippery and glistening in the cold sunbeams and a great stretch of empty sea. They all perished; the paintwork was scored and runnelled by their fingernails. 'Many waters cannot quench love.' That could be so; the sea nevertheless had taken them and there had been no help from God. Some of course said that it was a judgement; they should not have taken the boat. Mr McConochie was of this opinion; he had discussed the incident with her parents outside his church one Sunday morning: 'Aye, well, they kent the rules fine and they broke them. The commandment is there to be obeyed, whether ye be a floozy wee student or the Lord High Advocate. Ye'll recall the words of Knox "And if thou wilt not, flatter not thyself; the same justice remaineth in God to punish thee, Scotland, and thee, Edinburgh, in especial, that before punished the land of Judah and the city of Jerusalem."'

It did not seem to Janet that this was justice; it was a most cruel quenching of merriment, and there was little enough of gaiety or recklessness around those rocky shores. She thought of that moment when Lorna Doone's father, riding ahead of the family carriage up a mountain road in Italy, turns in his saddle, doffs his plumy hat and bows, laughing; then he spurs his horse into a gallop; round the bend they vanish, to plummet over a precipice. There seemed no place for gallantry or romance among Calvinists. They would say that he should have looked where he was going. Clearly he had not been one of the Elect who were distinguished by perseverance or grim stoicism, and were offered secret divine assistance. But another memory came to her. At the top of a great flight of rickety steps two small boys had paused; the sun shone down on them; they looked back at her and waved and then they vanished into a black void. She had felt no pity for them then, did not feel any now.

Two by two in their prickly tweed coats and their damp felt hats the girls of St Uncumba's marched in crocodile through empty streets back to their boarding houses. Bells were clamorous. Cynthia ogled the occasional male passer-by and sang a revolting song about babies,

> *Twenty tiny fingers, twenty tiny toes*
> *Two angel faces, each with a turned up nose . . .*

Janet was able to ignore her because she had discovered a beautiful new word in her Latin dictionary – *stillicidium*, the dripping of rain water from roofs and gables. It had stopped raining now, and the gaunt, steeply-pitched stone houses offered satisfying illustrations of the word's unique fitness for its purpose. How she wished she could share her pleasure with Cynthia; as it was she dared not even whisper the word aloud.

As they approached the War Memorial, Cynthia's pace slackened. 'Hang back,' she hissed at Janet. There was a small sweet shop open on Sundays and Cynthia planned to break the law. She would go in and she would buy a slab of Highland toffee. Janet was to keep watch; it would be worth it. The rest of the crocodile swung round the corner on to the cliff road. Cynthia sidled through the shop doorway. Janet stood with thumping heart, trying to look casual, certain that every distant figure was an oncoming member of staff. The penalties for breaking a school rule were severe; for going into a shop they could be suspended for weeks. They might be picking up germs which would spread through the school like wildfire. Most importantly they might be picking up the polio germ and bringing death and disablement. Besides, men went into shops and they must never, ever speak to men. The girls were given to understand that all men seethed with uncontrollable desire for them and the smallest encouragement would lead to murder. Or worse. Only their fathers might enter the sacred precincts of St Uncumba's. Uncles were out of the question. Janet wished Cynthia would hurry up. A group of people had gathered round the War Memorial. She watched them uneasily. They paid no attention to her; they were looking at something on the pavement. Janet edged nearer. They were laughing. A pigeon was walking in slow circles on the shining cobbles; it wore a little paper hat. How strange, thought Janet; perhaps it was a circus bird, a lawless Sunday entertainer. Then she saw that blood was dripping from its beak; its eye was dull, its gait unsteady. The top of its head had gone and what she had taken for a paper hat was the membrane which covered its brain. Someone picked up a stick and prodded it. It flounced sideways, toppled and regained its balance. Janet looked at the grinning faces; she looked at the bird, so meek and dignified, accepting its ruined life without complaint, silent and harmless.

'Get out of my way,' she yelled. Panting, she shoved her way through the throng and grabbed the bird. It settled passively in her cupped hands. She ran back to the shop. Cynthia appeared. 'Throw it away, Janet. It's going to die anyway.' 'There's a vet round the corner, we can take it there; we can't just leave it. Those people are hurting it.' 'Look, it's only a pigeon.' 'Shut up, shut up,' shrieked Janet; tears of outrage blurred her eyes. 'I'm going to the vet. Are you coming or not?' 'Oh for heaven's sake, all right then. But there's no point.'

Janet rang the vet's shiny brass doorbell. No one came. She beat on the door with the shiny brass knocker. She shouted through the letter box, 'Hurry up, please, please hurry up.' Suddenly the door was whisked open. A woman stood there glaring at them. 'How dare you make a racket like that. On a Sunday too. What do you want' Janet held out the pigeon. 'You've not made an appointment. You can't see the vet. In any case he's not here. You'd best give that thing a knock on the head. Now be off with you and stop wasting my time.' She slammed the door. The pigeon was soft and warm, nestled in Janet's hands, but blood flowed more freely now from its beak and it had begun to tremble. She could feel its tiny heart flickering. 'Well,' said Cynthia, 'either we chuck it over the cliff or we bash it on the head; it's worse for it to go on suffering.' 'Yes,' said Janet. 'Yes.' She looked at the bird and knew that she could not end its life, no matter how right, how necessary this was. She tried to imagine swinging it against a wall or smashing its brain with a stone and she felt all strength ebb from her limbs. She leant against the vet's railings, gasping. 'Oh *God*,' she wailed. 'Right, that's it. Give it to me,' commanded Cynthia. She took the bird and walked quickly behind the house. In a moment she was back. 'It didn't feel a thing, honestly.' 'But we must bury it,' sobbed Janet. 'Look, I've buried it; I put some earth over it. And we're going to be late back if we don't rush.' A bell tolled a single solemn note, a death knell. 'My God, it's one o'clock. Come *on*.' Janet did not believe that Cynthia had buried the pigeon but she was finished, without resource. Obediently she followed her. Cynthia explained their lateness by saying that Janet had felt faint and ill. 'I was really quite worried, Miss Smith. You can see how she's shaking now. Oh, she had a nose bleed too. Her coat's in a bit of a state.' 'Well done, Cynthia.'

Janet was packed off to bed where she continued to shake. She thought many thoughts, and the worst of all was that hateful Cynthia had had the courage to perform an act of mercy; she had failed through cowardice. 'Well done, Cynthia.' Her teeth chattered. She slept. When she woke it was still light. Downstairs someone was practising the flute. Four o'clock on a wan Sunday afternoon in March; a bad time, a time that was endless.

CHAPTER EIGHT

In April, when Janet returned to Auchnasaugh, she was astonished and overjoyed to find that Lila was there. In fact, Lila had scarcely been away. The shock of the journey to Edinburgh and the unfamiliar central heating in the little house had proved too great for Mouflon and for three agonising days Lila had watched him die. She ignored Maisie and her nervous fluttering cries, her pleas for help up the stairs, for tea and shortbread, for a friendly chat. She sat in her room with a bottle of whisky, feeding the old cat hourly from a dropper; she entered the kitchen only to warm milk for him. She left the house only to fetch more whisky, which she put down on Maisie's grocery bill. On the third day, when Mouflon was stiff and cold and dead she put him in the fridge, to await their return to Auchnasaugh, where he must be buried. Then she took the kitchen scissors from their hook above the sink ('A place for everything and everything in its place,' Maisie had quavered as she showed her round). She began to cut her hair off, sawing and wrenching at the resistant wiry locks. Long black hanks and twists drifted into the sink, blocking the drain outlet. The scissors were blunt. She hurled them across the room and seized a carving knife. Maisie heard the clatter and came creeping hopefully down the stairs. When she saw Lila her fey, small face lit up. 'Och that's good,' she said. 'Now you're settled in at last. We'll have a nice cup of coffee.' Lila stared blankly at her and went on slashing at her hair. Maisie, tremulously removing a bottle of Camp coffee from the cupboard, saw the sudden gleam of the knife in the neon strip light; she looked again at Lila, gasped and sat down. The bottle smashed to the floor. Maisie began to cry. In bustled her cleaning woman, Dora. 'Oh dear, what a mess. Never you mind, Miss Carstairs, it's only a wee bit of broken glass, dinna fash, we'll have it cleared in a minute.' She saw Lila. Her tone changed, 'And what may you be doing? I'll thank you to put that knife down. And if you'd be kind enough to move perhaps I could reach the brush and dustpan and perhaps I could get the milk for madam's hot drink.' Lila stood with her back against the fridge door. 'Go away,' she whispered, 'Go away.' 'I will do no such thing,' retorted Dora; she tugged at the door handle with one hand and grabbed at the knife with the other. Lila bit her arm. The fridge door swung open, revealing Mouflon's outstretched pinkly lustrous figure and sightless glare. Dora shrieked, slammed it shut and rushed from the room. She telephoned the doctor and the policeman before returning to the kitchen. Maisie was rocking from side to side on her chair; her eyes were shut; she sang a little ditty, beating time on the table:

> *Tompkin will you dance?*
> *Tompkin will you sing?*
> *Dance then, dance, you merry little men . . .*

Lila sat on the top of the fridge with her legs dangling down over the door. She still held the knife. 'I am in mourning,' she announced. 'I must go home.' 'Aye, that you must,' said Dora, 'And any minute now the car will be here. We'll give you a hand with your things. Lucky you haven't unpacked. Now just hand me the knife, there's a good wee lass.' Lila dropped the knife. 'Could you, very sweetly, pour me a tiny drop of whisky?' she asked in a soft, girlish voice. Dora's heart melted. 'Aye, gladly, and I'll join you. Just a wee dram; I think we both need it.' Then she remembered the approaching policeman and doctor. 'We'll take it in the breakfast cups. Just for the look of things, ye ken.' She glanced at the elfin, melodious figure swaying over the table. 'Herself won't mind. She's off in her own world, bless her. The best place tae be. Well now, here's tae us. And a wee Doc and Doris afore ye gang awa'!' Lila understood almost nothing of what she said, but she raised her cup and drank, although she could not smile, and did not speak.

Maisie was indeed in her own world, and farther than they thought. She was sitting on a lawn in Kashmir, under the greenish-black sweetness of a deodar tree. Her ayah's arms were tight and loving and rocked her; she wore her muslin dress with rosebuds and the pink sash. Beside them on the grass lay the sweeper's enchanting baby, clad only in a little shirt and a hat like a tea cosy. At a small distance the sweeper's wife sat cross-legged, her dark face tranquil and beaming. Maisie sang to the baby. The baby rolled and wriggled and laughed. How he laughed! Each time he laughed her ayah hugged her tighter and kissed her, and she laughed too. The heavy perfumed branches curved down and hid them from the house. The sun dazzled and spotted through them. So secret, so happy. Such memories she had, but no one wanted to hear them. And tea chests of sepia photographs, but no one wanted to see them. *'Dance then, dance, you merry little men . . .'* The sweet small feet beat the warm air; in the shining black eyes she could see her own reflection, and above, the great dark tree.

So it was that Lila returned to Auchnasaugh, silent and sedated, in the policeman's Black Maria. Grimly the kitchen staff brought in her possessions; they were relieved to find that the old fur coats had been left in Edinburgh. Dora, valiant and fortified by her unaccustomed morning whisky, had said that she would burn them. Later she regretted this and was obliged to take another wee dram before dragging them out to the patch of frozen garden. She soaked them in paraffin, stood back and tossed a lighted rag into the midst. A fireball shot towards the heavens, there was a mighty blaze and a dense pall of stinking smoke. 'It's a braw send off for the old cat,' she heard herself remark. This wouldn't do. No more whisky. She hurled the bottle on to the fire and went in for a good strong cup of tea with Maisie.

Meanwhile at Auchnasaugh Lila's rooms were being reassembled. Vera found some suitably moth-eaten and dingy curtains and a dank old roll of doggy carpet; thank goodness she hadn't yet painted the walls. What a waste of their time all that cleaning and fumigation had been. She was tense with fury. 'I don't believe she ever intended to make the slightest effort to build a life for herself,' she said to Hector. 'After all I've done for her. It is absolutely too bad.' Hector took a more philosophical view. 'It doesn't really matter. Truth to tell, I didn't feel too happy about her going to Edinburgh; she's never lived anywhere like that and she's too old to change her ways. Just let's leave her in peace. I'll sort something out for her.' By this Vera knew he meant that he would give Lila an allowance, to be squandered on whisky and cigarettes and tomatoes. She was too angry to argue, and at times she recognised in Hector a stubbornness greater than her own. This was such a time.

Lila had ignored everyone when she arrived. Her cat now rested in a deep drawer lined with blue velvet which she had removed from the Sheraton sideboard in Maisie's dining room, fancying that an indigo background would show Mouflon to advantage. No one had noticed when she carried it out, draped in black lace, to the policeman's car. No one noticed at all until it was too late. At Auchnasaugh Lila went straight down to the terrace garden, where animals were buried; erect and queenly, she glided over the hard-packed snow; she scarcely left a footprint. The policeman followed her, bearing the shrouded coffin. He laid it carefully on the frozen ground. Vera sent Francis down to help. 'Be quick. Otherwise goodness knows what she'll make that policeman do next. And if she makes the grave herself she's certain to dig up one of the dogs.' Francis appeared reluctantly, with a spade. The policeman departed. Lila and Francis chipped hopelessly at the unyielding snow. It was almost dusk and the crows and rooks were calling harshly as they drifted over a leaden sky, towards the woods. A cold wind stirred the ivy on the terrace wall. 'Maybe we could leave him until tomorrow?' suggested Francis. 'You can do what you please,' said Lila, giving him a long look of fathomless scorn. 'I know, I'll fetch Jim.' Francis and Jim brought the huge Aga kettles, full of boiling water. For an hour they clambered and slithered up and down the frozen path, filling and re-filling. Darkness fell. The snow melted away, hissing and steaming; at last the ground softened; they could begin to dig. Layer upon layer, the earth yielded to them. Now under the wavering beam of the torch, incompetently held by Lila, a capacious burial chamber lay ready. They had not disturbed the dogs' eternal sleep, but they had brought to the surface the skeleton of a goldfish; within its delicate structure lay the unmistakable spine of a smaller fish. 'Aha!' said Francis. 'One of life's mysteries is solved.' He turned chattily to his companions, 'I always thought there was something odd, fishy even, if I may so put it, in Hannibal dying on the day that Marius disappeared.' He laughed as a new thought came to him. 'Hannibal, posthumously known as Cannibal!' There was stony silence from Jim and Lila. Then, 'You can both go now,' said Lila. 'Not a word of thanks, of course,' Francis told Janet later. 'And we missed the only good bit. I was hoping for some serious liturgy. Or at least some keening and wailing.' 'You have no heart, Francis,' said Janet. 'That's as may be. Have you?'

April was a winter month at Auchnasaugh. The snow on the ground was dispersing, but all along the sides of the roads great frozen ramparts of it jutted out, discoloured and splattered with mud. It was an ugly, bitter time of year. Some days the windows were still blotted by whirling snowflakes, the glen muted. 'The last throes of winter,' they said, each time this happened. It was harder than usual to keep warm. The damp of the thaw crept through the stone floors, up the stone walls. They shivered by the fire, made endless cups of tea to warm their hands. The Aga sulked and fumed: Miss Wales emerged choking and spluttering from the kitchen and handed in her notice. No longer could she cope; her chest couldn't take it. Hector consoled Vera by reminding her that Miss Wales did this every year: 'As soon as she sees some blue sky, she'll be all right.' The bath water, never more than tepid, was now constantly cold, and flooding burns and reservoirs seeped rich red mud into the pipes so that the taps seemed to pour forth blood. A mean whipping wind whined and skirmished about the castle, now this way, now that, slamming doors, tearing at hats and scarves, whisking the dogs' ears inside out. The cats refused to go outside at all. It was a prime time for Jeyes fluid. Only the wild duck enjoyed themselves, swimming ostentatiously across the lawn or sporting upside down in the lagoons of the drive. Jim was deprived of his usual pursuits, both murderous and horticultural, for the tractor foundered in the deep mud and the earth lay waterlogged or snowbound; he gratified himself by laying poison for the rats. Their distended, bloated corpses began to appear in the puddles. You had to watch where you stepped in your wellingtons. One day a battlement, freighted with melting snow, fell off and nearly hit him as he spread dried blood on the grass.

Janet considered the matter of spring with a pang of longing. She remembered the vivid crocuses, purple, yellow and white, of her early childhood. Oh, for some colour in the landscape. Then she felt guilty; she could scarcely believe that she had made a criticism of Auchnasaugh. She squashed the memory. Soon, in May, there would be the daffodils, thousands of them. People in these parts did not use the word 'spring'. They said 'the end of winter' or 'the beginning of summer' or they used the month's name; winter ebbed into summer, there seemed no transitional period, none of the joyous awakening so favoured by verse and song. Janet felt that this season, as described by the English, brought out the worst in them.

> *Spring, the sweet spring, is the year's pleasant king;*
> *Then blooms each thing, then maids dance in a ring.*

Not here, they don't, not likely, she thought with grim satisfaction. Even Shakespeare was afflicted:

> *It was a lover and his lass*
> *With a hey and a ho and hey nonny no . . .*

and worse still,

> *When birds do sing hey ding a dong ding . . .*

She imagined herself coolly addressing the bard, 'And tell me, pray, just what birds do you have in mind?' Even Polly could sing better than that. In fact, Polly could sometimes sing '*Allons, enfants de la patrie*'. That was the kind of stuff you expected from people like the Dibdins, not from the author of *Macbeth*.

Lulu's birthday fell at the end of April, just before term time. Vera took them all to the zoo in her new car, a Triumph convertible. Janet didn't want to go. She dreaded the journey and she did not care to leave Auchnasaugh at any time. Nor did she take pleasure in other people's birthdays. This one had been more than usually provoking because Hector and Vera had given Lulu her very own shaggy black Shetland pony. Janet felt that ponies belonged to her personal area of expertise which she did not want to share with anyone. They were invading her territory. She also feared that Rosie might lose status to this upstart. So when Vera asked her to help prepare the pony for the great moment when Lulu would first see him, she refused. Vera was painting his hooves gold in the dining room; Janet said this was bad for him; poison would seep into his bloodstream. Vera hung red baubles and twined green ribbons in his mane and tail. Janet said the baubles would break and he would get glass in his feet. Janet also said that everyone knew Shetland ponies were totally untrustworthy; no one in their senses bought them for little children. Vera flung the dandy brush at her. 'Out!' she screeched, 'Just get out!'

Janet wandered off humming an insouciant hymn tune. Once she was out of earshot she sulked and brooded. She knew she was behaving horribly, she knew that she was indeed horrible, a despicable compound of arrogance, covetousness and self-centred rage. She was like one of those seething, stinking mud spouts which boil up in Iceland and lob burning rocks at passers-by. She felt guilt for blighting Vera's pleasure and excitement; she felt shame. Her shame and guilt only made her angrier. Where would it end? Her heart was pounding; any moment she might burst. And after everything, Lulu, in her ecstatic joy, pronounced that the pony's name was to be Blackie. Blackie! Not Satan, not Lucifer, not Pluto, not even Midnight, but Blackie! It was as well for her that Janet was speechless. Anyhow the morning's events should put paid to her presence on the zoo trip. But after lunch Hector drew her aside: 'I'm not going to discuss your behaviour. It is beneath contempt, as you well know. This is Lulu's day and you will go to the zoo with the others and put a good face on it. That is final.'

The zoo was in a fold of the hills about twelve miles away. It was privately owned and it was reputed to be run on the lines of Whipsnade. This meant, Vera explained, that the animals ranged with some freedom over woodland, grassy slopes or boulder strewn scree, according to preference. They had enclosures of course, but these were for their own protection. Wolves, after all, must be kept apart from deer. 'What, do you mean they don't have lions or elephants?' asked Rhona in disappointment. 'Oh yes, I think they do; I'm sure they do.' 'Well, how can animals from hot countries . . .,' began Janet. Then she remembered her outcast status and was silent. She was feeling a little more benevolent. She watched the clouds shift and the sun appear. A group of Highland cows were standing, sturdy and placid in the rough wet heather, by the roadside; beyond them the sky was palest blue and the watery sunbeams limned them in burnished light. They look holy, she thought, visionary. A vision of gentle beasts; she loved this idea.

Rhona had Caro firmly clasped on her knee. Her face was alight with warmth, affection and excitement. She was reciting to her '*Four* horses stuck in a bog, *Three* monkeys tied to a clog, *Two* pudding ends would choke a dog, With a gaping, wide mouthed waddling FROG'. Caro bounced up and down in time, squealing. Lulu wriggled forward, thrusting her elbow into Janet's stomach. She leant over into the front; it was her day after all. She took a deep breath and began to chant: 'High jump tomato, high jump tomato!' Rhona and Caro joined in. Francis was silent in the front; he was studying a map. Vera drove on imperviously. Janet unwound the window. The scent of wet turf and bog myrtle wafted up to her; she could hear a curlew and lambs crying. 'High jump tomato, high jump tomato!' 'Just fancy,' said Francis, 'there's a place called Balloch and near it there's a place called Luss. Gives one curiously to think, doesn't it?' 'Whatever do you mean?' asked Vera. Then abruptly, 'That's quite enough, Francis. Keep your schoolboy humour for your friends.' 'Do you really think,' inquired Francis, 'that they should be going on like that about tomatoes? You know how Janet is with tomatoes. And carrots.' Janet's mouth went dry; her stomach lurched. 'Please stop, quick, let me out,' she gasped. Bent double, heaving helplessly by a gorse bush she thought, 'He did that on purpose.'

It was cold at the zoo. The sky had clouded again and there was the bite of frost in the wind. Vera took the little ones off and left

Francis and Janet to look around on their own. Francis vanished into the snake house. Janet stood watching the monkeys. How dispiriting to think that these were close relations. On the other hand, perhaps this explained a good deal about human behaviour. They crouched on their branches picking fleas off each other and eating them. They were constantly on the move, changing places, slyly poking, pulling, jostling. They seemed unable to concentrate on anything for more than a moment. Then they noticed a blackbird trapped in their enclosure, desperately flinging itself against the netting. A hideous hunt began, with the monkeys anticipating every move of the bird, swinging and leaping, blocking its flight path. Janet shouted at them. She waved her arms about. They paid no attention. At last the bird sank in exhaustion to the floor. The monkeys crowded round it. The bird was motionless; only the faintest tremor in its breast showed that it still lived. The monkeys lost interest; back they went into the high branches where they resumed their scratching, pinching and intent scrutiny of each other's backsides. A man came with a wheelbarrow. He released the bird and, to Janet's joy, it flew at once.

Lions strolled lethargically on a muddy slope. They were tarnished by winter and dulled with boredom. A black panther glared from its den, so much a part of its enclosing darkness that only the two emerald chips of its eyes were visible. The lions stiffened, moved forward to their fence; suddenly they were alert and purposeful. Perhaps it was feeding time. Janet turned to see what they were watching. A group of nuns were coming along the path, their black habits billowing against the leaden sky. Were ancestral voices whispering to these lions, reminding them of what might be done with missionaries? Cheered by this thought, she moved on. An extraordinary creature confronted her from a small rectangular pool. It towered up out of the water, monumental and tragic. Its thick grey skin hung in flaps and folds, its great round face was a mass of whiskery wrinkles;

its brown eyes brimmed with yearning and sorrow. Sea lions frolicked heartlessly around it, slapping eddies of cold water up its flanks. It was a sea elephant, a manatee, a dugong, she read. She remembered that sailors were said to have mistaken these creatures for mermaids as they reared from the waves of far oceans, sunlit and turquoise. How could this ever be? The world must possess no creature more dolorous. Snow began to fall, fluttering and settling on the huge stony form. It did not move. Janet turned away miserably. She looked back at it once; it was still motionless, gazing unfathomably into the blizzard while the shining black sea lions leapt and played.

Woeful and cold she felt as they drove homewards. They passed the wolves, scrimmaging together in the dusk, rending and ripping at a small blue anorak. 'Well now,' said Francis, 'I wonder what they've done with the owner.' Lulu gasped; fearfully she clutched Rhona's arm. 'Don't be silly, Francis,' said Rhona, 'I saw you chucking that in to them.' 'Only something I found in a puddle. I thought it might cheer them up.' Vera sighed heavily. Janet sat in the front this time. Steadily the windscreen wipers fanned through the slush and mud. The snow had stopped but there had been a great burden of it on the canvas roof and now it was melting and dripping down all the windows like streaming tears, like the tears of the manatee. She shook her head hard, trying to dislodge the image. There had been a happy fish in the aquarium house. It was a skate, a pure white skate, and it had moved vertically, floating up and down on a little wake of bubbles, like a handkerchief or a small pale ghost. As it floated, it opened and closed its mouth, and it had seemed to Janet that it was soundlessly singing 'Hallelujah, hallelujah'. Its fluent effortless dance was a dance of praise, a joyous offering.

For most of the journey the little ones were quiet, but as they turned up the drive to Auchnasaugh and birthday tea and candles, excitement broke loose again. 'What IF,' they shrieked.

'What if a penguin rode on an elephant?' 'What if a pear jumped over the moon? No, a melon.' 'What if a slow worm?' 'No, Caro, that's not how you do it.' 'Water's dripping in from the roof,' said Francis. The canvas was sagging heavily inwards. 'Oh never mind, we're almost there,' said Vera, accelerating perilously. The car skidded, zigzagged, straightened. In the headlights they saw Jim pedalling laboriously towards them. He was on his way home; two rabbits and a pigeon dangled on strings from his handlebars; the rabbits' stiff hind legs swung against the spokes of his front wheel. 'I must just have a quick word with him.' Vera braked abruptly. The car lurched sideways again. There was a rending sound; an avalanche of slush and ice water engulfed Janet's head. 'The roof's split! Look at Janet!' squawked Francis. They looked, they squealed with laughter, they looked again and collapsed in helpless mirth. Vera wound up her window, waved to Jim, glanced at Janet and began to laugh too. Janet was speechless from the shock of the cold; her hair was saturated, water was still pouring over her face, on to her lap, soaking into her coat, trickling even into the capacious recesses of her padded preformed brassiere, bought to leave room for growth. (Growth, what a hideous word.) The car drew to a halt by the front door. 'What if,' proposed Francis, 'something extremely funny happened to Janet?' Blindly she rushed into the hall and up the stairs. The twin lagoons gurgled beneath her jersey. Far below she heard Caro trying again, 'What if a clown jumped into a bucket of socks?'

The summer term at St Uncumba's was almost bearable. Although the weather was always cool because of the sea breeze, the monotone grey dispersed and sky and water vied with each other in subtleties of blue and green. There was no more hockey, and you only had to play cricket if you showed promise. Otherwise there was tennis and swimming. Janet played tennis with her usual ineptitude, but because it was not a team game no one minded, except Cynthia, who would become exasperated and then furious and start hitting very fast and very accurate balls at Janet and the game would end. They swam in a huge natural pool among the rocks; the tide swept in twice daily and flooded it, bringing marine exotica, and not always removing them as it withdrew. Janet lost her pleasure in swimming here after meeting a six foot eel with goggling eyes. On sunny days when they went riding they wore their swimming costumes under their jodhpurs and Aertex shirts; they would gallop along the wet shining sands and then take the saddles off and swim the horses. This was marvellous. The horses trod warily into the shallows; they picked their feet up high and skipped sideways at the little waves. Then as they waded deeper they arched their necks and snorted, pushing their muzzles into the green swell. Their flanks grew wet and slippery. And suddenly with a wild forward lurch they gave themselves to the sea, wantonly plunging, surging and wallowing. The billows washed into Janet's face, the wind took her breath, she clung to the mane, elemental air and water, terror and ecstasy. She could die like this and never know the difference, horsed on the sightless couriers of the air.

One day Cynthia announced that she was going swimming in the sea. At the time they were returning from their Sunday afternoon walk, in crocodile as usual, marching along the shore road. On one side lay the dunes, crowned in spiky marram grass, on the other the lonely shards and splinters of the ancient cathedral. The roar of the strong wind almost drowned the distant peals of bells. 'Don't be ridiculous,' said Janet. 'It's freezing cold and the waves are all going in different directions. You'll be sucked under and that'll be the end of you. Not that I care, but I'll get the blame.' 'Shut up, you drip.' Cynthia twisted her wrist. 'Come on, quick, now, into the dunes.' Hopelessly Janet scurried after her; the sand blew into her eyes, her hat floated off down the beach. Gasping and choking, she retrieved it and crouched in the comfortless grasses. Before her lay the flotsam and jetsam of the retreating tide. The sea was swollen and evil. Only Cynthia could want to bathe at such a stupid time. It was like swimming on New Year's Day or across the Channel, which of course was exactly what she would have in her pin-sized mind. Why couldn't she just swim to Germany and be done with it? Germany would suit Cynthia very well, she reflected, watching the blonde athletic figure strike through the waves, turning her head from side to side in the absurd mechanical manner demanded by the crawl. Janet herself only floated or did breast stroke, keeping her head upright, well out of the water, and moving very slowly but, she believed, with a certain stately poise.

Suddenly she saw that Cynthia was not alone. Coasting and rolling, a couple of waves further out, were two round, bobbing heads. As Cynthia turned and swam along the surge of her wave so they swam along theirs, heads turned towards her, great dark eyes gleaming with merriment through the spume. A pair of seals were having sport with Cynthia, parodying her movements, coming in closer. Janet leapt to her feet and ran to the water's edge; she waved and pointed and shouted into the wind. Cynthia swam powerfully shorewards and strode scowling and dripping out of the water. 'What's the matter? Is someone coming?' she demanded, shaking herself like a dog so that freezing droplets flew all over Janet. 'Two seals were swimming with you. Look!' They stared out at the sea. The seals were gone, there was nothing but the whelming deep. 'You just made it up, didn't you, to get me out of the water?' Janet ignored her. They tramped back to the boarding house in angry silence, mitigated for Janet by the prodigy she had seen and Cynthia had not seen.

CHAPTER NINE

After that summer term all terms merged in Janet's mind. She had tried St Uncumba's in every season, months without end, fogs impenetrable, cold, windy sunlight – and she found it wanting, wanting in human kindness, in vision, in apprehension of the glories of the world. But the raw, sheer edge of her misery was blunted; she had learnt to cope, even to survive, by deviousness, by reading, and, as always, by daydreaming. She saw other, younger, girls become the persecuted quarry; although she was sometimes troubled by a perverse impulse to join their tormentors she never did so. Her reason for this was not honourable; it was simply disdain. She believed that she moved on a higher plane, beyond spite, beyond compromise. She had found a French word, *mesquin*; this she applied silently and liberally to the preoccupations of others. Her heart was hardened. Leafing through a magazine one day, her eye was caught by a photograph. For a moment, she took it to be a frieze from a Greek vase, nymphs and cupidons stepping through a graceful pastoral. Then she read the caption. It had been taken by a German war photographer and it showed Jewesses and their infants on their way to the gas chambers. Soon afterwards she came upon John Hersey's account of the destruction of Hiroshima and Nagasaki. She could no longer have faith in God or man. She transferred any religious impulse which might yet linger within her to the Greek gods who did not even pretend to care especially for humanity or to value its efforts and aspirations, being far too busy with their own competing plots, feuds and passions. Now when she prayed she stood in darkness, beneath the moon, and repeated her message three times, with rigidly clenched fists and unwinking stare, forcing all her strength upwards to the chilly disc or crescent which sometimes glanced slyly back at her, sometimes reeled drunkenly off into the torn clouds. She was in retreat from the world, in a state of numb and impotent horror. Francis told her that she was a boring monolith, concentred all in self. He was right, she thought, but she knew no way of expressing her state in words, no way of escaping her carapace. The lonely call of an owl, which once had thrilled her, now pierced her with apprehension. Man's inhumanity to man and beast dominated a world of vicious anarchy and disgrace. Only the trees and hills and the night sky held to their orderly beauty, 'O look upon the starry firmament'. She found an astronomical globe and took it to her room; she sat on the floor studying it and she wept. She did not know why she was weeping.

One day as she trudged up the drive at Auchnasaugh she came upon a squirrel, hit by a car. It lay in a semblance of repose, its head bowed in the meekness of violent death, its paws curving inwards. Its fur was sodden and dishonoured by rain and mud. Mechanically she picked it up and carried it off for burial. She could only find the big old gardening fork. As she dug, the wet red clods of earth clung to it so that she kept having to stop and wipe them off; her hands were sticky and sharp grit pressed into her palms. Suddenly on the prong was a frog, transfixed and splayed, kicking wildly. Janet's heart lurched. 'O son of man,' she gasped. She heard the words so loud they filled the rainy sky, louder than the wind which rocked the tree tops. Gently she drew the frog off the spike; it struggled into the nettles. Janet knelt on the ground. She buried the squirrel and then she sat by the small grave and was overwhelmed by grief. Pity, she thought, pity like a naked newborn babe, pity like the frog threshing on the fork, the desolate manatee, the melted eyeballs of the people of Hiroshima, the burning martyrs clapping their hands, pity was needed and was not in the world; if it existed, none of this could be. Divine pity. Human pity was not enough. A bleeding heart could only bleed and bleed. It seemed to her then that the nature of Caledonia was a pitiless nature and her own was no better. What use was it to be racked by pain for animals and the general woes of the world when she was unmoved by the sorrows of the people she knew? She thought again of the students drowning in the cold summer sea; they would have heard the church bells ringing out from the far invisible cliffs beyond the dawn mist, ringing and calling people to the love and knowledge of God; but not one of those people had heard their cries for help, and God had chosen to ignore them. Anger rose in her and merged with her grief, confusing her utterly. She had had enough, she could not cope. She placed a token frond of bracken on the grave, picked up the fork and plodded onwards up the drive. She passed the frog, spreadeagled and lifeless on the grey winter grass. Another burial; she could not bear it. She thrust the corpse into a heap of dead leaves. '"Nine peacocks in the air, I wonder how they all came there. I don't know and I don't care",' she remarked to the rustling, watchful Heracleum grove.

The empire of the winds is shared between the offspring of Eos the dawn and Astraeus the starry sky. Chill Boreas of the North and wild sorrowing Zephyr from the West were lords of the air at Auchnasaugh. Occasionally a mean blast blew from Eastern Eurus, straight off the heaving sea from the forlorn polderlands and farther barbarian territories, homes of the Goths and Vandals. The South wind Notus was a stranger to Caledonia, '*Ig*notus' as Janet said, making one of her boring, pedantic jokes. But most beautiful, most haunting and haunted, was the wind of dawn, which brought the next day, and whirled the past off into the breaking clouds: a wind thrilling and melancholy, tender and cruel, a wind of beginning and ending.

Janet lay in the darkness listening to it sweep and wail about the battlements. She felt weightless and abstract, almost the spirit she hoped one day to become. Then she heard her parents' warring voices down the corridor. She tried to switch on her lamp, simultaneously stubbing her toe on her cold stone hot water bottle. As she had expected, the lamp was not working. Hector and Vera had fused all the lights yet again. This had been happening all winter, since their acquisition of a Goblin Teasmaid. Vera had wanted one of these machines for many years, ever since she had visited Constance in her sterile apartment in Edinburgh and enjoyed the benison of solitary and effortless early morning tea, provided by a friendly automaton which required no gratitude. However, Hector's desire to wring six cups out of a system which believed that four were enough for anyone had dampened her enthusiasm and was now making her dislike the Goblin. The start of each day was nerve-racking. As Janet listened to the dawn wind, so Vera, tense with anxiety, listened to the Goblin swing into action. It sighed, puffed, panted, convulsed, hissed and then, if all were well and the day was to be a day of modest success, there was a hideous blast like a road drill and a lurid neon light flooded the room. Tea was ready. However, if Hector had overfilled the squat kettle, couched in homely conjunction with its squat teapot spouse, the Goblin would fall eerily silent in the midst of its heavy breathing, water would seep into the intricacies of the hydroelectric and as late as possible in the wrecked day a gloomy workman would arrive and restore light to the castle. What a good thing that they had kept the old Tilley lamps.

 Hector refused to accept that he was responsible for these disasters. He claimed that it was the fault of the hydroelectric and its minions; they had not wired the place properly. Although he was not a practical man, he loved gadgets. He had become deeply attached to the Goblin and would hear no criticism of it; indeed, according to Constance, he had identified with it, 'and I have to say, Vera, that this makes me a little anxious for you both'. Vera, looking into a bleak future of dawns shattered either by the Goblin's manic triumph roar or by Hector's fulminations, began to ponder the chances of some form of mutual extinction or electrocution as she lay awake, earlier and earlier, in dread of day. And so it was that at three o'clock on a summer morning she wandered silently in her dressing gown down the steep tower staircase, along the galleried corridor above the hall, down the great stone steps. The moon was still high and shining through the stained glass window. Her dark shadow obliterated the rubies and emeralds which it cast on the flagged floor. She passed through the green baize door into the passage which led to the kitchen. The back door stood wide open and a host of feral cats fled through it as she approached. She slammed it shut. No one ever locked the doors, but they could at least close them. In the kitchen she found the pony Blackie eating a geranium; wearily she pushed him out, ignoring his swishing tail and bared teeth. The geraniums had been another of Vera's attempts at domesticising Auchnasaugh, doomed as usual to failure. Miss Wales had been annoyed. She didn't want to water them; in fact she never had watered them and now most of them were shrivelled brown stumps. As she waited for the great domed kettle to boil on the sullen Aga, Vera was overcome by yearning for a normal house, of a normal size, warm and bright and cheerful, with doors which could be locked at night, and a cooker not subject to the wayward whims of the wind. Three friendly children (not one of them being Janet) would sit smiling round the tea table and her husband would go out in the morning and return in the evening. How tired she was. She made tea and set it with one cup on a tray. It was her intention to create her own tea-drinking scenario in her bedroom, in defiance and anticipation of the Goblin/Hector. With reluctance she turned away from the meagre warmth of the Aga and out into the draughty passages. Wind skittered about her ankles, lifting and flapping the hem of her pink silken gown, a garment ill suited to the climate of Auchnasaugh. Someone must have left the boiler room door open too, and now she would have to go and shut it. This was ridiculous. She put her tray down and hurried round the corner, just in time to witness Jim, the hunchbacked gardener, emerging stealthily from Lila's room.

Now Vera no longer felt cold. Her heart thumped; adrenalin pulsed through her body. Forgetful of the tray, she sped up the stairs, burst into her bedroom and woke Hector. Hector was not impressed by her news. He felt that it could have waited at least until the hour of the Goblin. 'She'll have to go,' shrieked Vera. 'This absolutely clinches it. We have the children to think of, let alone the boys in term time. How could she do such a thing, and under our roof.' 'Or Jim could go. After all it takes two to . . .' mumbled Hector. 'Don't be so disgusting. It doesn't bear thinking of. Of course Jim can't go. It's all Lila's fault. Anyway no one else would ever do a fraction of what he does. Though if his mother finds out she'll never let him near us again. No, you must arrange something with Lila. Or I will.' But where could Lila go? A sense of numbing hopelessness descended on Vera. Round and round in circles her brain scurried; Hector made the occasional monosyllabic comment. But there was no escaping the fact that she could think of no place for Lila. The room reverberated to the Goblin's cry of victory.

Neither Jim nor Lila went. For a while nothing much happened, as was so often the case at Auchnasaugh. Hector, staring at a point three feet above Jim's stooped head, told him that he believed he had been working late into the night and although of course he appreciated his selfless efforts, his duty after five in the evening was to be with his old mother. Jim, staring at Hector's conker brown brogues, nodded wordlessly. Thereafter he ignored Lila, even when he was working on the lawn outside her window and she was standing there, framed by her torn curtains, glowering at him.

Hector told Vera, untruthfully, that he had spoken to Lila. Vera, hissing with rage, made forays to Lila's room and, without mentioning anything so crude as factual evidence, informed her that she was a slut, an outcast, an unwelcome parasite who would be moved out at the first opportunity. And she was to keep away from the children: 'We both know what I mean.' Her fury fragmented her sentences. Phrases, 'abuse of trust', 'disgusting *urges*', 'flouting of protocol' winged off her lips and bombed like hornets about the room. Lila refused to speak. She turned her back and drank more whisky. But as the days passed her small reserve of appetite for life began to drain away. She no longer searched for mushrooms, no longer cared to paint her minute, intricate watercolours of mosses and lichens. Her face lost its contours and sagged, her eyeballs were veined in pink and yellow, fluff and dust gathered, unheeded, in her shorn locks. Sometimes at dusk she slipped out among the trees and howled like a wolf. Alone in her room she uttered strange cries and clawed her face into raw furrows so that she seemed to be weeping tears of blood. She played her John McCormack records at full volume to drown her own noise. All this Vera witnessed with grim satisfaction. She flung Lila's door open, without knocking. 'I'll thank you to turn that noise down. You might show just a little consideration for others.' Lila lay like a basilisk on the sofa; she stared at Vera without expression. Firelight flickered and gleamed on her whisky bottle, glittered across her black eyes.

> *O love is fair and love is rare,*
> *A little while when love is new,*
> *But when it's old, it waxes cold*
> *And fades away like morning dew*

intoned the gramophone. Vera stalked across to it: 'And that record belongs to me.' She switched off the control, wrenched off the record and slammed from the room.

Early one September morning Vera ascended the stone

staircase with her tea tray. She was in good spirits. Her campaign against Lila was going well. Her campaign against the Goblin was proving even more successful. Hector did not enjoy pouring his own tea (albeit four cups) and drinking it in silence while his spouse lay comatose beside him. His enthusiasm for the machine was flagging. Sometimes now he did not even switch it on at night. Her tiresome older children were both far off at their boarding schools; the boys' term had not yet begun. Life felt almost normal with Rhona, Lulu and Caro, Nanny and the pleasures of the nursery. With persistence one may achieve one's ends, she thought. She hummed an invigorating hymn tune:

> *Soldiers of Christ arise,*
> *And put your armour on,*
> *Strong in the strength which God supplies . . .*

Lila erupted from the shadows by the great stained glass window. She was swinging a wet towel, twisted into a rope. She walloped Vera across the face. The tray crashed down the stairs. Vera toppled, Lila swung the towel again and knocked her backwards. She rolled down the stairs, pursued by Lila in her flapping black garments. Lila kicked her as she went, lost her footing and fell over too. Horribly entwined they landed on the hall floor. Each sank her nails into the other's face. Lila suddenly let go. Vera pulled herself free and stood up, shaking. She grabbed the banister and heaved herself painfully up the stairs. Lila lay on the floor staring up at the dying cockatoo. She was laughing; her eyes were alive with merriment.

When Janet came home for the Christmas holidays she was horrified to find that Lila had been committed to a lunatic asylum, an appropriately Gothic establishment near the coast with the inappropriate name Sunny Days. Vera made it clear that Lila was to play no further part in their lives. Janet knew better than to argue, or even to speak of her. After Christmas she caught the bus from the village to Aberdeen, to exchange her Christmas presents. This had become an accepted part of Christmas ritual as they all grew older. Francis and Rhona did not care to travel with Janet; her frequent requests to the driver for halts and fresh air were a great embarrassment. Janet was inured to it; she did not feel quite so ill on the bus as she did in cars; there was no smell of leather upholstery to convulse her stomach. Now, jolting down the long winding road out of the hills, she felt wonderfully confident. Over her new tartan skirt she wore her new white duffel jacket. Beneath the tartan skirt lurked her romantic new paper nylon petticoat, tiered and flounced. It crackled loudly as she moved and swelled the brusque pleating of her skirt outwards into strange sagging contours like those of a homemade lampshade. Her ensemble was completed by ankle socks and the perennial StartRite walking shoes, laced very tight. On her knee she clasped a brown paper parcel containing six pairs of Celanese knickers, eau de nil, turquoise and sticking-plaster pink, cut like twin pillowcases. These hideous gifts arrived each year from one of Vera's many aunts and Janet was well aware that she would not be able to exchange them as, apart from anything else, they had been bought in Glasgow. But herein lay her alibi. No one would be surprised that she had done something so silly as to travel a total of eighty miles to change the unchangeable and had returned still burdened with it. 'Typical Janet', they would say, and that would be that.

Her plan was to leave the bus at the second coastal village and walk the short distance to the lunatic asylum. For the first time, Lila would have a visitor. Later she would catch the same bus back to the village where Hector or Vera would meet her as arranged. A foolproof plan, conceived and executed with daring efficiency, such efficiency that she had escaped without cleaning her shoes and without Vera noticing the presence of the paper nylon petticoat. ('For parties', she had purred, as Janet opened the parcel. What parties Janet asked herself. Rhona and the little ones went to parties but she did not. She remembered them from earlier days, without pleasure. She was always first to be out in games and she either became hectically over-excited so that she behaved appallingly and had to be spanked later, or was so consumed with shyness and nerves that she was sick. She had enjoyed the afternoon time before a party, however, with the electric fire glowing in Vera's bedroom at an unaccustomed hour, and the scent of starch as Nanny ironed their organdie dresses, and the lovely sight of Shetland shawls pinned out by their points across the carpet like a sequence of giant cobwebs.

Sunny Days had been built as a seaside hotel in Edwardian times. A glassed verandah ran the length of the building, offering an uninterrupted view of the bitter sea and bitter sky beyond the cliff edge. Little wooden balconies, their paintwork weathered and blistered, trembled outside shuttered windows. There was a lofty conservatory, starkly empty. The grounds were extensive, open and windswept. A few stunted trees pointed inland, signalling escape. There had been little demand for it as an hotel. The boulders and sharp outcrops of the shore made bathing impossible and the constant wind made people uneasy and fretful. There was agreement that its only possible use could be as a place of confinement for people who had already been disordered – by war, weather, humanity or what you will. As they were mad they would not notice its disadvantages. So it became a full house, and in constant demand.

Janet rang the doorbell, was admitted and directed along the hallway towards Lila's ground-floor room. A few people wandered about, looking normal if a trifle abstracted. A tall young man came towards her, smiling cordially. Janet smiled graciously back, making it clear that she was not one to be prejudiced against the deranged. As he drew level with her he suddenly bared his teeth and snarled. Janet's kindly smile disintegrated, her heart thumped. She hurried along the corridor, tightly clutching her parcel. She wished now that she had not worn her new petticoat; it seemed to alarm people; they recoiled and stared after her as she went crackling by. Lila occupied Room 24. In the middle of the corridor outside her door a mountainous and ancient woman was moored in an armchair. Her flesh lapped over the sides; her manifold chins bristled like St Uncumba's. One of her eyeballs was rolled upwards so that only the white showed; the other swivelled sharply towards Janet. 'Fit like, hen?' she enquired. 'I'm very well, thank you,' responded Janet, banging on Lila's door and simultaneously opening it. Lila lay in bed staring at the ceiling. 'Hallo Lila, I've come to see you,' Janet announced. 'Oh,' said Lila. 'Hallo,' she added. There was silence, broken by a series of squawks from the corridor, beyond the closed door. Janet tried to think of something to say. 'How are you, Lila? Do you like it here?' 'It's all right really,' said Lila, still looking at the ceiling. 'I'm just very tired. In fact I must go to sleep now.' She closed her eyes. The room was very small and white, the bed was white, Lila wore a white garment like a grocer's overall, but back to front. There was no furniture, apart from a chest of drawers. Beyond the uncurtained window a great stretch of bleached grass ran down to the cliff edge. At least the sea was out of sight. A clothes-line festooned with dusters and dishcloths flapped and flopped at the empty sky. Janet felt silly, standing there with her parcel. She wondered whether she could sit on the chest of drawers. Lila looked strange and small, asleep in the white bed, as though nothing had ever happened to her, she had never been anywhere, as though all her existence had contracted to this point and would proceed no further. The door burst open. In rushed a beak-faced little woman with stubbly hair like a *collaborateuse*. She wore a child's black velvet party frock, undone down the back and exposing a sweep of yellowed flesh.

Janet looked at her with distaste, then was smitten with sudden pain by the innocent moulding of her spine. Her legs and feet were bare, and mottled with cold. 'Gie us a fag,' she cried. 'Come on Lila, gie us a fag.' 'I think she's asleep,' ventured Janet. 'Och, rubbish.' She shook open a drawer and seized a packet of Craven A. She stared at Janet; her eye fell on the parcel. 'Fit's in yon? Ye've brought us a giftie; awfy guid. Gie us.' She snatched the package and ripped it open. 'Knickers, knickers, knickers. Knickers, knickers, knickers. These are for me; ye see I've nane.' She pirouetted, lifting her skirt. She spoke the truth. Janet averted her eyes, appalled. Nudity had no part to play in her life. 'Please do have them, if they're any use to you,' she began. 'Oh Lady Bountiful, oh how too too kind.' Beakface was mimicking Janet's voice; then she resumed her own. 'I'll have them whether you like it or no. *Milksop*!' she yelled and ran from the room. Janet heard her negotiate her way round the wheezing armchair woman. 'And haud yer wheesht, ye muckle great sumph.'

Janet wondered what to do now. She wanted to go; she wanted very much to go. But if Lila woke and found her gone, she might be disappointed and hurt. She gazed gloomily out of the window. Someone had taken in the washing. Would Lila care if she went? She was distracted by voices outside the door. The mountainous sedentary woman, not unlike the manatee, now she thought of it, seemed to be engaged with a nurse. Said nurse, brisk but kind, '*Of course* you're not a snake.' Mountain: 'And hoo dae ye ken, can ye say that for a fact?' Nurse: 'I most certainly can. Snakes have scales. You have lovely soft skin.' Mountain: 'I'm no a lass. Ye ken, I'm no a lass nae mair.' Nurse: 'Well, you're not a snake either.' Mountain: 'Then wha's the snake? *Ye* maun be the snake. Aye, it is yersel'.' A series of squawking gasps. Nurse: 'For heaven's sake, Mrs Farquharson. I'm getting the doctor.' Then, meaningfully, 'I think you'll have to Go Downstairs.' There was a click of retreating heels. The squawks rose to a gruff choking climax, then subsided. They were replaced by sonorous mutterings. Janet looked again at Lila. She lay there like an effigy, the sheet scarcely rising as she breathed. She looked out at the blank sky. There was still one object hanging from the washing line. It was a tiny black velvet child's party frock, pinned by its lace-trimmed sleeves, as though Beakface had shrunk like Alice in Wonderland, and evaporated into the bitter wind. For a moment Janet thought she had caught the madness or crossed into a realm where all was possible. She pulled her left pigtail hard. It hurt. She was Janet, and the thing on the line was a clothes-peg bag, made perforce in some heartless handicrafts session, by a person of tragic destiny. 'Goodbye, Lila,' she said. There was no answer. Out in the corridor the woman in the chair was lying back, breathing heavily, eyes half closed. Now both eyeballs showed only white. As Janet warily skirted round her, she mumbled, 'Rabbits'.

The bus toiled noisily into the twilit hills. Janet reflected on her expedition. Strategy apart, it could not be called a success. She had imagined Lila's ravaged face softening into her rare sweet smile at her arrival. Her black eyes would glow with pleasure as Janet told her of the infant Heracleum which she had dug up and transplanted to adorn the grave of Mouflon. There would be talk of animals and trees, of fungi and the great draughty castle, but not of its inhabitants. Lila shared Janet's distaste for the Teutonic and she had hoped to describe St Uncumba's German nativity play and reproduce the turgid gutturals of Gabriel's message to Mary. It seemed curious to her that the Germans, who had murdered so many Jews, should be widely regarded as a people appropriate to proclaim, in folksy manner, the miraculous birth of the doomed and Jewish babe. Why not perform a Latin play about the slaughter of the Innocents? It would be more honourable and at least it would sound beautiful, apart, of course, from the yells of the Innocents. The hideous short 'u' which occurred in so many

English words of disparagement, insult or plain dreariness, she ascribed to the Teutonic influence. 'Rut,' she thought. 'Ugh. Lump.' And there were worse, far worse. Such sounds did not exist in Latin or Greek. Francis claimed to have found an especially satisfying and characteristic German word: *Ein beutelattengittenwettenhof.* 'In other, simpler words, a kangaroo shelter. Current among ex-Nazis, hiding their shame by farming kangaroos in the Australian outback. Their wives take the Joeys, or Johanns more properly – baby kangaroos to you – into the house and dress them in *lederhosen.* Sometimes they don't notice as they bustle about attending to *Kinder, Kirche und Küchen,* that little Johann has grown up and is now nearly six feet tall. Sometimes *Hausfrau* and Johann meet in a rather unexpected manner in the corner of the kitchen. But this is not for your girlish ears, Janet.'

She was aware that she was trying not to think of the asylum and the people she had seen there. Later, there would be a time for this, and she feared its coming. One lovely thing had happened. As she walked away from Sunny Days along the cliff road, she had been followed and escorted by a great white bird, a fulmar. It floated just below her, beneath the edge of the cliff, dipping and drifting, its inscrutable disc face turned towards her. She thought that perhaps it was Lila's soul, briefly escaped from her little white cell and narrow bed and slumbering physical being, and ranging free on the back of the wind, a phantom presence come to wish her well.

Vera met her off the bus. As they drove up the glen road she questioned Janet about her day. Janet talked with animation for, as part of her strategy, she had researched intensively in *Vogue* and *Woman's Journal.* She described the cup of coffee she had taken in Watt and Grants, and the haughty mannequin who had glided up and down between the tables, expressionlessly flinging a fur wrap over one shoulder, revolving like a mechanical doll so that the pleats of her Gor-ray skirt fanned out above the ruler-straight seams of her stockings. She spoke of A-line dresses and pencil skirts, of shot taffeta ball gowns and fashion's hideous new colour, shocking pink. She claimed that she had tried on a pair of shoes with Louis heels, 'just for fun, of course. I know I'm not old enough to wear heels.'

Vera was astonished and delighted. Perhaps at last Janet was growing up, becoming more feminine. How she yearned for a companionable daughter. Rhona was always a pleasure, but she was still rather young. What fun it would be if she and Janet could exchange girlish confidences, complicit glances, enter into the powerful freemasonry of the female against all that was uncouth, barbaric and disruptive (well, masculine) at Auchnasaugh. 'Shoe kicking time', she thought, in happy anticipation, imagining the two of them, lounging and lolling on Janet's bed, chattering and giggling late into the evening, perhaps over mugs of drinking chocolate. Of course she would have to provide Janet with a different bedside lamp, some floral affair in china, with a rosy silken shade. This scene could not be enacted in the harsh light of her Anglepoise. Janet, aware of her mother's new warmth of spirit, ventured to ask whether she might just possibly, as an end of holidays present, have a copy of the *Collected Poems of W. B. Yeats*. Vera frowned, remembering the books stacked slithering and topsy-turvy all over Janet's bedroom floor. Why add to them? 'All right,' she said, 'I'll ask them to send it straight to you at school.' Janet eyed her distrustfully and saw that it was best to drop the subject. 'Where, incidentally,' demanded Vera, still ruffled, 'are the things you changed for whatever it was?' 'Oh,' said glib Janet, 'it was the Celanese knickers and they wouldn't swop them. Oh goodness, oh dear, I must have left them on the bus.' Vera sighed. 'Your poor great aunt. What a waste,' she said. 'Typical,' she said.

That winter lasted even longer than usual. In late March Janet walked slowly up the drive; her feet were beginning to ache with cold, but she could go no faster for fear of falling on the dense sheet ice. The air was hushed and clouded as though it too were about to freeze. The rhododendron leaves hung stiff and shrivelled, the trees loomed black and still. Nothing stirred. It seemed a dead landscape, imprisoned beneath a colourless sky. Great icicles hung below the bridge over the burn. The water moved wearily, obstructed by tangles of frozen branches and random chunks of ice; the glen was drained, exhausted. Janet thought of Tennyson, 'I dreamed there would be spring no more.' As the words formed in her mind, a kingfisher shot from under the bridge and sped in brilliant zigzags down the dreary burn, glorifying the winter world. Janet was exultant. She had been accorded a vision. '"What, though the field be lost, all is not lost!"' she cried aloud to the silent hills and the echo returned, giving her the lie, 'Lost, lost, lost'. Unheeding, she hobbled on to Auchnasaugh; a spring of crystalline joy was leaping in her heart. *Wherefore let thy voice Rise like a fountain in me, night and day.*' She thanked God, she thanked the moon, still visible in the midday sky. The pale sun and the pale moon hung opposite each other in that white sky. It was like the Book of Revelations.

Over lunch she related the miracle to her family. Hector and Vera became bored as she described, with unnecessary detail, her progress up a drive whose every tree, bush, ditch or frozen puddle they knew as well as she. 'Do get to the point Janet, you're just blethering.' She got to the point. There was a moment's silence, then everyone spoke at once; Francis' voice was loudest. He and Rhona were exchanging a meaningful look. 'I won't say it's camp,' said he, 'but it's tantamount. And of course, purest Disney.' 'Drip, drip, drip little April showers,' sang Rhona gleefully. Francis joined in, so did Lulu. Caro squealed with delight. Hector and Vera subsided into mirth. Janet wanted to cry, but she would not give them that satisfaction. She had been trying to read Proust recently and she had pounced with relish on his phrase '*l'étouffoir familial*', the family suffocation chamber. Vengefully and silently she repeated it.

Late in the afternoon she did something which even she regarded as criminal, albeit an act of retribution. She slipped into Francis' room, haven to his bizarre collection of cacti. Some stood in sandy desert land, a miniature Arizona, curvaceous and, as cacti went, normal-looking. Others were veiled by tawny tresses or wispy white beards; some sported jaunty and unconvincing scarlet flowers as though trying to pass themselves off as South Sea Island beauties. Some pointed stiffly with odd truncated limbs, reminding Janet of the amputees among the war wounded, so long ago. There were tall ones like trees and little ones like hedgehogs; and there were succulents. Janet disliked the succulents. Their complacent, smooth green flesh bore witness to ugly subterranean greed. She could imagine them feeding off blood. They were dewy and plump. They were repulsive. With care, she selected her victim. The rising moon assisted her, illuminating the spectral throng. She stooped over the tallest, broadest succulent. It was crowned by a moist jade leaf, a new leaf, the product of many months of self-regarding ingestion. She plunged her thumbnail, filed to talon sharpness, deep into its thick flesh. She stabbed it through in one deft movement, leaving a crescent-shaped wound. With a sigh of satisfaction she turned away. She paused to look at Francis' slow-worm, known to him as Montgomery, known to all others as Gloria. In his huge vivarium, Gloria was contemplating his prey. Sometimes he did this for so long that even slugs moved out of his reach. The moon rippled across his burnished pewter back and lingered on his azure spots. Janet stroked his ancient forehead. He ignored her, gazing balefully into his litter of earth and leaves.

Within a few days the succulent's proud new leaf had withered, etiolated and fallen off. The wound gaped. Francis was mystified. Eventually another leaf took its place. On its bland surface it bore a crescent-shaped mark and as the leaf grew the crescent cracked open, until this leaf fell also, fatally wounded. So began a long sequence of doomed leaves, always growing singly in that same spot, always stamped with the crescent of Janet's thumbnail. She felt no guilt. She believed it was the moon's revenge.

That year the daffodils would wait no longer. They forced their way through the earth's chill carapace and bloomed in the tarnished snow. At once a wild wind swept in from the west and whirled them into crazed confusion, snapping the stems, tearing off the golden trumpets, tossing and flattening the survivors. The cats paced and hovered by the back door, uncertain whether to risk the outdoors; with wrinkled muzzles, they tested the wind. Among the swirling daffodils the old labrador lay out, in the heart of the gale. Her head was raised, her ears were pricked; alertly she snuffed the air; she watched the world turn, the new season approach. Looking at her, Janet thought in sharp sorrow, 'I will not see this again,' for now the labrador could scarcely walk; her hind legs were emaciated and she had to be helped in and out and up the stairs. Yet she was couched out there, unafraid, welcoming with dignity whatever was to come, among the reckless, gaudy flowers whose time was even briefer. *'Fair Daffodils, we weep to see You haste away so soon.'* Fair Labrador. Sometimes Janet thought that life's sole purpose was to teach one how to die. As in most spheres, so in this, animals did better than people.

She mused upon her own remote and unalarming death and the arrangements for her funeral which she had for a long time now been inscribing in the back of her special notebook, adding new pleasures as they came to mind. The place was, as always, up in the hills, among the pine groves above the brown and secret pool. There would be bagpipes and there would be

Gregorian chants. The Papal Count might be present, as a disembodied voice, singing 'Danny Boy'; she was not entirely sure about this. For a little time one faithful dog would sit beside the grave, while others ran and skirmished in merry insouciance along the shadowed woodland paths, possibly flushing out the capercailzie. This was another point of uncertainty, for although he was a kind of *genius loci*, his demeanour might lower the dignity of the occasion. The word preposterous, she thought, could have been coined especially for the mighty caper. Cats would be stretched, couchant and motionless along the tree branches, staring down with glittering eyes. She saw no people there. If John McCormack could be disembodied so could the piper and the chanters. But in time to come an occasional ghostly visitant might make his way through the trees and pause by her stone and think of how she had loved him, furling his cloak against the winds of dawn. At present these pilgrims would include W. B. Yeats, Catullus, Virgil, Alfred de Vigny, Rupert Brooke, John Donne, Racine, Alain Fournier, Henry Vaughan, Sophocles and Tacitus. Shakespeare would be too busy. She would have liked to have had Baudelaire, but she could imagine no circumstances, ghostly or otherwise, which would have persuaded him to come. If only she were an *affreuse juive*. Oh well, *tant pis*.

CHAPTER TEN

Janet lay in bed in the sanatorium at St Uncumba's. In the distance she could hear the girls' voices, jostling and raucous like birds, the thud and bounce of tennis balls, the click of a cricket bat, cries of seagulls. Through the drawn curtains watery light washed the room, forming and reforming intermittent bright splashes which trembled against the walls and ceiling. She felt weightless and immaterial, deliciously remote. With great caution she moved her head, moved her eyes; the headache had gone. She rolled her eyes in all directions. There was no answering pain. The iron vice which had been clamped about her skull for days on end had dissolved into thin air, just as though it had never been. Now she could scarcely imagine it, had almost forgotten how she had been walking and seen rain about her but had felt none, so that she had moved forward like a blind person, with hands outstretched trying to catch the bright droplets, until the sudden agony had gripped her head and she dared not make one step further, dared not cry out for help. Motionless she had stood, engulfed in pounding pain while the crazy rainstorm flashed about her and her lips moved silently. Girls wandered past, unsurprised by her behaviour, nudging each other or tapping their foreheads. Break ended, lessons began again and still she stood there. Far away in the black pulsating torture chamber of her skull she perceived the form of the weeping manatee, and the word humanity and the word manatee merged in dolour. At last someone had come and led her in to the matron.

She remembered little after that. But now she was well, miraculously reprieved, and she was to go home for several weeks, perhaps even for the rest of term, and rest. They believed that she had been overworking. Her eyes were strained, the middle finger of her right hand had developed a permanent ink-stained bump from too much writing. Twice she had behaved strangely in class; they had been reading Propertius' poem about the springs of Clitumnus and when they reached the lines which describe the great white oxen wading through the shallows Janet had burst into tears, uncontrollable, flooding tears which she had been unable to explain, apart from saying that she found the image moving. Then there had been the mortifying and hideous moment when, in her solitary Greek lesson, the mad old prophet Tiresias' description of fat floating in the blood of sacrificial beasts had caused her to vomit hugely across the room. And besides, Miss Smith the housemistress, while exercising her trio of Skye terriers in the gloaming, had observed Janet, who was supposedly supervising the younger ones at their prep, emerging furtively from the Catholic church beneath the windswept headland. Great was the fear that she might be succumbing to the blandishments of the Scarlet Woman of Rome. In fact, Janet sometimes went to this lonely church because she loved its glowing banks of candles and the heavy perfume of the air, and the mysterious altar, shrouded in purple draperies in the sad days before Easter. She did not like the statues, saints ecstatic or agonised, blood spouting from every visible orifice. But the place had a powerful feeling of sanctuary; it made her think of the lost traveller's dream under the hill. And she felt for its abandonment, remote from the life of the town, almost forgotten; she was angered by remarks she had overheard about popery and its works and the triumph of righteousness, which meant that the little church would one day soon slump down the eroding cliff face and into the whelming Protestant waters.

Some of this she told the various people who took it upon themselves to reason with her and warn her of the corruption which threatened her soul. As usual they paid no attention; if she had informed them that she was a pagan, and a moongazer, they would have continued with their obsessive anti-Catholic tirade in just the same way. She let them rant and rave, and thought instead about albatrosses, the doomed bird in the 'Ancient Mariner', Baudelaire's haunter of storms and rainbows, reduced to clumsy crippledom on earth, object of mockery to man, and the albatross who had been swept off course into the wrong hemisphere and now dwelt on a barren peninsula in the far north of Scotland, obliged to consort with kittiwakes; there it was waiting in vain for the high thermals which might waft it back to that unattainably distant south. As she imagined the plight of this bird her hands clenched, she bit her lip, and she stared hard ahead, willing and praying for its release. People mistook this for the outward show of inner religious turmoil. All in all, it would be best for her to spend some time in the carefree, relaxed atmosphere of her home, concluded Miss Smith. 'And not too much of the old bookwork,' she twinkled. 'Gosh no, golly, you bet not!' agreed Janet, pretending to be a different sort of person, as was clearly required.

Vera, initially depressed by the prospect of a summer shadowed by Janet's presence, remembered her dream of girlish camaraderie and decided that now was the moment to implement it. When Janet arrived home, she was astonished to find that her bedroom's bleak cream walls had been transformed by sprigged wallpaper. Coral pink curtains billowed at the open window and in one corner, confronting a coral-seated stool, there was a dressing table, bridally veiled in swags and festoons of net, as though, thought Janet, her direct reflection might cause the mirror to crack. But her bookcase was still there, and her table, and although there was now a pretty rosy lamp by the bed, her Anglepoise hovered like a lone heron on the wide margin of wooden floorboards at the edge of the coral carpet. She could soon put things right. In fact, she reflected, it might be interesting to live in a new environment, so long as she could see to read and had room for her books.

There was a new tin of Field's French Pink talcum powder on the dressing table. Recklessly she flung some into the air to impart feminine fragrance. It drifted down like chalk dust and lay in blotches on the carpet. Chastened, she rubbed it in with the sole of her shoe; she must think before she acted. For a long time she had affected to despise what she thought of as the world of women, its preoccupations with clothes and spring weddings (and hey nonny no) and needlework and babies. While she still had no interest in any of these matters, there were other aspects which drew her, as a lighted window glimpsed in a house unknown can rouse in the passer-by a sense not only of obscure longing for other warmer lives but also of sharp exclusion, harsh as a door slammed in the face. The delicious tracery of scent pervading the upper regions of a house, so that as you climbed the stairs you felt that you were entering a domain of excitement, romance and opulence, where silks rustled, where there was soft conspiratorial laughter, the easy understanding of those who speak in the same idiom, knowing nothing of painful silences – all this Janet had apprehended but never achieved; it seemed beyond her personal reach; a heavenly version of Fuller's.

Little did she know, and astounded she would have been to know, how this longing of hers echoed that of Vera. Janet could see that Rhona would have no difficulty in entering this realm, just as automatic access seemed granted to the girls at school; for herself it was otherwise. She seemed to lack some essential quality of girlishness. She pondered the phrase 'young girl' which she had observed gave rise to so much sentiment, rather like 'spring, the sweet spring': she thought that she had never been a young girl, never would be. She wondered what a young manatee looked like. Then she checked the thought; she was feeling increasing kinship with this creature, and it troubled her. She had discovered that if she gazed into her own eyes in the mirror for long enough her features would alter and resolve into those of another person, and she feared that she might one day find a manatee staring back at her.

Vera was gratified by Janet's pleasure in her room, although she was less pleased a few days later to find books littered across the floor in their usual fashion and the Anglepoise lamp reinstated by the bed. However, she reminded herself, she had always encouraged the child to read; it was the disorder and the unsocial nature of her reading habits which were depressing. Indeed there was something peculiarly irritating about the sight of Janet reading. She sat bolt upright at her table on a plain wooden schoolroom chair, ignoring the chintzy armchair which had been provided. Her eyes protruded as she read and she breathed heavily. She was unaware of anything happening around her; she turned the pages in a voracious, feral manner as though she were rending the limbs of some slaughtered beast. Immersed in this solitary, private and obsessional activity, she reminded Vera of a girl she had known once, who was said to be a pathological eating maniac.

Janet would be sixteen in the coming winter. Vera decided that it was time she stopped being a child and became an adult. She bought her a good tweed suit, badge of the grown Scottish female, a cashmere twinset, shoes and pretty cotton dresses. It was clear that something must be done about her hair. Janet refused to have it cut. She tried to pin it up; it fell down again at once. She wound her pigtails round her head. She looked like a menacing *Hausfrau*. Vera insisted that a short, boyish style would be best: 'Carefree for summer. Think, you'd only have to run a comb through it.' Janet's face grew heavy with anger. She didn't want to think about combing her hair; she didn't want to be a grown-up; this was all a boring waste of time. She shut herself in her room and read Baudelaire. Vera, alarmed by the prospect of a wardrobe full of unworn new clothes and a huge daughter in ankle socks, made a compromise. She must have her hair cut, but only to shoulder length. 'Then you'll have the best of both worlds. It will look long, but be much more manageable.' Janet unwillingly agreed. She despised compromise, but was tempted by some of her new clothes and the possibilities they offered for wearing her paper nylon petticoat.

An appointment was made with a famous hairdresser in Edinburgh, a great distance to travel, but then, as Vera said, this was an important moment in the life of a young girl. It was a dank, misty day and Janet wore her new tweed suit. It prickled incessantly and drove her to such a point of irritation that she did not feel car sick on the journey. Her legs felt strange and suffocated in their wrappings of twenty-denier nylon. She longed for it all to be over. Vera, who had begun the journey in high spirits, feeling that at last they were off on a mother and daughter spree together, became fretful and depressed after long hours of lugubrious silence on foggy roads. As they waited for the ferry to bear them across the Forth, each had a vengeful fantasy of the car overshooting the pier and engulfing the other for ever.

The salon reminded Janet of the lunatic asylum. People came in, looking normal and cheerful. They were ushered by white-coated, unctuous attendants into a neon-lit inner torture chamber of throbbing machines. There they sat, gowned and scarlet-faced and in no time at all they had lost their identity, their features had lapsed and swollen in the intense heat, their hair bristled with small metal daggers or their scalps were packed with wiry cylinders. Glassy-eyed, they gazed into the mirrors. Hope ebbed from the day. The place reeked of sulphur and brimstone, like hell. As Janet, swathed in billowing pink nylon, followed Monsieur André down the gleaming corridor, she glimpsed her fearful reflection. 'To what green altar, O mysterious priest, Lead'st thou that heifer lowing at the skies?' Well, she knew the name of that altar, the dim, blood-boultered altar of womanhood.

When she emerged she looked worse than she could ever have anticipated. Vera and Monsieur André had chosen to discuss what was to be done when Janet was helpless, her head forced backwards into a stream of scalding water while a smiling sadist clawed her scalp into ribbons. Far from being shoulder length, her hair now scarcely reached her collar. They had curled it and baked it and lacquered it and now she looked old enough to be Vera's mother; indeed she looked not unlike the Queen Mother. As a final insult she was handed a shiny green box which contained her severed locks, plaited and coiled like a treacherous reptile. 'For a chignon,' said Vera. 'Isn't this fun!'

Zephyr the west wind roared like a mighty ocean through the rhododendrons. In the sheltered sunken garden the azaleas' scarlet blossoms tossed and curvetted for a moment, then dreamed again in the perfumed haze of early summer. Janet lay on the grass in a little glade among the azaleas, listening to the roar fade to a sigh, recede and retire. She stared at the sky and remembered how she used to watch the fleeting gold chasms between the clouds for glimpses of God or the dead. She could imagine the spirits of the dead disporting themselves on such a wind as this. She thought of George Peele's astonishing line 'God, in a whizzing summer wind, marches upon the tops of mulberry trees'. Such a day this was, such a wind. It filled her with yearning and exhilaration; the shining leaves were charged with poignancy. Tendrils of ivy flickered down the wall, curling into the grass among the starry flowers of wild strawberry.

A tiny bird was there; it watched Janet. Janet watched the bird. Its eye was bright and anxious; it opened and closed its beak, beseeching, soundless. Gently she picked it up. It was a jackdaw nestling, not even fledged, and its beak was crossed. It had been flung to the ground to die. Janet thought that there was little hope for it, but she took it indoors to the warmth of a haybox on the back of the Aga. To her surprise and delight the bird survived. Soon she was able to move the box to her bedroom where she tended the incessant cheepings night and day. She decided that he was a male bird; his name was Claws. Now when she entered the room he came hopping to meet her, wings outstretched in welcome, beak agape. She took her old doll's house from the nursery. At last it had a purpose. She had never played with it and its only previous use to her had been on the long-ago occasion when a friendly rat had sauntered up to Francis in the woodshed. He had brought it in, and he and Janet had installed it in the doll's house, where it crept about on its belly, peering balefully out of the latticed windows and gnawing the staircase. They secreted liberal quantities of mince and stew in their table napkins and ferried them up the stairs to the voracious and grateful rodent. Lulu had become suspicious of Janet's sudden interest in the despised mock Tudor residence; she opened the house when no one was around, saw the rat with delight and stroked its tremulous snout. It sank its teeth into her plump pink thumb. She was rushed to hospital for injections against Weil's disease and the rat was banished back to the woodshed. Word spread through the village; rats teeming in the very nursery at Auchnasaugh. Just what they would have expected. When Francis and Janet took their rat its evening meal beneath the fragrant wood pile, they found it murdered, ripped apart by other rats, maddened by the taint of mankind. 'Like King Lear,' pronounced Janet. 'Someone says, "O let me kiss that hand" and he says, "Let me wipe it first; it smells of mortality".' 'That's not what he means,' said Francis. 'Yes it is,' said Janet. It was what Lear meant, and it was what she meant too.

When the doll's house had been scrubbed out and flooded with Jeyes fluid, it was handed over to Lulu and Caro who could be trusted to use it sensibly. Now they shrieked with fury as Janet tipped their furniture on to the floor and contemptuously shook out their apple-cheeked happy family. 'You're far too old to play with it. What do you want it for? I'm going to tell on you.' 'Shut up, it's mine,' snapped Janet. It was just the right size for Claws and his personal furbishments, at this stage of his development. She left the windows and doors open so that he could come in and out as he wished. The house needed a name. She loved addresses; she had memorised the St Uncumba's list of five hundred, imagining each one, furnishing it, in some cases providing gardens or parkland, in others, lamplit alleyways where assassins prowled. Her favourites were the ones which sounded suburban. She imagined soft, deep wall-to-wall carpets, imitation log fires which gave out real heat and did not burn holes in carpets, divan beds, perfumed bathrooms with pastel accessories en suite (unlike the looming, glacial Elderslie Washdown which clanked and gurgled in the mildewed nursery bathroom at Auchnasaugh); in such places the feminine mystique might flourish like the green bay tree, which would be growing in a neat tub by the diamond-paned porch. As usual she felt guilty and treacherous for these thoughts. Her allegiance was to Auchnasaugh. But there was no reason why Claws' residence should not be named for that discreet, charming and muted world. Carefully she painted '8, Belitha Villas' above the front door.

Alas for human aspiration. Claws grew apace and although he could stalk about quite comfortably in his villa he made it clear that Janet's whole room was to be his territory. He skittered about the floor and clambered, flailing his wings, on to the bed. He was fascinated by the dressing table and spent much of his time grimacing in the mirror and overturning the shiny little pots and bottles which Vera had bought for Janet on their day in Edinburgh. At feeding times he nestled in her lap while she dropped squamous delicacies down his throat from a silver salt spoon. She stroked his stubby, growing feathers. Soon he must learn to fly and to feed himself. She worried about his crossed bill.

He taught himself to fly, launching himself from the gable of his villa and hurtling on to Janet's shoulder as she sat reading. Each fine afternoon she took him down to the terrace garden where she had found him, so that when the urge came he might go, take up the life of a jackdaw, forget her. He hopped about, pecking at the earth, and she was glad to see that his damaged beak was only a slight handicap. He could fend for himself. He flew farther now, sometimes out of sight among the trees, but he always came back, fluttering and drifting down to the azalea bushes. The day came when he did not return. With heavy heart, Janet tramped up the steep path; she had dreaded this necessary parting and although she knew she must be glad for him she could not restrain her tears. Listlessly she began to reassemble her ravaged bedroom. Claws hurtled through the open window and skidded across her Greek dictionary. 'Kya,' he observed, settling on the Anglepoise lamp.

After this they were seldom apart. When Janet walked up the great staircase, Claws hopped beside her; he could have flown up the stairs but he never did. She carried him along the corridors, fearful of the cats. Out of doors he would fly to great heights, turn and plummet out of the clouds to her shoulder. He came to her call. To call a bird from the sky! It seemed beyond a mortal's lot. If he was outside and she was inside he would search for her, peering in through every window until he saw her; then he hovered, knocking on the pane with his crossed beak until he was admitted. If she went off in the car he would follow, making darting swoops at the car windows so that they had to stop and take him back and shut him in his villa. Janet could not understand how he knew that she was in the car at all, for on many of these occasions he had been indoors when she left, in the care of Rhona or the boys. On walks or rides he flew far ahead, exploring; sometimes he hopped companionably alongside her or perched on the front of the saddle. He was free to range wherever he wished; always he came back to her and at night they repaired to her room, where he roosted like a guardian spirit on the iron rail of her bed. He was a magic bird. She loved him more than she had loved anything, anything or anyone.

Her room looked like a rock in mid Atlantic.

> *Miss Buss and Miss Beale*
> *Cupid's darts do not feel.*
> *How different from us,*
> *Miss Beale and Miss Buss.*

declaimed the girls. On Saturday evenings they danced together in the boot room to the strains of someone's record player. 'Catch a falling star and put it in your pocket' or 'Once I had a secret love'. Janet remained aloof from this, as always, but was now surprised to find herself stirred by romantic impulse. It was as though her intense love for her jackdaw had unlocked her heart and left it open to the weather. 'Set me as a seal upon thine arm', she wrote in her book, 'Set me as a seal upon thy heart. For love is strong as death'. She also inscribed the closing lines of *Medea*:

> *Many are the Fates which Zeus in Olympus dispenses;*
> *Many matters the Gods bring to surprising ends.*
> *The things we thought would happen do not happen . . .*

The gods whom Janet had chosen played tricks on mortals for their pleasure; this she had not considered. She believed that she could control her destiny. She dreamed of unutterable, unearthly love, passion of the spirit, not of the flesh, a pure and searing fire. She did not expect to find an object. She brooded upon poets distanced by death, heroes of legend, demon lovers, powerful yet insubstantial.

Her life seemed to have entered a period of calm, a stretch of slow, clear-flowing water, illuminated by her love for her jackdaw and quickened by her apprehensions of romance. It was her last year at school and she was able to spend most of her time in the library, an ancient building overlooking a garden of weeping trees and lavender. The scent of rainy leaves hung in the mild air. Another window looked down on to the street. On the sill stood a wide glass carafe, half full of water, and in the water she could see the miniature and upside-down reflection of everything that happened far below and out of sight. Columns of girls passed through it, hurrying to their houses. They looked like swarms of midges. Once a bride and her attendants came from the church and drifted like petals across the greenish depths. When dusk fell, the street lamps were golden sea anemones. Janet was happy there, working on into the evening. When she came out, the frosty night sky filled her with excitement; she felt intensely alive. Her hair had now grown long enough to touch her shoulders and it crackled and stood on end as she brushed it; electric sparks whirled about her head.

Vera was planning to launch Janet into society that winter. To this end she had arranged a fearsome programme of subscription dances, commencing unfortunately with the event which should have been its climax; the hunt ball. Janet was appalled; she had looked forward to spending the holidays in her room with her books and her jackdaw. To her huge relief Claws had not been seduced by the charms of Rhona's room, where he had been an unwelcome and unwilling lodger during the term. By day he had been thrust out of doors, and at night when he flew back, always to Janet's room, he had been shut firmly in his villa. 'You see,' said Vera, 'It's perfectly simple to keep a bird and still have a fresh, pretty room.' Janet ignored her. '8, Belitha Villas' resumed its role as a place of safety in the dismal event of outings by car. Claws roosted on Janet's bed by night and kept her company by day. Sometimes, when the wind was wild and other jackdaws flocked and shrieked across the racing clouds, he flew out to join them. They drove him off and sent him plunging headlong back to the battlements and Janet's window. She was glad that he too was an outcast. '*Nos contra mundum*, Claws,' she told him. She wondered whether she could teach him to say this. But first he must learn to say 'Never more'. If she were given any money for Christmas, she planned to spend it on lengths of purple taffeta which she would nail to her walls as a start to redesigning the room in the manner of Edgar Allan Poe.

Vera declared that Rhona should also go to the hunt ball. There had been trouble over Janet's choice of an evening dress. She had refused to be guided by her mother or by the lady in Watt and Grants. When they had peeped into the fitting room to see how she was faring in the white chiffon they had selected, they found her sitting on a chair, sucking her thumb. She had not even taken off her coat. With the thumb hovering a fraction outside her lower lip she announced, 'It's no good. It doesn't fit.' Vera was speechless, doubly mortified by the thumb and the blatant lie. The thumb was about to be reinserted. Hastily she said, 'Well, have you seen anything you really like?' Janet brightened. 'Yes,' she said, 'the purple one.' Vera had also noticed the purple dress; it was uniquely hideous, festooned with massive bows and encumbered by a bizarre scalloped train like a dragon's tail. It might be worn with panache by a mad old person whose brains had been jumbled by hunting accidents, and who was indulgently regarded as 'game', but by a young girl never. 'Never. Never. Never,' she said aloud, surprising herself. Janet leered at her. 'Tricolonic anaphora', she remarked in her most irritating, pedantic voice. The familiar sense of numb despair began to creep over Vera. 'Oh all right then, try it on.' Surely even Janet would see how monstrous it looked. Janet emerged from the fitting room with flushed cheeks and shining eyes; she looked almost pretty for a moment. 'It's absolutely beautiful. Exactly right.' It was then that Vera decided to take Rhona to the ball. At least she could find pleasure in the appearance of one daughter. And although Rhona really was too young, she was tall for her age and naturally elegant. She would look delightful in the white chiffon, a winter rose. And Francis was always presentable, if annoying.

In view of the great frozen distances to be covered, from diverse directions, they were to meet with the rest of their party at the ball itself. Hector and Francis were resplendent in kilts and jabots. 'I shall be fiendishly handsome,' Francis had prophesied. 'Like Clark Gable in *Gone With The Wind*. There will be quite a flutter in the dovecotes.' *Gone With The Wind*: Janet could only remember the piled dead and litter of wounded in the great square of Atlanta, and far up against the blue sky the Southern flag flickering in the breeze like the tongue of a snake. Rhona looked like a nymph from a Greek vase. She was incandescent with excitement. Vera and she had spent the whole day in girlish conspiracy. Janet was envious and contemptuous; she wished them to know of her contempt. 'What is the late November doing, with the confusion of the spring?' she asked Vera. Vera paid no attention. She was sorting through boxes of old lipsticks, sharing secrets of the past with Rhona. 'And can you imagine, this is the colour we all wore in 1946.' Janet slunk off to her room.

Now as Hector drove them northwards, sipping occasionally from his hip flask, Janet was in good spirits, for she felt like the queen of the night in her purple dress. The queen of air and darkness. Perhaps she would meet a kindred spirit: 'But one man loved the pilgrim soul in you.' This was just what she wanted. But how did anyone recognise a pilgrim soul? She had sat for a long time in front of her mirror turning her head about and twisting her features into soulful expressions. Nothing was quite right. Face turned to three-quarter profile, raised chin and upturned eyeballs gave an impression of an ecstatic pre-Raphaelite maiden, but she could hardly walk around like that. Vera had once said that in infancy Janet had beautiful eyelids. She felt that little could be made of this. She recalled that one of the bad-tempered Greek goddesses shared this meaningless asset with her. Hera probably, the worst of the lot. Calliblepharous; an unappealing adjective. And there had been the occasion when a friend of her parents had told them she thought Janet had a lovely face. Vera had reported this in accents of astonishment. Janet's delight had rapidly turned to fear. She must never again meet this woman in case she changed her mind.

'And don't forget what I told you about your gloves,' said Vera suddenly from the front of the car. Janet could remember nothing of the decorum and etiquette of these gloves, long, limp and white with exasperating tiny pearl buttons. She resolved that she would lose hers as soon as they arrived. She began to feel nervous. Francis was silent, doubtless brooding on his conquests. 'You'd better not talk the way you usually do; they'll think you're mad. Or showing off,' she advised him, from bitter experience. 'Nonsense,' said Francis. 'They'll love it. They don't like it when you go on about things because you're a girl. And of course you are extremely boring. Girls need to know when to keep their mouths shut.'

The hunt ball was held in the Master's house, enormous and Georgian, surrounded by rolling acres of snowy lawn and cedar trees. 'More like an English country house,' said Vera approvingly, and certainly it was unusually well heated. On each side of the lofty entrance hall were vistas of long rooms opening into one another, each with a blazing log fire. The ballroom lay beyond the hall, brilliantly lit by chandeliers, pillared and mirrored. The Master, clad in hunting pink, greeted them warmly and seemed not to notice that Janet gave him both her hands to shake, having entangled the buttons of her gloves in her desperate attempt to get rid of them. They found the rest of their party. The grown-ups greeted each other with ecstatic cries, kisses and handshakes. The young exchanged muttered introductions and eyed each other in silence. Janet had met two of the three girls before, but she knew only one of the boys, from long ago at Auchnasaugh. Francis and the boys moved off towards a drinks table. Vera watched them with narrowed eyes. The girls studied one another's dresses. Janet was pleased to see that these were all rather similar, demurely pretty pastels with full floating skirts. 'Very *jeune fille*,' she thought. She wriggled her hips so that her dragon tail swished from side to side. The shiny purple bows trembled like gigantic moths. Quite a few people were staring at her. She felt elated. Each of the boys, except for Francis, and each of the fathers asked her for a dance. Carefully she pencilled their names into her tiny pink programme book; she noticed that there were still a great many dances left to be filled in, but no doubt her partners would return to her. Or of course she might meet her demon lover.

Spinning about in an eightsome reel, she began to have doubts about her dress. People kept stepping on the train; sometimes it flew up behind her and caught on a sporran. Once it knocked a glass out of a woman's hand. She noticed the relief with which her partners escorted her back to the rows of gilded chairs along the side of the room, where the dowagers sat in speculation and gossip. 'Exquisite little thing,' one of them was saying now to Vera. Hope rose in Janet. 'And the one in purple is your eldest girl?' Hope subsided. 'Such an unusual dress. Most sophisticated.' 'Yes,' said Vera. 'One might say that. She chose it herself.' 'And does she still ride? I remember she used to be so keen.' 'She still rides a little,' said Vera. 'But really she's more interested in her books.' She had to justify Janet's appearance somehow. 'She's rather dreamy, the academic sort, you know.' 'Ah. A pity about the riding. Keeps them away from the boys. I always say, who needs a fella between their knees when they could have a good hunter. Mind you,' the harridan added, 'from the look of her that may not be a problem. A different matter with your younger girl. You'll have to watch her like a hawk. A honey pot.' Vera was tight-lipped. 'Excuse me one moment, please.' She rose and summoned the young females of her party, 'Come along girls. Time to powder our noses.' In an obedient drift they followed her. They were like tugs in the wake of a majestic, sleekbowed liner, thought Janet, hastening after them. Others saw it differently. A couple of very old men sat by the fire in the hall; they leant close over their sticks and their eyes were bright and roguish. As Vera's company rustled by, one observed to the other, 'The hens go marching off to the midden.' A burst of wheezing laughter dissolved into prolonged coughing.

The seventh dance was a waltz. This was the moment Janet dreaded, for she would be obliged to speak. Talk was not possible in Highland dancing, and thank goodness for that. She was booked for this waltz by a pale-faced boy called Keith; she reflected that this must be the worst name in the world. She did not intend to use it. They set forth on their circuit. Keith cleared his throat, frowning. 'Have you been to many of these sort of do's?' he asked, sounding half dead with boredom. 'No,' said Janet. She thought of a whole sentence. 'This is my very first.' 'Oh,' said Keith. Janet trod on her train and lurched sideways, colliding with the couple beside them. Keith grabbed her before she fell, and heaved her into the vertical with such force that she bumped her nose against his shoulder. Her eyes watered. 'Oh dear, sorry,' said Keith in his monotone. 'Do you have a dog?' asked Janet, trying to look sparkling and keenly interested. Keith ignored this. 'Let's go and have a drink,' he said. They manoeuvred their way off the dance floor. He seized two glasses of champagne from a passing waiter. Janet glanced round uneasily. Vera was nowhere to be seen. She gulped it down in two draughts. Her palate prickled; her eyes watered again. 'You'd better have another,' droned Keith. This time Janet sipped in a ladylike manner. Keith looked disappointed. 'It's hellish hot,' he said. The words rang a warning bell in Janet's mind, but she could not place them. 'Let's have a breath of air.' He led the way to a french window which stood open on to the terrace. The night was deliciously cold, like the champagne. The moon glittered across the untrodden snow. Keith took her hand: 'Come and look over the balustrade.' Janet was horrified. She hadn't held anyone's hand since she was four years old and she certainly didn't want to now. How ridiculous. What was she meant to do with it? It lay limply wrapped in her own like some awful dead thing. 'What a beautiful body you have,' drawled Keith. She couldn't have heard correctly. 'I beg your pardon?' she squawked. 'I said, what a beautiful body you have,' reiterated the lifeless voice. Janet snatched her hand from his flaccid clasp and careered back into the ballroom. Where could she go for safety? If she went to the ladies' rooms she would have to pass those two evil old men. She decided on the dining room. To her relief it was almost empty. With shaking hands she took a bowl of trifle from the long buffet and sat panting at a rickety table. Luckily she had thought to bring a book with her. From her evening bag she extracted Carcopino's *Daily Life in Ancient Rome* and propped it against a vase of snowdrops and holly berries. Her heart stopped thumping. She helped herself to another mound of trifle and read on. Cream dribbled off her spoon on to the tablecloth, on to her dress, down her front. She did not care.

Towards midnight she returned cautiously to the ballroom, peering this way and that like some quaint woodland creature. She inserted herself among the ranks of seated dowagers. It was still stiflingly hot. The band was playing a quickstep. Pallid Keith whirled past with Rhona in his arms. Rhona's face was flushed and vivid; she was talking with animation. Over her shoulder Keith winked at Janet. There was an unpleasant smell in the air; Janet associated it with Keith. Her neighbour was fanning herself with her programme card. 'A distinct whiff of the farmyard,' she said. 'Wherever can it be coming from?' They stared around them. 'A cow byre I'd say,' said someone else. 'Or a midden. Surely he hasn't put a midden right by the house. Let's shut that window.' Janet leapt up, remembering her manners: 'I'll do it.' As she moved she realised that the powerful smell of dairy produce emanated from her, from her bosom to be exact. The blobs of double cream which had trickled into her cleavage had turned sour with the heat. Briskly she closed the window, and made her way, smiling vaguely, in a wide arc past the dowagers. Once in the hall she ran for it, bolting up the staircase to the secure haven of the ladies' room. Unaware of her pungent passing, the old men slept in their chairs.

As they clattered and clicked at last over the frosted gravel to the car Janet trod again on her train. She seized it and wrenched; there was a pleasant sound of rending. She tugged it; she dropped her evening bag and with both hands twisted and pulled, spinning round like a mechanical ballerina, stamping on it as she heaved. 'Do let me help,' said Francis, looming up behind her. Off came the dragon tail, ripping away part of the skirt as well. Janet hurled the glinting bundle on to the lawn. There it was found the next day, giving rise to wanton speculation and establishing Janet as a woman of easy virtue. For her dress had been, as she had hoped, distinctive.

CHAPTER ELEVEN

Thus began and ended Janet's social life, apart from a brief excursion on Hogmanay, when at Vera's insistence Hector took Janet and Francis first footing. They were to visit a widower who lived in the nearest coastal village. 'He's always been so kind to us, and taken such an interest in the children, and with his wife dead only two months ago he'll be dreadfully lonely. I doubt if he knows many people round there. They never went out.' It was thrilling to step out of doors just after midnight into the first new day of a new year. The stars were brilliant, the heavens luminous and expectant. They paused on the way to watch the northern lights. Their eerie flickering was a portent. All will be well and all manner of things will be well.

They parked near the church and walked down the narrow street to Mr Neville's cottage by the breakwater. Their footsteps echoed in the frosty air. Old people came hopefully to their doors as they passed and retreated in disappointment. Through lighted windows Janet glimpsed tables laid out with black buns and trays of glasses and whisky, and anxious faces peering out into the darkness. She could not bear it. Where were the heartless young? She clenched her hands and prayed with all her might that each house would have at least one visitor, one traveller bearing memories of love and loyalty and the irredeemable unquenchable past.

Clutching their pieces of coal, they knocked on Mr Neville's door. It was whisked open. Hector stepped carefully, left foot first, over the threshold. A genial hubbub greeted them. The lonely widower was not alone. Holding on to the wall with one hand, he came to greet them, lurching and weaving but none the less dignified. Hector set his coal carefully on the fire and joined the throng around the table. Francis followed him. Janet stood still, overwhelmed with shyness. She did not know what to do. The moon spread a dazzle of silver on the sea; she wanted to go to the window and watch it but she dared not move. She was still holding her piece of coal; she could not put it on the fire. Someone thrust a glass of whisky into her hand and before she could say 'No, thank you' moved on. The little room was very hot and full of noisy people. Slowly and carefully, trying to make no sound, she put down her glass and her coal and took off her heavy coat. Then she picked up the coal again, and the glass also, so as not to seem rude or ungrateful. She prayed to the moon that someone might come and talk to her, release her from this tranced immobility. The moon gave her a leery look and sidled behind a cloud. A moment or two later it relented and reappeared; but Janet thought its expression malign. Perhaps she was mistaken, for here was a man standing at her elbow with every sign of convivial goodwill. 'I know you,' he was saying. 'I met you long ago, when your family lived at the manse. You were just a wee thing then; you won't remember. Your grandfather was always very good to me.' He gulped his whisky. Janet smiled encouragingly; she was still speechless, but she was beginning to feel less estranged. 'Aye,' he said, 'a long time past. And now you're grown up.' He stared at her from unfocused eyes. 'Indeed so. Quite the young lady.' Suddenly he was pinching her left bosom with a hand which had no fingers, only a row of wizened purple stumps. As suddenly, his hand dropped, he turned on his heel and walked away. Janet stood there. Again, she did not know what to do. Nothing she had read, nothing she had been taught, nothing in her life had prepared her for this. If she kept very still perhaps it would turn out that it had not happened; or perhaps she would cease to exist. She stood motionless, but her offending bosom rose and fell. She must not breathe. She held her breath. Now she was truly motionless. She fainted.

March was mild that year, and the snow melted earlier than anyone could remember. The gentlest of winds stirred the wild cherry blossom against a soft blue sky. Daffodils and snowdrops bloomed together. Janet's jackdaw was behaving strangely. He would climb into her pocket and peer up at her, twisting his head in a beckoning manner, his eye bright with meaning. She became worried and searched for a jackdaw book. In Konrad Lorenz's wonderful *King Solomon's Ring* she found the explanation. He wished to lure her into her pocket, and there they would build a nest together. He had chosen her as his mate, his true and everlasting love, for jackdaws are monogamous. How strange that the creature who offered her all this should be a bird. How strange for him that she should be a human. What a merry little joke for the gods. She felt honoured and glorified, but she was glad when summer began and the nesting season was over. One day as Claws paced along the roof of 8, Belitha Villas, he spoke. 'Never mind,' he said. Janet was overjoyed; but surely he meant to say 'Never more'. 'Never more, Claws,' she said, 'Never more.' 'Never mind,' he repeated, and this time he sounded like Francis.

'I thought it was a more useful expression,' said Francis. 'But I've been teaching him to say "Never more" for almost a year.' 'Well, I've been teaching him to say "Never mind" for about three weeks. I think we may draw certain conclusions about our respective teaching methods. I also think that Poe's poem would have been a lot more fun if the Raven said "Never mind" and I shall be emending any copies which come my way.' Janet glanced anxiously at her guano-encrusted bookcase. 'Don't worry. I've sorted yours out already.'

Janet's last summer term at St Uncumba's passed swiftly, as examination terms always do. She completed her 'A' levels and attempted Maths 'O' level for the fifth time. There was a total eclipse of the sun on the day the 'A' levels ended. The girls believed it was a cosmic confirmation of their new adult lives; they sat out on the grass in the ghostly light and vowed that come what may they would meet together in seventeen years' time, when the next total eclipse was due. There followed a period of elegiac lazing; the blue skies and the blue sea shimmered with the poignancy of farewell. The staff invited girls to tea, plied them with cakes and revealed themselves as warm, witty human beings. Everyone suddenly liked everyone else. Cynthia and Janet, buoyed by the happy knowledge that they need never speak to each other again, wept and embraced at the prospect of their separation.

Just before the end of term Miss Wilson, who taught Latin, took Janet to a classical verse speaking competition at Glasgow University. Janet recited the passage from the Georgics which described Orpheus' final loss of Eurydice. She was nervous beforehand and shook uncontrollably when she was on the stage. She spoke her lines over-emphatically so that they seemed to be a harangue rather than a lamentation. Her teeth chattered in the pauses. Mortified, she sat with bowed head beside kind, comforting Miss Wilson and listened to the other speakers, many of whom were even worse than she. People sniffed and coughed and shuffled. There were too many entries. The air grew heavy with apathy. Janet longed for tea. Then suddenly there was absolute silence; the atmosphere was electric. Janet sat bolt upright, her spine tingling, her heart leaping. A boy was speaking Greek, Hector's farewell to Andromache. Mournful and tender, cruel and foreboding, beyond all else noble, the beautiful voice rose finally to the tolling invocation of the gods and died away. People jumped to their feet, applauding wildly. Janet still sat, transfixed, staring at the boy's dark face. She had fallen in love.

It is said that those who are visited by a vision are not to be envied, for they are thereafter haunted. So it was with Janet. She learned the passage of Homer by heart and nightly repeated it to herself, trying to conjure up the boy's voice. She knew his name, for of course he had won the competition. She discovered that he had a cousin in her year at St Uncumba's. In the genial atmosphere of the end of term she persuaded this cousin to give her a photograph of him. She also found out his address and wrote to him – a simple, objective sort of letter expressing her admiration for his recitation and her hope that one day they might meet to discuss classical matters. He did not reply.

Back at Auchnasaugh the blue days of earlier summer were now obliterated by a pervasive mist which hung all day long, every day. In the evenings it dispersed, revealing a watery sky and fitful shafts of pallid sunlight. Janet was unconcerned. She kept to her room, reading love poetry and dreaming of Desmond (for this was his pleasing name). From her window she could see only a uniform whiteness, with the occasional spare suggestion of a branch. The glen was blotted out and silent but for the sound of dripping trees. When a bird sang out of the fog it startled her. Claws was depressed and stayed in with her; sometimes he shredded a page of her book to create a diversion. He could sense that she was abstracted. He sat on her shoulder and tweaked her hair, crying 'Never mind' at her unresponsive back. One day he noticed the photograph of Desmond protruding from the *Iliad*. He pulled it out and threw it on the floor. So it was that the creature who loved her most brought about her destruction.

Vera and Hector were suspicious of Janet. Not only was she more than usually reclusive, but she had lost weight and her eyes had a feverish shine. Vera went to examine her room for signs of depravity and found the photograph lying on the bird-stained carpet. She carried it off and showed it to Hector. They resolved to have it out with Janet.

'We don't know what you're up to, Janet, but we know you're

up to something. What we do insist on knowing is the name of this young man and your connection with him.' A great tide of fury surged up in Janet. 'I'm not going to tell you,' she said. 'And please give me back that photograph. It's my property.' 'Don't be insolent. And do as you're told. We want his name.' 'I'm not telling you,' Janet said again. They began to shout at her. Their faces were distorted with anger. Hector tore the photograph in pieces and flung them on the fire. Janet burst into tears and slammed out of the room. She locked her door and barricaded it with chairs. Then she sat weeping on her bed. She cradled Claws on her lap and rocked from side to side. 'Poor little bird,' she sobbed. 'Poor little bird.'

The next day she refused to unlock the door and she would not answer when they spoke to her. They were all supposed to be going away for a couple of days to the west coast, where the sun was apparently shining. 'If you don't come out this minute, Janet, you'll have to stay behind.' 'Good,' said Janet silently. 'Right, that's it. You're a very silly little girl. And you won't like being here by yourself one bit. On your own head be it. You're old enough to fend for yourself. We'll see you on Monday. Meanwhile you had better think one or two things over.' Janet listened to the retreating car engine. She waited for half an hour to be sure that they had gone and then she took down her barricades. How wonderful to have all Auchnasaugh to herself.

The day passed pleasantly. She wandered about the castle, entering rooms which were usually out of bounds because they were dangerous, or because they contained important documents. She particularly enjoyed the circular attic room above the circular nursery. It contained a huge wasps' nest. She found a battered old suitcase full of Lila's flappy black clothes. These she decided to wear for the family homecoming. How angry that would make Vera. She would persist in wearing them and eventually, with any luck, Vera would ask in exasperation why she always had to wear black and she would reply like Nina in *The Seagull*, 'I am in mourning for my life'. For some time she had been looking for a chance to use this line, and it would make Vera even angrier. With difficulty she dragged a tall mildewed mirror down from the attic to her room and admired the greenish quality it gave to her skin. In the afternoon she and Claws walked down through the mist to visit the ponies. She decided that she enjoyed moving through this vaporous element. She felt weightless, as though she might fly.

When the mist cleared in early evening the sun shone down from a clear blue sky for the first time in weeks. She fed the cats and then she fed the dogs. Claws and she shared some digestive biscuits and a pot of tea, making a horrible soggy mess which she resolved to clear up later, not now. The kitchen was an enjoyable place without Miss Wales and Jim. She supposed they had been given the weekend off since no one was meant to be here. In the nursery she changed the parrot's water and gave him some more sunflower seeds. It was growing dark, and the evening suddenly seemed to stretch out endlessly before her. She would go and read in her room. But she could not settle. Restless, she paced about. She went down to the drawing room and drew the curtains. She was beginning to feel vulnerable and exposed, a single human being in this great empty place, and not another soul for miles. Not, of course, that there was anything to fear. It was just a strange sensation, like being an ant crawling across a globe. Owls went shrieking by in the blackness. The rose branches fingered the windows. She thought she heard footsteps outside on the grass; she stood rigid. Then a cat mewed. She had forgotten how much noise animals can make at night. The moon had risen; she went outside to look at it. It was almost full and sailing swiftly through great banks of cloud. She felt cold and returned to the drawing room. She decided that a sensible thing to do was to have a drink. It would calm her nerves and warm her. Perhaps then she wouldn't mind being alone, but at present she was not enjoying it.

She selected a bottle of malt whisky on the grounds that it was almost colourless and therefore, she hoped, harmless. She sipped it with misgiving. Crystalline fire flickered through her veins; she gasped, then was warm. She walked about the drawing room with the drink in her hand, feeling worldly. She finished one glass and poured herself another. She put a record on, a Bach violin quartet. Then she went upstairs with her glass, turning the music to full volume so that she could hear it. She rummaged about in Vera's dressing table; she found lipstick and rouge and mascara. Peering into the mirror, she applied them liberally. Then she hung her head upside down and brushed her hair hard; she shook it back from her face and was pleased to see the electric sparks like fireflies dancing around it. She felt strong and bright and beautiful. Perhaps it was worth being female after all. She anointed herself with Chanel's Gardenia, spilling a drop or two into her whisky. Oh well, it would make it taste nicer. It did; she was drinking flowers and fire. No wonder bees worked so hard. Now she lifted Vera's black lace evening dress down from its hanger. It was fastened by a series of tiny hooks and it took her a long time. At last she went to her own room and looked at her reflection in the submarine murk of her new mirror. She was amazed; she was unrecognisable. She closed the door firmly on the protesting jackdaw and set forth down the stairs towards the distant music. When she reached the stone flight she held tightly to the banister, for Vera's high-heeled shoes were slippery and treacherous. But as she passed the stained-glass window thoughts of this or anything else were routed by the wild spirallings of the violins. She was walking down into music made palpable; it swept upwards like a tidal wave and broke over her and engulfed her. In the drawing room she pulled off her shoes and flung them into the corner. She drank some more gardenia-flavoured whisky and sat brooding, suddenly melancholy. 'O who would inhabit this bleak world alone?' she said aloud. She yearned for her love. She had suffered for him. Surely she deserved him. She switched off the violins; they were steeped in pain, torn heart strings of the suffering hopeless world. The moon was high and flooding light through the staircase window. She turned off the hall lamps and watched the crimson and blue and green wash over the grey steps, and the cockatoo cast his rubies over the flagstones. Once again she prayed to the moon. Help me; bring me happiness; bring him to me. The moon beamed on her as she stood below the window. She felt hope revive. The moon had given her a thought. In the drawing room was a copy of Theocritus and in that book was a magic spell for a girl to call her lover to her side. It was addressed to the Moon. The girl was supposed to be spinning, but *tant pis* to that; she could find something to take the place of a spinning wheel. She ran back to the drawing room and found the book. Should she have music? She glanced at the stack of records. The top one was Orpheus and Eurydice. This could not be coincidence. Her hands shook as she set it on the turntable. She took a crystal sphere from the mantelpiece for her substitute wheel. She turned the music high and ran up the stairs to the wide windowsill. There she sat, turning the crystal in her hands as she chanted the spell. The moon lit the pages of the book. The spell was long and complicated and some of it she did not understand. She repeated the choral lines, read the verses, repeated the choral lines, turning the crystal over and over.

> *Shine clear and bright, Moon goddess . . .*
> *O crystal, bring my beloved to my home . . .*
> *Think, dear goddess, of my love and how it came about . . .*
> *Bring him hither, bring him home . . .*
> *Shine clear, shine bright Moon goddess . . .*
>
> *What is life to me without thee,*
> *What is left if thou art gone . . .*
> *. . . What is life without my love?*

lamented Orpheus as Janet muttered away in the shadows. The further reaches of the hall lay in profound darkness, intensified by the moonlit staircase.

So it was that Janet first saw the male figure as it emerged from deep blackness into lesser blackness. The Moon had granted her wish, had brought her happiness. Crazed and joyful she careered down the stairs and flung herself passionately at the dark figure. There was a dreadful cry of outrage and disgust; she heard a voice hiss, 'You filthy wee whore', but she did not feel the knife as it stabbed again and again and again. Only a great langour seemed to draw her downwards, slowly falling as Orpheus cried out for her, falling towards the roar of the waters of Avernus.

Jim wiped his rabbit skinning knife on his trouser leg. He had come in to turn off the music and the lights and so he turned them off. Then he went into the outer darkness. For a long time the castle was silent.

The wild winds of dawn beat about Auchnasaugh, moaning through the treetops and rattling the windowpanes. At last they retreated northwards, bearing with them Janet's spirit, far north of love or grief, until their withdrawing was no more than the sigh of the sea in a shell.

SHORT STORIES

IN VAGLIAGLI

Long before I ever went to Tuscany, which was once Etruria, I saw in Rome the Etruscan Apollo of Veii, with his loving and pitiless smile. This was not the sun god of the Greeks or Romans: this god presided over human sacrifice. I understood him better after a summer in Vagliagli.

Vagliagli lies north of Siena in the hills, surrounded by steep, dense forest of scrub oak and pine. Above, narrow white dust tracks climb to a bare, lunar landscape. The people of Vagliagli are called the Vagliaglini; they are swarthy and inscrutable, they do not speak to strangers. For those who wish to be serious about wine there is a famous Enoteca in the village, much frequented by Saxon plunderers. Their Volvos whirl in and out in clouds of dust. Otherwise it is a silent, lonely place. In late summer pregnant vipers hang from the forest trees of Vagliagli.

Below the forest line, on gentler slopes, are vineyards, and there, in a tall old house with thick walls, steep stairs and tiny windows, overlooking a hamlet, we stayed one summer. Sitting in early evening on the terrace we watched land and sky merge into one darkness, lit only by a bell tower whose arched window became at last a glowing doorway into the black hillside; the air was fragrant with thyme and fennel, cicadas sang in the vineyard and we felt blessed indeed. But the next day Patrick became ill, and day after day he grew worse, unable to eat, unable to cope with the stairs, suffocating in the infernal heat of a densely walled south facing room. All the rooms in this house were hot. It seemed that the sun never really left it. Doctors came and went, reassuring, all specialists in heart and respiration; injections and drugs marked out the days' bright hours, impersonal and implicit with menace as the radials on a sundial, and bearing the sundial's urgent message, *Tempus fugit* and *Carpe diem.*

One night I sat outside to watch an eclipse of the moon. As the earth's shadow finally overcast it, I noticed that the rhythm of the cicadas had changed, slowing and labouring. I thought of Ecclesiastes 'And the sound of the grasshopper shall be a burden, For man goeth to his long home.' The frail rim of light struggled, wavered against the engulfing blackness, burst out again in agonised pangs of sullen red, then suddenly was gone. The cicadas were silent. In panic I rushed up the stairs to our room. But he was alive, he was breathing steadily and indeed the next day he seemed stronger and was able to come downstairs.

The house at this time contained many people, too many people, of the wrong age for each other. The two tiny children, worn out by the heat and unable to play on the thistly scrub outside, quarrelled and wailed unceasingly. Their intense pleasure was to feed the starving cats which slunk up the outside staircase into the living room. Soon fifteen starving cats were crouching behind sofas, leaping on tables, licking plates and saucepans, vomiting soundlessly on the cheerful rustic rugs. Two of them mated in the pot of basil. Fast as they were driven out by flailing adult arms, legs and brooms, so fast they returned. Annie had a special cat, so stunted and emaciated that it lay limply on her lap or shoulder, doing no wrong, and passively enduring dolls' tea parties. She dressed it in a long baby gown and rocked it to sleep in a cradle, droning a tuneless lullaby. Later she found it there, stiff and dead in its pink ribboned bonnet. The boys buried it, with difficulty, in the hard, dry melon patch. After that no one would eat the melons. The boys too were having troubles, missing other boys' company, but they were inarticulate in the face of the noisy competition from the little ones and the teenage girls. The girls wanted only to meet boys, older boys, Italian or British, no matter, so long as they were romantic and had transport. But there were only two of them, they spoke no Italian, and they didn't feel confident enough to travel the fourteen miles to Siena on their own. By day they slept, or seethed about the house, and each night, when the moon rose, they would put on their most beautiful dresses and run out into the vineyards, Titian hair and golden hair flying behind them, in search of an Endymion. But by daylight or by moonlight one man only walked along those white dust roads. He was the village priest; he had suffered a terrible and disabling illness; and was performing an autocure; between the hamlet and the next village and back again he trudged, his head askew, his twisted arms held strangely to the left, unable to speak, intent only on reaching his goal and starting out again.

Then there were ourselves, and our host and hostess who gallantly maintained the idioms of a cheerful family holiday, with excursions and picnics, swimming and endless shopping and assurances that it was a joy to have us there, and no trouble at all to fetch drugs and doctors and have a sense of doom in the house. We drank a lot of wine.

On the day after the eclipse of the moon ('only for noctambules' proclaimed the local paper), we took Patrick and the wheelchair to Siena, to the cathedral and the marble floor of crazed Sibyls, Hermes Trismegistos, and the slaughtered Innocents. Among the votives hung five motorbike helmets. Patrick tried to reach the holy water in the great font by the entrance, dragging himself out of the chair, clutching the brim and sending showers out over other visitors. He could not see the stone fish lurking smoothly in its depths. Outside in the steep, hot streets, people stared at the wheelchair, and grotesque Fellini faces leered from shadowy doorways. Our economist host explained that Italy had achieved an economic miracle, *il sorpasso*, and no longer felt any need to be polite to foreign visitors. I pondered on the inscription over the cast archway in the city walls, which declares that Siena opens its heart to all who come. Siena keeps its sombre volcanic heart for its own. And rightly so.

Back at the house, exhaustion and anxiety were as usual pervading; the children had begun to quarrel again, when we were surprised by visitors, Jenny the faith healer and her psychotherapist husband, old friends of our friends. They were staying nearby. Jenny was a tall, fierce woman with wildly curling hair. She hated me on sight and I hated her too. When she heard of Patrick's illness her angry features reassembled into an expression of possessive fervour. She must give him a Healing.

'Well, it's worth trying anything,' I said wearily, incurring an X-ray blast from her cold, grey eyes, grey-green really, glaucous, probably the colour of the eyes of the disagreeable goddess Minerva, who was, I then remembered, the goddess of healing. Trying to improve our relations I told her this. It didn't work; there had been no call for elitist and depraved classics in the schools of her childhood in bleak northern England. Up the stairs she went. After a few minutes I looked round the door; she was crouched over the bed, her hands hovering like pallid birds of prey over Patrick's stomach. She was muttering about blue being the colour of stress, she saw blue, she saw anger and fear. Tiny bottles were laid out in meticulous rows on the table. Patrick appeared to be asleep. When she came downstairs she told us that because of the gravity of his illness she had given him her special amethyst crystal. She had bought this in a shop devoted to the sale of crystals, and as she stood, waiting for the assistant, she had heard a high, constant ringing sound and all the crystals on all the shelves had beamed a great white light at her. I was longing for her to go because the doctor was due to arrive. She went, assuring us that she would be sending telepathic healing from her house to Patrick, and also, she added, to me.

That night rain and wind swept down over the hills and sheet lightning exploded about the house. In the morning the skies had cleared and the sun again shone brilliantly. Patrick tried to get up, slipped and fell heavily on the marble floor. Back in bed, he could scarcely speak, he could scarcely hear, let alone breathe. The doctor came again, with an electrocardiograph machine. As I watched the giddy peaks and troughs of his heart pattern, I noticed the amethyst crystal on the table, complacent and viscous as a jellyfish. I removed it to a drawer. Patrick had to go to hospital.

Hurtling in the ambulance down the white hill roads, pitted now and grooved with shining rivulets, my head was filled with monotonous refrains, 'Will he live? Will he die?' over and over, banishing thought. Then, for the first time, I saw the hospital. Behind it, a perspective of distant hills, winding waters and towers, delicate as a quattrocento painting, and there, in the foreground, where once there would have been a crucifixion, a colossal structure of concrete blocks, united in a grid system, monstrous and shocking, but holding such hope as there was in the world. Where once there would have been a crucifixion.

Swing doors crashed, trolleys sped over acres of gleaming grey corridor, green overalled doctors emerged, shouted instructions, vanished. The usual chaos of hospital admission wrought its usual despair. Patrick lay still, speechless and twisted on his stretcher, like one of the terrible contorted figures found in the streets of Pompeii. At last I was called to see the doctors. They sat in a row, young and glamorous, smoking and flirting with giggling nurses, behind a long table. There was nowhere for me to sit nor any suggestion that I should. I became aware that the insect bites which had turned my legs into swollen twin bolsters had burst and poison was trickling into my sandals. They went on smoking and giggling for a while, ignoring me. At last they spoke. Patrick was very ill. He should not have come to Italy. Why had we come to Italy? 'Chiantishire,' sneered one adventurous linguist. Useless to protest scorn and loathing of this expression and all that it stands for, useless to do anything but let them have their revenge on Englishness until they tired of it. I stood there meekly in my squelching sandals, a sacrificial heifer. And soon, indeed, they relented. Patrick had a fair chance of recovery; they would take good care of him. He could now go to his ward.

Many hours later, leaving Patrick in his bed, wonderfully restored to life, able to speak, hear, even laugh, and surrounded by kind and courteous older doctors, we went to dinner in a small restaurant a couple of miles from the house. The telephone rang. We sat rigid with fear, and, sure enough, the waiter came straight to us. But it was not the hospital. There had been a fire in the house, we must come at once. In the hamlet all the old people had emerged from their houses, the cats were crouched like a Greek chorus at the foot of the outside staircase and the children, huddled in blankets, were weeping in the street. Everyone was safe, but inside the house there was a dense miasma so suffocating that you could only rush straight out again into the sweet night air. Earlier, the little children had gone to bed as usual with their windows and shutters closed against the insects. They had a dim lamp in their room but tonight they complained it was too bright, although they would not have it switched off, so one of the boys had propped a large floor cushion against it as an improvised shade, not, of course, touching the bulb. Hours later he had by chance gone upstairs and smelt terrible fumes coming from the babies' room. They were sound asleep, the cushion was blazing, the floor was smouldering and thick smoke, pungent and murderous, billowed out as he opened the door. Too choked to shout for help, he had pulled the shutters apart, dragged the windows open, and hurled the foam-stuffed cushion into the street, blindly stamped his way through the flames to the little ones' bed and pulled them down the stairs. The others beat out the burning mats. So they were safe, but nearly not. That night, when at last the fumes had dispersed, we slept, or tried to sleep, with every window open, and the mosquitoes and hornets and phosphorescent beetles joined the cats in wild marauding and no one cared.

Meanwhile in the hospital Patrick had been taken off his drip and settled for the night. He woke in darkness knowing that he was in a South African prison camp. Stark naked, this man who had been unable to move only a few hours before, leapt out of bed and fled from the ward, pursued by Hassan, the Iranian in the opposite bed. Hassan had pneumonia. Down the silent corridors they sped, past the night nurse who was dozing; Patrick shot into the lift, leaving Hassan clutching at the blank doors; he found another ward and took a shower, then, dripping wet and skidding perilously on the grey linoleum, he neatly skirted a prison guard advancing with a syringe and bolted again out of sight. From ten at night until five in the morning he maintained his mad career around the hospital, visiting among many places the ophthalmic ward, the spare mattress warehouse, a deserted cafeteria, and finally an operating theatre where he was captured by astonished surgeons. High rails were placed about his bed, but these proved no obstacle to the chameleon poet: he vaulted lightly over them; this time though, he could go no further than the ward doors. The day staff had come on duty.

So it was that when we came to visit him, the three others in his room were laid out flat in deep sleep. He himself was both frightened and exhilarated by his adventures and claimed to be looking forward to the next night. However, for the next night and a couple after, I stayed there with him in a bizarre reclining chair and these nights were without incident. I say without incident, but I will not forget the restlessness and palpable fear which accumulated in the very early mornings, in the hours before dawn, when the old men would whisper and call out to each other to make sure they were still alive; and then they dared not sleep in case the darkness took them. When the sun rose there was such joy. 'Allah has brought us another day,' said Hassan beaming. And they would prop themselves up and gaze out at the towers and the far hills and the cypresses still scarved in mist beneath the green, translucent sky.

Patrick grew stronger and the days assumed their own slow rhythm in the world outside a world that is a hospital. I read to him and I read the Italian newspapers. At first, I could only cope with local news, the Palio and the pole cats which were wantonly ravaging a village near Vagliagli. 'A new ecological disaster' and 'Paura nelle Case'. They hurtled from roof tops and they had consumed a Persian cat and a Pekinese dog. Becoming more ambitious I studied a photograph of a monstrous fish like a squashed banana skin with a skull's face; it had been found in Cornuvaglia, perhaps another outpost of Vagliagli, pullulating with vitiated nature; in fact it turned out to be Cornwall. But as in Britain, so in Italy the greater horrors were the human ones. Immigrant negro labourers were being subjected to conditions of the utmost squalor and brutality and then viciously murdered as they worked on the tomato harvest. I thought of all those cheerful blue and red tins of tomatoes that brighten the murk of British country kitchens with their suggestion of honest toil and laughter under a cloudless sky where the benign sun confers natural goodness. And the Camorra had been busy, gunning down little girls whom they had mistaken for middle aged Mafiosi.

One evening when I returned from the hospital we went to dinner with Jenny the healer and her psychotherapist husband. I didn't want to go, but I was told that this was very rude, in view of her intense interest in Patrick's health and her continual sending of telepathic healing. So off we went up the moonlit trails, beneath the viper-garlanded branches. A thin fox slunk

IN VAGLIAGLI

across the car headlights and a small owl glared malignly from a rotted stump. It reminded me again of Minerva, and her constant companion, the very little owl.

The house was huge, square and sinister, full of Chirico archways and airport-style furniture hand crafted by its owner, a Dutch museum curator. The electricity quivered and quavered but didn't go out. It was costing Jenny, her husband and two other friends, two thousand pounds a week. But then there was a swimming pool, albeit quarter of a mile away and in the viperous woods. We sat for a few minutes on the terrace over a single glass of wine before we were driven indoors by a new variety of droning, devouring insect. In the dining room, one more glass of wine was poured, then the bottle we had brought was corked and put aside.

As we masticated our red cabbage with apple, and mushrooms with pistachios and minimalist pork I asked Jenny whether she had met any pregnant vipers doing hydrotherapy in her pool. There was a small silence about the table while she dismissed this with a glaucous glance and a magisterial wave of the hand, turning in intense communion to her neighbour. Chastened, I ate my pudding silently, longing for another drink. Suddenly, Jenny's friend Sue was hugging me. 'I feel so sad for you,' she said. Well, I thought things weren't good, but they could be worse; however, in this world one must be glad of anything affectionate and so I hugged her back. A moment later things definitely improved. A stout bottle of brandy appeared on the table, accompanied by a tray of tea. We sat in our neo Bauhaus chairs round a modestly smouldering fire. Talk turned to education, then to the middle-class ethic of postponed pleasure, then to how much danger children should be allowed. At this point, I remembered that in Il Messagero at the hospital that morning, I had read of the sudden death of the famous psychotherapist R. D. Laing. Knowing that they only read several days' old copies of English newspapers, and thinking it might be a topic of mild interest, at a pause in the theme of whether or not to let children climb trees, I said casually, 'By the way, did you see that R. D. Laing has died?' There was silence, so I added, 'Yesterday, in the south of France, a heart attack.' More silence. 'Aged 58, I think.' The silence ended. Five people were on their feet shrieking, wailing, embracing. Jenny was foremost. 'To have heard it like that! From someone like that!' she yelled, burying her head in her husband's black leather bosom. Then, advancing to the table, hieratic and deadly, she seized the brandy bottle and hurled it on the fire. A bolt of lightning ascended to the heavens. 'Goodbye Ronnie!' she cried. 'Goodbye Ronnie!' echoed the others. I noticed there were a great many black grasshoppers with red spots on their backs leaping about our feet and even onto the rows of empty airport chairs beyond the mezzanine. It was time to go.

A few days later Patrick left the hospital. We cried as we said goodbye to his three room mates. We cried and they cried and we all embraced again and again. 'Tanti auguri, tanti auguri!' they called as we set off down that grey gleaming corridor. They stood in the room doorway, waving and smiling, and they reminded me of the souls on the bank of the Styx, stretching out their hands in longing for that further shore. Outside the hospital the sun beat down again, astonishingly brilliant. I knew then that the sun god of Tuscany is not the Greek Apollo, not the Roman Phoebus Apollo, but the Etruscan Apollo of Veii with his warm and pitiless smile. It was autumn then in Vagliagli. The hunters had gone and the birdless woods were silent. Small vipers slipped from the trees to burrow and nest in the soil of ancient Etruria.

DOGS OF ATHENS

It was in Athens airport that I saw them first. They sat close together, very upright on their airport chairs, all knitting. Or were they all knitting? As I walked past it seemed out of the corner of my eye as though only one was knitting and the others were straightening the wool, holding the ball, but each taking her turn with the needles. Three ancient crones, wrapped in black. The three fates, Clotho, Lachesis and something. Why couldn't I remember the third one's name? It is depressing to survive for fifty years only to begin to forget things you have always known. 'Well,' says the voice in the back of my head, 'if only you hadn't drunk so much ouzo at Iraklion before you got on the plane things might be different.' 'Rubbish' I tell it. 'Flying is awful, crazy, degrading to human dignity. Remember Icarus drowning in the sea we've just crossed. There are warnings everywhere and we should take some notice.' 'Flying is the safest form of transport' says the voice. It says this often. 'Qantas has never lost a passenger,' it adds. 'What's Qantas got to do with flying Crete to Athens, or Athens to London, come to that?' I demand. I peer anxiously at the three fates, for tomorrow is another flying day. They ignore me, intent on their skeins of orange wool. Ravelling and unravelling. May the Lord preserve us. Anyway, I have outwitted them for now.

  I become aware that there are a number of cheerful dogs about, apparently unattached, trotting around the concourses, greeting pilots and vigorously enjoying the business of international arrivals and departures and casual disposal of airport food. How they smile and swish their tails; east, west, dogs are best and I am missing mine. Tomorrow I will see them.

Today and now there is the hotel and then Christina.

I didn't know Christina very well although I'd seen her on and off over many years. Back in England it had seemed a good idea to stop over one night in Athens, meet, have fun. Christina hadn't actually sounded very enthusiastic down the phone, but her laconic and curiously well preserved Texan drawl had often misled me. Now she was in hospital and I'd no idea what was wrong. She had sent a message to the hotel saying 'Come this minute, bored, bored, bored'. The hospital was up in the hills outside Athens and I was pleased to have discovered the bus station and the bus despite the intense pall of mid afternoon heat and the major handicap of my 5th century BC Attic Greek. One of the people I had accosted for directions had insisted in only slightly American English that no one had used the rough breathing since 400 AD. That wasn't going to stop me.

As the suburbs fell away the bus gathered speed into dusty scrubland. The sky hung heavy and dull over slopes littered with unfinished breeze block structures; in the hazed light they seemed like ruined temples, parched and skeletal. I looked forward to the cool of evening and the hotel roof garden where I might sip a Bloody Mary or two and gaze out at the ghostly Parthenon. I realised that not knowing what was wrong with Christina had no relevance; she probably wouldn't tell me anyway. If she even knew. She had a dismissive attitude to the woes of the body. I remembered her galloping through the woods on a huge grey horse, her skirts bundled up round her thighs, one broken arm in plaster and sling. She admitted to hangovers; nothing much else. And she disposed of hangovers with a slosh of brandy in the morning's second cup of coffee, followed by a spot more on the hour throughout the day. Despite her alcoholic intake, or perhaps because of it, she was able to make a reasonable living from freelance journalism, even contriving to write satirical pieces on London social life from her Athens apartment. She was consistently unkind to her lovers who never lasted more than a week or two. She would shout at them in public places; if one had really irritated her she would pick him up in a sort of fireman's hoist, sling him over her shoulder and carry him down the street. I wondered now whether I even liked her, whether this visit might not be a wretched mistake. But beyond the drinking and ranting she was funny and generous and I admired the relish she took in her odd, lonely life.

The hospital was huge and parts of it were still being built. The hillside was gouged with quarry workings, and great grey bulldozers and cranes and diggers toiled slowly back and forth, changing places, revolving, realigning in a complex and enigmatic pavane. Dust thickened the air and clouded out the sky; the colour had leached from the landscape, leaving it lunar and featureless. A no place. I thought of the word Utopia and its literal meaning of no place and how strange it is that this no place is always taken to be a desirable one.

Shining rivers of grey vinyl wound my way to Christina's room. I hesitated at the doorway, scanning the four beds. She wasn't there. Then 'Hey DUDE!' shrieked the weird person at the far end by the window. Christina was in disguise; she had dolled herself up as some kind of invalid Country and Western lady. Her hair hung down in blonde ringlets, her décolleté nightdress bore a huge pink satin bow just beneath the bust, strongly suggestive of Easter eggs. Over it she wore a pink feather boa, wispily attached to a fluffy angora bed jacket. The boa flipped about, involving itself with a dangling tube hooked up to Christina's left arm. God, I thought, it's a blood transfusion. My Bloody Marys made a swift and shameful appearance in my mind; lined up on a silver tray, they reeled into darkness. 'So what's the matter with you?' I demanded, sounding bossy and curt, cutting through Christina's babble about the *awesome* horror of hospital food. She was making me feel pedantic and English; she was making me hold tightly onto my handbag handles and sit with my feet in symmetrical parallel. 'Nothing much'; she sipped some water or possibly vodka. 'I had a pain in my stomach but it's gone now. They just won't let me out yet because they want to do some tests. Anyhow I'll lose some weight.' I felt reassured by this non reply and told her about a recent visit to an English casualty ward where I overheard a doctor interviewing a youth behind closed curtains.

Doctor: 'So you have taken a number of tablets. Did you mean to kill yourself?'
Youth: 'Dunno, maybe not really, don't know.'
Doctor, keenly: 'Ever thought of cutting your wrists?'
Youth: 'No.'
Doctor: 'Do you have a garden shed?'
Youth: 'What?'
Doctor: 'A garden shed with weedkiller in it. Do you have access to weedkiller?'
Youth: 'No. For goodness' sake, what is this?'
Doctor: 'Are there firearms in your house? In an unlocked cupboard?'
Youth: 'Please go away. Just leave me alone.'
Doctor: 'So you haven't been tempted to shoot yourself?'
Youth: 'Oh fuck off.' He begins to sob.

Christina enjoyed this tale and laughed a lot. An eyelash detached itself and drifted down, iridescent and eddying in the late afternoon light. I remembered the harbour at Réthimnon and the kingfisher; it dipped back and forth among the boulders of the sea barrier, brilliant against a sullen, windy sky. Off it flew westward and all its colour was quenched into blackness before the pallid spot of the sun. The sea was swollen, pounding and dragging the shingle, the cafés were deserted, the tables stacked, the umbrellas furled. The melancholy of the changing season whined through the wind's skirmishes and the groan of the shifting shingle. All things are passing.

Christina was staring at me; I felt a pang of terror. Her eyes seemed to have receded into her skull; she gazed out as though from a cavern, withdrawn from the rest of the world, unreachable. And then she was back, complaining about the nurse who had confiscated her vodka bottle from her sponge bag, addressing her as Little Lady. 'Bloody puritanical Yanks,' she said. 'I'd be better off in a Greek hospital. Anyhow I've a story to tell you too. I've been thinking about this a lot since I've been in here. Maybe it's the best thing that's happened to me; or maybe not the best, but the thing I've liked most.'

Once upon a time Christina lived in Chicago. She was fourteen years old and her parents' marriage had just broken up, so that she and her mother had come from Texas to live with her grandmother. Christina hated it; she missed her old home and her father and her friends, and most of all she missed her ballet lessons. Her mother promised that when they were more settled she could take them up again, but Christina didn't believe her. Like everything else here, promises were nothing, air and water. Rudolf Nureyev had recently defected and was coming to dance in Chicago. They had promised tickets for this but of course nothing had been done and now there were no tickets left. She felt intense panic at the real facts of time passing and having nowhere to practise; she was getting taller everyday and could soon be too tall to be allowed into ballet class. Or too fat, for she was bored and lonely and she ate too much. She seemed incapable of sitting down without having to eat simultaneously. Partly to avoid sitting down, and partly to make herself more miserable, after school each day she would walk for hours in the bitter late winter winds. Or was it early spring? The snow had gone, but the sky remained colourless, and the buildings were grey and the waters of the great lake were grey, whisked to a constant mean turmoil by the crazy, buffeting winds. Air, water, nothing and noise, aircraft, sirens, traffic, fog horns, construction work, wind booming round the corners of the blocks.

So there Christina went, trudging along in her tight red woolly hat and her unmatching gloves, her winter trousers and boots. She dragged her soles along the concrete walkway by the lake, head down, doubled over against the roaring, idiot enemy. Her eyes stung and her chilblains itched. In the near distance a dark figure was moving rapidly, purposefully, towards her. A man. She peered round; there was no one else in sight. Her heart began to thump; God, she prayed, if you don't let him kill me, I'll stop going on these stupid walks. A flight of geese rose shrieking off the lake and passed in formation high above her, darkening the sky with omen. Their wings creaked as they went. Now the man confronted her; he stood still. Christina stood still. He wore a black cloak which puffed and billowed towards her, as if to envelop her. Speechless she stared at him, and the breath caught in her throat. It was Nureyev. He swept off his floppy black cap and bowed in a deep curve of sinuous grace. Her eyes still fixed on his face, Christina sank into a curtsey. Their gloved hands clasped as he raised her to her feet. Then they walked on in their opposite directions. 'And I didn't look back,' Christina concluded, triumphant, glowing. But a moment later her eyelids drooped and the colour had faded from her cheeks. 'I'm really sorry but I have to take a rest,' she said. 'I've had it.' I thought then that she meant she was exhausted; perhaps she did. I kissed her goodbye and I went. 'And I won't look back,' I said.

She died that evening, but I didn't know this until I was home in London. I sat out then on my balcony in sultry October dusk and watched the planes stacking and sliding past the pinnacles of Westminster Cathedral and I thought of Christina and the crones and the dogs of Athens, sleeping by their own cathedral, littered in shaggy heaps about its glassy forecourt. I remembered a flower seller appearing in the early morning square, making his way round the café tables. In seconds the dogs were up and barking; they saw him off and returned to their slumbers. Later I saw them dispersed through the streets, sleeping again, by dark shop doorways. At the airport they were busy as before, seeking companionship with no great urgency, amiable and bright of eye. The three crones sat knitting in their row of chairs and one of them dropped the orange ball of wool. It rolled out across the floor and a sheepdog bounded towards it. I moved fast to intercept it but it had gone. I could not tell whether the dog had seized it, the woman had picked it up or someone had kicked it off under the chairs. In my head there was an image of a pomegranate rolling across mosaic tiles and a hand outstretched to catch it, the hand of a person unseen, something from a half forgotten poem two thousand years old.

THE DRESS

Long is the route from very rural Norfolk to the urban pastoral of Belsize Park, and longer still is the infernal transit of underground London between Liverpool Street and that promised land, involving vertiginous and hip-wrenching changes, bewilderment, and sequential folly, and a deep yearning just to turn round and go home. Nostalgia is the old Greek word for this powerful impulse and it may occur not only after ten years battle on the plains of Troy but after a few hours of public transport, albeit confined to one day. The final entry to the promised land is achieved in a fearsome lift which shudders, halts, cries out, shudders again and eventually is cranked up to the light of day. The travellers, packed in unwilling conjunction, eye one another, assessing the range of God's good will, glance at the notice which warns of overcrowding, do a headcount, pray or study the floor, invisible beneath too many feet.

But one late summer afternoon I was in this lift and an extraordinary thing happened. A stranger – but of course we were all strangers – a mythic stranger came last into the lift. She was not as others. People instinctively made way for her. She stood in a light-filled space, both stately and glamorous as only a goddess may be. Her hair was wild and black, her gaze abstracted, and her dress was green. This was the world's most perfect green, platonically perfect green, beyond viridian, emerald or jade, intense and yet translucent, fathoms deep. And the dress itself flowed exquisitely, neither long nor short, bias-cut, three quarter sleeved; romantic but formal, sculpted and flounced, flamboyant and entirely *comme il faut*, self-contradictory. In brief, it was the most beautiful dress in the world and I forgot the long journey and the steep walk ahead of me, and my purpose in coming at all to London in my absolute need to possess it.

Safely delivered to the upper air, I ventured to address the goddess, stating that this was a literally fabulous dress. She was pleased and so I dared to ask where she had found it. Norfolk. Unbelievable auspice. We parted, and I moved onward to my baby grandson, dreaming still of the green dress and haunted by Lorca's wonderful lines,

Verde, que te quiero verde . . .
Green, how I long for you green,
Green wind. Green branches.
The ship upon the sea
The horse on the mountain.
With the shadow on her waist
She dreams on her balcony . . .
With eyes of cold silver.

And there is mention of the gypsy moon, *la luna gitana.*

Outside my daughter's house a mulberry tree's leaves fling glimpses of the bluest sky and its fruits splash in wanton scarlet across the pavement. The fierce and simple joy of primary colours, compounds with the bliss of the baby's shining eyes and conspiratorial smiles. He is my favourite ballroom partner, and after quite a few circuits of Brahms's lullaby, he retires to his dreams and I to mine. Of the dress.

And there are more delights to come. I am woken in early morning by the delicate pacing of a horse beneath my window. A soldier riding down the Crescent, his horse sheened in light. And then the sound of a mighty cataract, incomprehensible and overwhelming. Sixty-three horses pass by, stepping in harmony, three by three, one ridden, two bareback. I run down the stairs in my dressing gown, which looks much like an archaic summer dress; round the corner I rush, into the villagey square. It is thronged with horses and the early shopkeepers have set out buckets of water. Quite a few star-struck women in déshabille are milling about, some attached to small children. The soldiers, dismounted, stand modestly by their horses as they drink. In the warm sun steam rises from the shining flanks and there is a fragrance of tarry smoke, most delicate, like Lapsang Souchong. Everyone wants to speak to a soldier, everyone wants to stroke a horse. Everyone is happy. The horses raise their heads and sigh; diamond drops glitter on their muzzles. We are all outside time, in perfect accord. And then the riders are up and gone, and the great waterfalling noise of hooves recedes into such stillness that we hear a cock crowing far, far away.

So, back in Norfolk, trapped again in the unremitting blankness of a wet, failed summer, I telephone the creator of the green dress and arrange that she shall make one for me. This is an *enormous thing for me to do*. I am a person devoid of disposable income and I never buy clothes. What is the point, when I'd be best in a burkha? The last time anyone made me something to wear was in my own early childhood. Nanny's customised bibs – purple ribbon binding – pinafores and smocked dresses belong in that neverland of thumb-sucking and proper summers and paddling in rock pools and planning to be a princess. When one grew up. I realise that this is exactly what I am doing now. I, who have always reacted badly to remarks like 'that's really you' in sartorial circumstance, believing that clothing's purpose is to conceal or transform the raw material into the unrecognisable, am now helplessly submerged by the pathetic fallacy that in achieving and wearing the green dress I shall become the desired one in Lorca's poem, the mythic creature up from the underworld, the princess of my infant aspiration.

The creator, whose voice is identical to the voice of someone I love, commands me to take measurements of utterly inaccessible bits of myself. Nape of neck to back of waist. Waist to lower shin or something. How? No-one but I and she must know these terrible truths. The final statistics suggest that I am a hexagonal wardrobe.

In due course a huge parcel arrives by special delivery. The creator has told me that it contains not only the dress but a hat and a necklace and an insouciant wrap. I am very frightened. For days the box sits looming reproachfully across my bedroom. People ask me if I have tried it on. Yes, I say, it's perfect. I have talked too much about this and I am resolved that even if it fits not at all the die is cast. The dress and I must go forth together, specifically to an oncoming family wedding.

But what if the most beautiful dress in the world has now become the most hideous? I ponder the possibilities. Perhaps I'll never wear it again. Perhaps I will wear it for my funeral. Or for gardening. Or if it is still the most beautiful dress in the world, perhaps someone will be so beguiled by it that they will mistake me for the princess and I will be wearing it for a wedding of my own. Currently the only person who wishes to marry me is my black Labrador, who of course is almost perfect. But the vicar wont hear of it. O dress, are you me? Am I you?

So time goes by and the day of the wedding is with us. Even then I postpone my rendezvous with the dress until the last possible moment, painting and repainting my nails, according great and unaccustomed attention to mascara and poking the wand into my eyeball. Almost blindly the dress, the hat and I are united. I glance in my darkling mirror and see nothing but a vague and tarnished spectre. I don't really want to see more. The hat is small and coquettish, echoing here and there the dress's green; it is plumed and veiled. I have never worn a veil before, but it definitely seems a good thing. On the way to the wedding through marshland and cornfields and wet skies which will be struck by vast revolving shafts of sun as the bride enters the ancient church, my escort makes favourable comment upon the ensemble. However, as he often tells people, he is a Scottish, Irish, Roman Catholic, homosexual, orphaned, working-class poet. So what does he know?

As the service begins the veil seems a less good thing. During hymn number one, it becomes fatally entangled with my reading spectacles. I shouldn't have been wearing them anyway, as I know every item in the hymnary by heart.

My panicked daughter and I struggle tearfully and silently against the fragile but very stubborn black lace. Eventually my useless specs are disentangled, just in time for the first prayer. As I don't know the prayer, I need my specs again. Nonchalantly I cast the veil aside. I can see at last.

At this point it occurs to me that actually no-one is looking at me anyhow and the wedding is for the bride and groom. They stand together in archetypal beauty beneath a window of sea water glass beyond which rears the tree of life. In that church there is always the stirring of wind, even when the surrounding cornfields stand dazed and motionless in summer heat. Once I saw a pair of pigeons hatch on a stone windowsill and stretch their skeletal wings to dry in the sighing air. It is said that Anne Boleyn's remains were taken from the Tower and buried secretly here beneath an anonymous slab, in the church built by her family. Her spirit haunts it, sometimes in the form of a hare, a witch's familiar. She too wore a green dress, celebrated by her wilful spouse in the song Greensleeves.

Later, out in the graveyard in the windy sunlight, the bells clamour and everyone is joyful. I no longer care whether or not my dress is beautiful. I am not a dress. A dress is not me. The idea has leapt and flamed and burnt itself out. I look as from a great height at people happy among the ancient tombs. There is the bride and the tower and the whirling birds. Far over there in the shade of a yew tree someone is laughing, someone in a green dress. A ghost? Myself? It doesn't matter now.

CARBORUNDUM

She was perfecting her wintry smile in a hand mirror tarnished with verdigris. The face that looked back at her was white as snow, or chalk rather, her own powdery chalk. When she ran her hands down her cheeks, smoothing away the excess, it settled in a fine dust over her shoulders. The wind whisked long hanks of grizzled hair across her eyes and a cold sun dazzled her. She reached beneath the tarpaulin and withdrew her mother's old magenta jumper. It was shrunken now and felted with the years of damp and dews, but it provided just enough protection for this November afternoon. Carefully she lowered her legs over the edge of the platform and began the slow descent, breathing a little heavily now as the soles of her boots tested, then found purchase on the slippery ladder rungs. As always, she felt a flicker of relief when she reached the carpet of beech nut husks and sodden leaves.

She dragged the high old pram out of the shed and set forth along the cliff track, gripping the handle tightly, bent against the wind. Beneath, the sea prowled back and forth, complaining.

When she trudged along like this, she was able to think, or, more importantly, remember. Up in her trees she was too busy; life hung on a concatenation of infinitely laborious small tasks, and as she grew older, everything took longer. This was how she wanted it to be. She was eking out existence, waiting to go. For others all things might be passing, but for her all things long since had passed. And the fact that she generally remembered the same things did not trouble her. For so long things had been the same, two separate samenesses, one more detailed than the other. Thirty years rotting away with mother, thirty years in the trees. Was there a story at all, a shape? Is there ever?

The lofty rocking motion of the ancient perambulator had perhaps been a foreshadow of the swaying beech tree branches, systole and diastole of wind and weather, the rhythms of her world; for as an infant she had occupied this very vehicle, propped on lace-edged pillows of cambric, propelled back and forth by adoring relatives. Who had all died. Except, of course, for Mother, who had died later, far too late and who had certainly not adored her. Even now, the thought of her mother made her knuckles strain white under their carapace of rough red skin, brown blotches, veins serpentine and glaucous. 'Won't you ever take pride in your appearance, Marjory?' demanded a ghostly voice. 'Look at your hands. Anyone would think you were a skivvy.' Her heart then had cried out in silence that she was indeed a skivvy, enslaved by a cold and cruel despot who had tricked her into servitude and would not ever release her.

The summer when she had finished boarding school and was about to go to university she had found herself consumed by a great weariness, headaches and shooting pains, so that she could scarcely get out of bed, could not eat, could not speak. The doctor said she had brain fever and she must rest for a long time or it would not go away. How mother's eyes shone; she was sharpening her knives. 'Just you stay in bed, darling, and I'll look after you. It will be fun to have you properly at home after all these years I've been on my own. While *you've* been off being *educated*' she added with a tinkly laugh. 'And what an expense that was' she said a few weeks later. 'Really I have to say I'm quite glad that university is out of the question now.' 'Only for this year, surely?' mumbled an alarmed Marjory, capable now of speech, less capable of enduring interminable afternoons by the unlit drawing room fire, gazing out at the merge of pale sea and pale sky. 'Time will tell' said mother, her eyes no longer bright but dull and critical. 'Certainly you won't be going anywhere at all unless you put on some weight'. How could anyone gain weight on a diet of calves' foot jelly and tripe, borne grudgingly on trays to her room? She was forbidden to eat downstairs; she realised that this was because Mother was eating normal food and would find her company and the sight of her not eating her invalid food unbearably irritating.

So began the sequestration, the erosion of possibility and aspiration, stretching into years, into forever. For when at last Marjory was well again, mother chose to retire to her bed, suffering from some unidentifiable malaise. 'Perhaps I've caught that nasty disease off you, after all that time nursing you. Dr Fox is baffled of course. So lucky for me that you're here, darling.' This was the second time in two years that she had called Marjory darling.

As she reached the outskirts of the village, a shower of pebbles skittered against the pram wheels and ricocheted off, stinging into her ankles. She stopped stock still and turned her chalky face towards the jeering children; slowly, deliberately, she smiled her frozen smile, her eyes expressionless. The children melted into the dunes and marram grass. The village shop smelt of paraffin and apples as it always had done, and no one flinched at her appearance. They packed her box up as usual and it was only after she had laboured out with it to the pram, refusing offers of help, and had moved into her return journey that one rolled eyes at another, heads were shaken, voices lowered. Just for a moment; there were more interesting topics with novelty value, winter holiday tenants, the tideline of wreckage left by the half term break, the occupants of the bus shelter. Marjory plodded on, up to the clifftop path and the stir of the wind. Already the light was fading and the bleached grasses shivered; the sea was ruffled, metallic grey in the chill of evening. An occasional poppy still trembled on the dunes' edge and as the path climbed she could distinguish the small pale stars of camomile, but colour was leaching from the landscape, into a dying winter world. She looked back at the lit windows of the village and was unmoved. Once she would have envied the lives she imagined in those lamplit rooms, familial meals, exchange of the day's events, a loving kindness reserved for those within, implicit in the shrug and glide of curtains drawn against the outsider. Exclusion was now her natural state; no doubt it always had been, but then she had not recognised it, then when she still had small hopes of a normal life and believed what people said.

The summer Mother had gone, there had been a song blaring endlessly from the wireless in the shop and from people's cars; most of the words were unintelligible to her, but there was a single line refrain, 'The day the music died.' That was the summer when one life had ended and another begun, the day his letter had come and the wedding was off, the dining room full of presents which she would never use, the accoutrements of a real house, an undiscovered place waiting to be realised. The wedding dress in its shrouds of tissue swayed and twisted in the draught from her bedroom window; it watched her, the faceless ghost of her trusting self; and she thought it mocked her. 'How could you think you could ever be a bride?' it whispered. 'Be loved and cherished and make golden perfect toast in the toaster, wake to the welcome of the Goblin Teasmaid, iron crisp, fragrant linen on that pristine padded ironing board. Share your life in the warmth while the sea wind batters the windows.' There might have been a dog, and cat, even a child. All gone that day, the day the music died, the day she took to the trees.

She stood on the cliff edge, where you could see nothing but sea and sky and the curved rim of the horizon, and heard the hushed roar of water ceaselessly shifting stones. All things were temporal and passing; the cliff itself, perilously layered, would slither some day soon into the heave of ocean, and the white birds floating beneath her now, untroubled, would find themselves new sanctuaries on the raw exposed rock face. Turning away, she was aware of sharp pain in her hips and in her knees where her old bones scraped and ground each other into rough jagging surfaces. The stones were better served by the sea; it left them smooth and shining. Cliff and sea, hip and knee; a cheerless little grindstone song. Near to shore on a post, a cormorant was drying his outspread wings, densely black and cruciform against the swelling tide.

At the back gate she glanced into the letterbox. Nothing but snails. Beyond the parched winter grasses and shrivelled stands of dock leaves the house loomed, blinded by shutters. Sometimes she played with the notion of going in there; sometimes she crept around it like a thief, peering through cracks in the shutters and cobwebs at vistas and sepia rooms lined with bookcases, heavy mahogany tables, grimly upholstered armchairs. But when she saw the wedding presents still there in the dining room, and when she thought of the dress performing its twirling dance upstairs, her heart would thump and she would begin to shake.

That night, in the tree house, her eagle home, she could not sleep for the pain in her hips. Each morning she would wake colder and stiffer. In the light of day she knew the rooks were watching her. It was too late now for it to matter where or whether she lived or died. This pain and cold would also pass. All those years of falling leaves and rooks nesting and spring's return, distant foghorns, drownings and foundering ships, wind and weather, had purged her, bleached her like driftwood. She was memory now, nothing more nor less. One day, maybe this day, in a flurry of shining leaves and eyes and beaks she would have gone and then the rooks would have her. So let it be; her story was over.

DOWN BY THE SEA

Breathing heavily, the Morris Minor toiled over the crest of the coastal ridge. Mary gripped the steering wheel tight, veins bulging on her gnarled old hands, and inched cautiously onto the track ahead which glittered in frost light, straight as a Roman way far down to the cliff edge; beyond, sea and sky merged, grey into grey. Blanched by winter the headland grasses stood stiff and motionless. In summer this was a joyous landscape, a profusion of primary colours, crayon blue sea and azure sky, green cropped turf, scarlet poppies. Where did colour go? Once an emerald moth had balanced, quivering on her bedroom window frame, the purest, deepest translucent green, a platonically perfect green, fading imperceptibly through the days to pallid lettuce. Sorrow, like winter, leaches colour from the world. For a long time after Peter died, Mary moved in a blur of neutral tones, very occasionally offset by a bloody sunset. So it was today, sky and land and sea mournful, hushed, as though waiting for resolution. A storm cloud of lapwings lifted off the headland and darkened the air with omen.

   Sidney's house was a garish brightness in the dreary day. He had painted it cornflower blue and it stood defiant on the edge of the high, crumbling cliff. Most of its garden had gone over years ago. Every now and then another yard or two would silently detach and plunge to the shingle sixty feet below. The lower parts of the cliff face had become gelatinous, involved in a mysterious marine process of liquefaction. Soon the house would go too. Sidney was untroubled by this prospect; he believed it would outlive him. Mary doubted this, but she too was untroubled. She saw herself floating downwards, like an inverted parasol, an airy scrap of flotsam, to be absumed by elemental wind and water. This was the brink of the world. Nothing but sky and sea, flint stone and the drifting sea birds. Fulmars nested in holes in the upper cliff face; they glided past, their flat faces enigmatic and preoccupied, the tips of their wings almost brushing the grasses. Sidney had called his house The Lobster's Return in anticipation of its watery destiny. Mary imagined the migrant lobsters even now marching in phalanxes over the murky ocean floor, through depths illuminated only by a shafting and fitful sunspot, guided by instinct towards their sunken palace.

Picking her way up the slippery garden path above the grind and groan of sea on shingle, she heard the urgent wails of Sidney's dogs. At once she wished she hadn't come. In the early morning she had been seized by a resentful need for the gardening books she had lent him perhaps four years ago, and had not even thought of since. Vengeful and waspish, she had set forth on a journey which she saw now was pointless. The return of borrowed books was no longer a matter of principle to her; nor was she, or Sidney, come to that, likely now to be planting any of those shrubs, bulbs, perennials, middle or back of the border subjects. *Heuchera Stormy Sea*, heliotrope, mulberry, quince or medlar; *rosa mundi, rosa versicolor, Belle de Crécy*, the strangely named masculine roses, *Parkdirektor Riggers, Rambling Rector*, or *Robert le Diable*, whom she had brought once as a gift for Sidney because it resembled him: 'procumbent in habit with a vinous flush'. The litany had lost its power to move her; those days were gone and her garden could go with them. How long before it reverted to bramble and nettle and wilderness, seeding grasses, dandelions, thistledown? Before Sidney's house went under the sea? Before her own demise?

She pushed the front door open. 'Come up to the drawing room,' cried Sidney from above. Warily she skirted the kitchen; it was worse than last time, with even more bread. Every flat surface was a litter of mouldering slices, crumpets lurid with verdigris, tureens and platters overspilling pockmarked loaves, carbonised toast, rolls turned to rock. She had asked him why he didn't throw it all out. 'I'm keeping it for the peacocks,' he said absently. The last peacock was long dead and the peacocks' tamarisk walk lay under water now. She pointed this out. 'Well, the birds then.'

But not even Sidney could wreck the drawing room. Three tall bay windows overhung the sea and on the walls between, great mirrors drew in the light so that at sunset the room was a spinning vortex of pink and gold and azure, and then a phoenix's nest of molten fire. In the cold gaze of this February morning a shift of clouds suggested changing weather, soothed her, confirmed the mutability of all things. Who should care about the bread and the birds?

Sidney hadn't done much about getting dressed. In his floor length red brocade dressing gown he tottered about the room looking for sherry glasses and wheezing. Mary declined the sherry and he ignored her. Dog hairs clung around the rim of her glass. She placed it on the nearest small table, one of a sequence which stood in inconvenient positions across the room, bearing tiny troops drawn up in battle formation, rearguards, vanguards, pincer movements, cavalry and infantry and artillery; awaiting their high command. 'Is it still Waterloo?' she asked politely. 'Absolutely not. Oudenard. If the dogs don't get in we could have victory by nightfall. And then I'm moving on to Malplaquet. What larks!' he said, rubbing his hands together. God, thought Mary. Five minutes more of this and she could go. There was precious little likelihood of victory by nightfall. The dogs had two purposes. One was to gallop about the headland, terrorising ramblers; then they would collapse and sleep noisily in the back kitchen. But, when bored, they would work their door latch loose and come crashing up the stairs. Well, one of them crashed; the other scrabbled. Both were spoilers of the fortunes of war. With one mighty swing of her tail, the Newfoundland despatched battalions piecemeal about the room; the Pekinese pounced among the fallen, snuffling and dismembering. Sidney would be lying helpless and breathless in his armchair, toppled by the Newfoundland's ecstatic greeting, high leap of embrace, fervent licks and jocular toss of the head. Stalactites of slobber slouched shining down the walls. When he had caught his breath, Sidney would make his joke. 'O, my America,' he gasped, 'my Newfoundland.' He had called the dog America for this purpose. The Peke was called Frean after Peek Frean, a biscuit firm which had long ceased to trade, so that no one was amused. Not that they would have been anyhow; and according to Sidney only two people had ever recognised the America allusion. He used it as an intellectual benchmark, he claimed, exonerating Mary's failure to respond by saying that in her very distant youth no girl would have been allowed to read a poem so shocking. Actually, Mary thought, he was even older than she was; and the close of girlhood did not signal an end to poetry reading. She intended now to leave before this all happened again.

As she drove down the coast road to Cromer, she realised that she had left all the books behind. She left the Morris tucked into the taxi rank by the church and hobbled through the great oak door. Bonily she settled into a hard, polished pew. She was tired and jangled. But then the familiar, enfolding peace came upon her, conferred by high windows of sea water glass, through which she could just discern the shadow forms of pigeons tumbling from the tower. *A pigeon tumbling in clear summer air, a laughing schoolboy without grief or care.* She remembered that summer feeling from childhood, running with arms outflung through the silver birches, head back, eyes dazzled, almost flying. To swoop, to soar; all things then were possible. She closed her eyes and slept and dreamed of white feathers falling like winter round her.

Meanwhile Sidney, snugly wrapped against the cold, sits out on the cliff edge and stares at his soldiers. They lie in a heap of disorder on a folding table which is topped by an artful tray depicting Balmoral. He can think of nothing to do with them. Far below the sea prowls and sloughs over the shingle; the tide is full and the noise of sucking and disgorging drowns out the shrill yaps of the Pekinese and the baritone boom of the Newfoundland as they race about the headland, drowns out the working of Sidney's brain. He sips a gin and tonic and chews his lower lip. He gathers his coats and dressing gown about him; the late afternoon chill intensifies and the sky which for an hour had been a tender blue, a fickle promise of spring, has whitened. Time to go in, he thinks, heaving himself up. But it is already too late; the turf beneath his feet buckles and wrenches and slithers forward and downward. Sidney and his soldiers are gone, pitched in a headlong welter of earth and rock and sand and startled birds whose wing tips buffet him as he hurtles into darkness.

The dogs have noticed nothing, but after a comfortless night, tomorrow at low tide they will retrieve some of the soldiers and chew them up. Small children will find more and take them home in pockets clammy with sand and shells, dead crabs and starfish; but no one will find Sidney for a long time. He has been rolled far out on a rip tide, and will emerge, eyeless and shrouded in bladderwrack, one bright summer morning, miles down the coast on a Blue Flag beach, forever blighting the lives of a pair of ramblers.

MISSING

'*C'est un beau chien,*' said the Frenchman. Mary and he stared at the black lurcher curvetting and galloping in and out and round about the vast cylindrical straw bales, zigzagging almost horizontal to the stubble.

'She's a bitch,' said Mary. 'Actually,' she added, so as not to seem rude, although she felt like being rude. Why was he here at all, when he was her daughter's friend? And why wasn't Ellen here?

'*Chienne alors,*' shrugged the Frenchman, '*même chose.*'

Rage mounted in Mary.

'It's not at all the same thing; perhaps it is in France. Here we look differently at dogs.'

Woodpigeons cooed and mourned in the heavy August trees, tarnished already with the ebbing days of summer. An exhaust backfired, scattering the pigeons out against the clouded sky. Ellen's car jolted up the drive, roaring and revving. A Cromer Carnival pennant clung to the wireless aerial and two huge grizzled dogs glowered from the windows. Thank God for that, thought Mary. Now perhaps he'll go. In the sharp shadow cast by the bales he looked like Louis Jourdan playing Dracula. Or the man on the old Gitanes packet. Or was it Gauloises? She was too old for all this. Now Ellen stood beside him in her dreadful paramilitary trousers, and they were beaming at her. Extraordinary behaviour. The low sun dazzled her eyes.

'We've something to tell you, Mother,' said Ellen. The Frenchman nodded vigorously.

'You say,' he urged.

'No, you.' Ellen pushed him forward.

Mary's heart lurched. Surely they weren't planning to marry. Not *Ellen*.

He cleared his throat.

'I have found the grave,' he pronounced, each word slow and careful. 'I have found at last the grave of your husband.'

Ellen's mother Mary had learned a few things in her time, as she sometimes told her unfriendly daughter. One of these was to live with grief, or rather to live without it, beyond it. She had been alone a long time now, existing, Ellen thought, not only beyond grief, but also beyond love. Mary's husband had died invisibly in the Normandy landings, missing, presumed dead, a couple of months before Ellen was born. These days Mary didn't think about him much. Sometimes, but not often. And she had never thought much about Ellen. She was old and dusty and almost immaterial, shrinking her way out of life. She tried to live in abeyance from mortality. She preferred the evanescent, brooding endlessly on wind and weather, hunched over her wireless. If she considered life or death she became weighed down, oppressed: there had been too much of both and she could not succumb to either. The passing moment exacted all the strength she had left. 'I'm tired of living and I'm tired of dying,' she sang to herself. That wasn't right and she couldn't remember any of the other lines and she didn't care. Words came uninvited and tangled in her brain and set themselves to music. They would hang about for weeks, until they were replaced by something else, a phrase or two of poetry, an advertising slogan, some old time ribaldry.

Even on this strange evening, when Ellen and the Frenchman had gone, and dusk and owls had invaded her garden, her skull was buzzing with a sprightly jingle:

It's a fine tanking day
And as balmy as May

And the crew to the tank parks have hurried.

She persuaded herself there was nothing she could do about it, and it was better than thinking, when there was time to pass before any hope of sleep. So, humming briskly, she moved her frail body about her house; her bones clicked and creaked like knitting needles. The air was cold now, so cold that she sipped it, rather than breathed it in, a chill presaging the bleak East Anglian winter. Draughts skittered through the window frames and lifted the edges of threadbare rugs. As darkness gathered through those unlit, unpeopled rooms, she could almost believe that she had attained the ghostly state of her aspiration. There but not there. Intimations of the past lay all about her and in her solitude she might choose to remember, to forget, or to rearrange. Only very rarely, as now, was she caught unawares, overwhelmed by a great, retching pang of agonised grief, which left her shaken and gasping, clutching at the walls for support, slithering to the floor.

She sat there very still and stared at the runnels on her finger tips. where dust and skin cells merged, ashes to ashes. An old familiar image lingered in her head, a heave of sea the colour of muddy milk, waves racing and breaking under a dingy sky, frameless, boundless, implacable. And with it a sense of absolute terror. Slowly it receded. She breathed more steadily and concentrated on her becalming method, a memory of a house from her Norfolk childhood, the home of her cousins. It was damp and half derelict, and when they had got round to making it habitable, after many years of habitation, a slab of rotten plaster had crumbled from the wall, revealing a staring, ecstatic eye, a web of golden hair. Soon a colonnade of saints and heavenly bodies gazed out in troubled piety from the dining-room walls.

'All the way round too', grumbled Uncle Randal. 'What on earth are we to do?' The planned rewiring would cause grievous injuries. The mighty, smoking fire would discolour and desiccate. Worse was to come. In the upstairs corridors and largest bedroom an ancient hunting scene emerged, all swishing tails and stabbing fangs and spears. A boar at bay snarled and a crown rolled beneath the stamp of hooves, just where the socket for Aunt Ruth's electric fire should be.

'Wheesht,' said Randal. 'Aye, wheesht's the word,' agreed the workmen. Within days the figures were again immured, sealed in by thick layers of plaster and distemper. As a nervous small child, Mary had found the thought of those saints and horsemen, vigilant but invisible, wonderfully comforting. Now she imagined herself joining them, becoming part of that house, fading slowly into the plaster, into self-effacement, there and not there. Thus fortified she accomplished without effort the three hotwater bottle evening ritual and retired to bed.

But this night was different. Peter has been found. Or, more likely, bits of Peter. She thought again of that muddy sea, breaking forever on its forlorn strand. She had gone to that great curve of beach once, years ago, with her friend Josephine, trying to imagine what Peter had seen, last seen before he fell. Josephine had said it would be good for her, a laying of a ghost. Mary didn't find it good at all. Josephine had brought a picnic to enjoy at this maritime charnelhouse. Mary walked down to the sea; the tide was far out and the sands shone under a pallid, fitful sun.

She was remembering the first time she met Peter. He was dressed in cricket whites, waiting to bat. He leaned slightly forward on his bat and she saw a crusader leaning on his sheathed sword. A perfect, gentle knight in a world then crowded with possibility, a future in which the past would renew itself, complementing and deepening the present; no opportunity would ever be cancelled, no prospect rendered void. One would grow a little older, but not to any irretrievable degree. There had been a day in Oxford when they had wandered together through water meadows thronged with cow parsley and birdsong. Mary was intensely happy. So many years later, how well she recalled that day. It was warm and uncertain; spring sunlight glanced through rain soaked leaves and the air was blurred and pungent with blossom and earth and damp, charged with an erotic excitement and poignancy which Mary had noticed then and since in ancient university cities. An exhalation compounded of hundreds of yearning springtimes, aspiration thwarted, unfocused desire, urgent joy and mild, pastoral melancholy. She felt a quiver of fear.

'You want to watch this place,' she said. 'It's an ambush, isn't it? Toils of enchantment. Toil and moil, warp and weft. Funny that; could you say it warps you?' She eyed Peter sidelong, hoping to provoke him. But he wasn't listening; or rather he was listening to the bells, clamorous as always, and the cuckoo calling over the high walls. Spring-struck, he moved, tranced as a pilgrim through the scent of wallflowers and then of bluebells as they turned into woodland along the river. A path, freshly hacked through undergrowth, led them to a clearing, and in the centre of the clearing a scowling priapic statue squatted, one arm extended as if grudgingly to shake hands. As they drew closer they saw that in fact the arm was pointing them back towards the river. Beyond stretched an overgrown garden, starred pink with campion and bramble. The sun shone strongly now and insects hummed and buzzed through the tall flowering grasses, nettles and elder. The house at the top of the garden was smothered in creeper; vine and clematis clambered to the roof edge, felt their way under the tiles, still dark from the early rain, and curved luxuriantly down again. They had wrenched the balconies from the wall and suspended them in airy cages of leaf and tendril. Above the porch an odd rectangle of brickwork remained bare, shadowed randomly by the faintest of markings, like ancient drawings or a forgotten script.

'Look,' said Peter, 'just watch this.' The markings were gaining in definition; they resolved into imposing Roman capitals, they grouped, they formed a word: PARADISE, they proclaimed. Mary sat down abruptly in the sodden grass. She was frightened and hot and something had bitten her on the eyelid. Her heart thudded. Peter was smiling down at her.

'It's all right,' he said, 'don't look like that. It's meant to be a surprise. And I didn't know if it would really happen.'

'What on earth do you mean? How did you know? Have you been here before? What is it *doing*?'

Peter pulled her up and hugged her. 'It's lichens.'

Lichens. Mary had never heard this word pronounced. *Lichens.* She was overwhelmed with love for him.

'This place used to be a pub or an inn or something and it had metal letters on the wall. You get these lichens left underneath them and they develop just for a few minutes when it's hot after it's been raining. Then they fade away again. Wait and see.'

Mary could not bear to watch the fading.

'Let's go, quick, and then it'll always be there.'

It was too late; the space was blank again and an ancient, angry face glared down from an upstairs window. Squashed and distorted against the pane, its bulging cheeks resembled the gargoyle features in the clearing.

So it had been.

She became aware now of the chill of the sands; she was shivering. She glanced back at the picnicking Josephine and could only make out a huddled form, intent on its Tupperware boxes. The shore and the dunes and the further cliff line were blanked out by a low hanging thick white fog. Looming here and there near the waterline, the tractors which dragged speedboats down to the sea might have been the rusty skeletons of tanks, and occasional distant figures were visible only in parts, a head, a glimpse of torso, a flailing arm. The tide crept swiftly inshore, the colour of her imagining, muddy milk. Fear gathered, thudding, in her head and heart.

So on that cold August night, Mary lay awake; she thought of Peter and his grave and all the half life lived since he had gone, the surprising resolution of middle age into old age and her relief then that soon it would all be over. And her guilt now at so many years wasted, that others could have cherished. But if Peter had not been taken from her, how different it would have been. She might have loved Ellen, instead of finding her a dismal encumbrance. Ellen might have grown up to be pretty and loving and marriageable instead of going around in army surplus clothes and breeding weird curly coated dogs with webbed feet.

'As mentioned in Shakespeare. *Water rugs,*' she claimed.

Everything that had mattered was so long ago; she thought her feelings had all leached away and she had nothing left. Nothing but that intermittent pain of missing Peter, of missing being loved, of the abiding loss of her share of the world.

All that summer a comet had hung in the sky above Mary's garden. Ellen claimed that it was also suspended above the shanty town ensemble of wirenetting pens and corrugated iron huts which comprised her kennels, but Mary had certainly not seen it there. She enjoyed the comet's strangeness, its air of preoccupation, as if it were brooding upon its imminent departure into unreachable black voids for another four thousand years. She felt personally privileged by its coming and she treasured its unmatchable evanescence; it made her bold and dismissive and untruthful.

'What then is life?' she asked it. She was seized by an irrational fear that it would disappear while she and Ellen were in France at Peter's grave. The night before they left she stood out on her dewy lawn, hands clasped tight; staring up at it she recited silently a rhyme half forgotten from childhood:

Star light, star bright
First star I see tonight
I wish I may, I wish I might
Have the wish I wish this night.

But she didn't know what to wish. The comet dreamed on, impervious. Somewhere across the river a goose was laughing.

They drove to Portsmouth in Ellen's rackety, dog smelling car. Tufts of fur eddied down shafts of sunlight and strewed themselves delicately over the padded shoulders of Mary's severe grey coat and skirt, still very serviceable after fifty years of wardrobe and mothballs. On the boat, out on deck and hanging on to the rail, she shut her eyes and tried to will herself to push through time and emerge on the far side, a forties sweetheart, a forces sweetheart, Peter's sweetheart. But her legs were too wobbly and her hands too gnarled. The bright breeze made her cheekbones ache; her eyes watered.

Ellen had rented a house near Caen. It was unnecessarily large, and gloomy; on the walls were tattered, blackened copies of ancient funeral notices and Ellen announced proudly that it was here that Charlotte Corday had stayed in the weeks before she murdered Marat.

'It's dead cheap because of that,' she said.

But it had a large and beautiful garden where apples hung red and gold from trees swagged with mistletoe. At night shooting stars plunged from the heavens, but Mary looked in vain for the comet.

On a brilliant blue day of Indian summer, Ellen took Mary to the graveyard. Slow and silent, they walked together up the long, green slope between the crowding multitude of white stones. Mary leaned heavily on Ellen's arm; she had no thoughts at all, no feelings, only a thudding heart and a great weariness. But as they turned down the avenue of Peter's grave her step quickened. She let go of Ellen's arm; she pushed her hair back and smoothed it, she shook out her skirt and moved forward, head high, serene and eager, a ghostly bride advancing to her lover.

In late afternoon they returned to the house. Ellen's friend François brought tea out to the garden. Mary took her cup and smiled at him, surprising him.

'Thank you, Peter darling,' she said, surprising him more. She studied her tea, its swaying disc of surface. It was reminding her of something, but she could not focus on it; she saw a pinpoint of sunlight reflected and she heard the roaring of the sea. She slipped sideways from her chair to the grass and lay there, staring unseeing up at François, her hands still clasping the delicate cup.

They cremated her in Caen and Ellen took the ashes, a rosebush and a trowel back to the war graves. She laid the ashes in Peter's oblong of turf and above she planted the rose. She walked away down the green slope to the gateway. Poppies trembled there in the long grass and she thought how strange it was that they should be the flowers of remembrance and of forgetfulness. She believed then, and not for the first time, that she had inherited her mother's cold, passionless nature, for she felt nothing but a powerful longing to be done with all this, and never to return. Several days later she found beneath a carpet in Mary's house a dusty brown paper bag. In it was a photograph of her parents as she had never seen them, he in his uniform, she in a flowered dress, laughing and young and ardent, gazing at each other.

'Before my time,' Ellen thought. Out in the twilight sky, the comet was tilting away into renewed aeons of solitude. She was overwhelmed by desolation, a longing to arrest the moment, to declare that love is as strong as death; but this she could not do. Anyhow, it was time to feed her dogs.

THE DANCE

Jennifer was a mordant child. Her first memories were of biting and gnawing. Her teeth came unexpectedly early, 'before even the first snowdrops' said her mother, who was romantically inclined but passed her days fashioning loaves in the form of lobsters, crabs and indeterminate sea creatures armoured with crisp antennae. The broken antennae were kept for Jennifer and these were the secret of her precocious mandibles.

They lived above the bread shop; the house was thin and old and the windows looked out on the heaving grey North Sea. On winter afternoons, when sky and sea merged and the rain beat down on Cromer, her mother would draw the curtains and shiver. Then she would talk of another sea, peacock blue and peacock green, lapping white sands. A castle overlooked that sea, a castle alone on its promontory; no town, no bread shop. There she had lived, there still her mother lived. One day she would go there with Jennifer. 'You will see the sun as you have never seen it,' she said in her oddly formal English.

Once on the promenade, staring at the whitening sea, she wept, but went on staring at it. The rain slashed down and mixed with her tears. Jennifer began to cry too. 'In my beginning is my end,' said her mother. Jennifer pulled her sleeve with numb starfish fingers and they trudged up the cliff path. The house seemed warm to Jennifer, then, and welcoming, with the scent of the bread which was always baking, or steaming and brown on racks, and her father in his white overall waving through the misted pane in the kitchen door. But her mother would pull her coat collar up as if she were even colder now she was indoors, and she ducked her head down and ran up the stairs with her nose wrinkled. There was no escape from the doughy fragrance. On the sitting room table, heaped on her mother's great Portuguese platter, azure and white as her far seas, were the day's failures or unsuccesses. 'There is no such thing as failure. There is only unsuccess,' said her father. Jennifer found this statement meaningless, but could see that it annoyed her mother. Anyhow, there they were for her tea time delectation, broken bread lobster pincers, and crab claws, antennae and small warped crustaceans, and for her this was home, the smell of the bread and the crunch of the crust, the coal fire sizzling as the rain spat down the chimney, the curtains drawn and outside the great roaring sea and the lowering sky. And her mother was happy when she could not see the sea.

Later in life she could remember no summer on that northern coast, but summer must have come and gone, five times in fact, when her mother took her to Portugal. They had to fly there and then travel a whole day in a bus. Jennifer was sick a number of times, but because of her mother's excitement she was able to rise above her lurching entrails and the awful quivering, quenching heat. 'Rise above it.' She had heard her father shout this at her mother when she herself was tucked up in bed, had been asleep even in the warm alcove by the chimney breast above the oven. In the darkness she imagined her mother floating and lost as a seagull over the icy whelm of ocean and she clenched her fists tight and prayed for her, as if she were one of the lifeboatmen or fishermen, who went in peril on the sea.

Now the bus was bumping off the white dusty track into a village square; her mother had seized both her limp hands and was squeezing them and staring into her face with wild shining eyes. 'I am happy. I am so happy,' she whispered. They hugged each other. Jennifer was glad for her, but most of all she was glad to clamber off the bus and stand unsteadily in the shade, while a great shrieking gaggle of women in black flapping clothes embraced her mother and wept and embraced her again.

Then they were swooping down on Jennifer. 'Ah, the little beautiful.' 'Ah, it is at last Ginevra.' The tree's low branches trembled and its leaves which were like hands waved and fanned the hot air. Fat little purple fruits plopped through them and burst in carnal crimson against the ground. The aunts trampled over them. Seeds spurted and stuck to their heavy black shoes.

The castle stood on a headland up a long hill from the village; you could not see it until you were almost there. Parts of it resembled the massive fortresses Jennifer had seen in picture books; elsewhere it was dazzling white, like some of the houses in the village. There were arcades and galleries, courtyards and fountains. Most of the fountains didn't work. Lizards basked in the stone basins and thin cats pounced and played among the fallen leaves which choked them. Jennifer lay in a canopied swing in her grandmother's special courtyard, high above a little bay and the sea which was so bright she could not look straight at it. Here water played gently from an upturned urn on to a splashing cherub and behind her she could hear women's voices, a continuing murmurousness from upstairs windows, half shuttered now against the morning light. That was what they did all day, her mother, her grandmother, her aunts. They talked and they sipped iced tea and they laughed in that shadowed room as they sat over their embroidery. Aunt Rosa was going to have a baby, perhaps tomorrow, perhaps this very day, who knew? Each evening Uncle Adriano came back from his work in his pale, crumpled suit, looking excited, and they would all smile and shake their heads. Her grandmother said, 'A baby chooses his own time. Is that not so, Ginevra?'

Jennifer had no idea how babies made their plans, but she nodded fervently, for her grandmother was the wise person, the queen of the castle; even though she was smaller than any of them and wore very plain clothes. There were a number of other older people about, mostly her grandmother's sisters or sisters-in-law. They were all widows and they looked frightening when they sat out together on the courtyard terrace, a flock of birds of anguish, although they smiled at her and stroked her hair as she sidled past. The only young aunt was Aunt Jezebel who was eighteen. Her name wasn't really Jezebel but this was how it sounded to Jennifer. Jezebel spent all day with the other women in the cool upstairs chambers or on the terrace, but she was not paying attention to them. Her round dreamy eyes stared out over the ramparts, her heavy brows contracted and her mouth turned down. She did not want to be there; not one bit. She shredded eucalyptus leaves and ground them under her heel; she moved about in an aura of camphor. This gave Jennifer a pang of wintry longing, for it reminded her of having colds in Cromer. She thought she liked Portugal, but it was very bright and it wasn't home. Soon her father was coming, and she looked forward to that, although she had the feeling that her mother did not. She had heard her mother referring to Cromer as Cromer Sur Mer and there was something not quite right about this.

Jezebel took Jennifer to the village to meet her father off the bus. They rode down the hill on Jezebel's bicycle, with Jennifer sitting in a pannier on the back. Jezebel was happy; she sang loud melancholy songs as they went, trailing her foot round the bends instead of braking, so that the dust blew up into their faces. In the square she left Jennifer at a table under the fig trees and disappeared into the bar. By the time the bus at last came throbbing in, Jennifer was feeling very hot and very embarrassed. She did not like to sit all alone as though she were a friendless orphan; people stared at her and some children came up and spoke to her but she could not answer them and after a little they ran off, looking back at her and giggling. She chewed at her fingers and she bit her nails and she studied the ground beneath the table.

Suddenly Jezebel was leaning over her, lifting her up, pretending to be a loving aunt, and there was her father and there was a woman walking beside her father; he did not look well. His eyes glittered but his face was white. The woman was jauntily swinging a bottle by its neck. When she saw Jennifer looking at it, she stuffed it into her handbag. Her cheeks were puffy and pallid like fermenting dough; her bobbed blond hair was streaked with damp. There were subdued hugs and handshakes. Jennifer's father said the woman's name was Amicia; they were fellow travellers. He laughed after he said this, but no one else did. Jezebel had stopped looking happy and was glaring at Amicia. 'Well, I guess I'll love you and leave you,' she announced. 'See you later alligators,' she added over her shoulder. They watched in silence as her high heels wobbled across the square to the pale green portico of the little hotel. A group of men had emerged from the bar and were watching her too. A cat with a lizard protruding from its jaws slunk round the wall of the well, snarling to itself. It looked as if it were smoking a cigar. Jennifer longed to be back in Cromer.

At lunch, in the shuttered upper room, her longing increased. Her father had been odd and quiet in the taxi from the village. 'Not feeling too good; it's the heat,' he said, sighing and mopping his forehead. He had to borrow clothes from Adriano; his own were far too heavy. There wasn't much conversation. Usually the women spoke simultaneously and incessantly, sometimes in English, more often in Portuguese, even at times in French, for one of the great aunts came from Normandy. Although her mother had seemed pleased when he arrived, now, sitting next to him at the long table, she turned the other way, towards her own mother, and engaged in a discussion of embroidery silks suitable for the dress she was making for Rosa's baby. Nor was her father enjoying his plate of salt cod. He was pushing it around, nonplussed, trying to hide the glimmering and rigid fish tails under his potatoes. From her high alcove above the Virgin Mary eyed him with displeasure.

Things seemed better the next day. Colour returned to her father's face and although the sun shone bright as ever a breeze diffused the heat. In the evening there was a party in the village square. The tables were laid out in the open and everyone danced, even the old people. In one corner bumper cars were flashing and colliding, and merry-go-round horses rose and sank and rose. The air boomed with different kinds of music and was hazy with smoke from the spits of tragic roasting piglets. Candles and bottles shone on the white tablecloths. Amicia appeared, weaving through the dancers, and joined them. She wore scarlet lipstick and she had an orange flower in her hair. She was drinking out of her own bottle, not very carefully. Pungent amber drops trickled down her chin and on to her throat. She flicked them away with a faintly grubby hand, shook her blond hair about and pulled off her jacket. The ancient aunts sighed and looked away from her. They had smiled at her and inclined their heads. They would not do this again. At the far end of the table Grandmama's face was expressionless. Only Jezebel stared unwinkingly at those twin rotundities which heaved and quivered beyond the merest strand of black and yellow dotted nylon. Only Jezebel and the men. The men who came swarming, touching Amicia's bare arm, entreating her to dance, pulling at her hands. They surrounded her, black as flies in their shiny suits. As Jennifer and her family left the square they could see her spinning about, still clutching her bottle, while the men formed a circle round her, clapping slowly, a measured clap like the beat of a funeral drum.

The old aunts went home then, but Grandmama led the rest of them down the cliff path to her terrace, a vast ledge overhanging the bay. The tide was full and tranced in the moonlight, almost inaudibly lapping and swelling far below. A surprise awaited them, a table laid out with plates of lobsters and salads, apricots and wine and iced lemonade. Adriano had brought his wind up gramophone and for a while they sat and watched the sea and the moving heavens, and listened to a woman's voice in lamentation. 'Remember me. Remember me,' she pleaded, and

Jennifer saw that the clouds and the moon were still and the whole night silenced, attentive only to that desperate cry. Then Jezebel was on her feet, changing the record, winding. 'We will dance,' she declared. She stretched out her hands to Jennifer's father, but he shook his head and sat back with his shy smile, clasping his glass of wine. Jezebel revolved slowly, furling and whirling her petticoats. staring now at the sea, now at the dark hillside, half angry, half yearning. Jennifer's mother pulled her and Grandmama up. They danced in a circle; their linked hands formed a grave and tender coronal of love. Jennifer forgot everything but this place, wished only to be here for ever. Rosa and Adriano were dancing too, very slowly; she could see that Adriano was afraid of colliding with Rosa's huge stomach. Rosa rocked from side to side and Adriano held her at arm's length as though she were some unmanageable agricultural implement. Their shadows all mingled, separated, flowed, pacific as clouds.

And then there were other shadows, an alien blot which spread into the centre of the terrace. Amicia was there, and she was wrapped about a man. At least she had her jacket on again. But the man was Jennifer's father. She saw Amicia's face sagged against his, her red mouth smudging his collar. She saw Adriano gaze wistfully at them and Aunt Rosa looking savagely at Adriano. For a moment as they whirled round she saw her father as she had never seen him, a small man, sly, afraid and greedy. Then the music stopped, the dance was over. Amicia lurched to the table. The feral cats were scrabbling among the lobsters. 'Fucking bloody cats,' she yelled. 'Disgusting. Where's the music?' No one answered. They all stood still. She saw the gramophone. 'Aw, for Godsake. Come on then, I'll give you some music.' She grabbed a whole lobster and flung her jacket at the cats. Moving backwards she wrenched at the claws. The wilted orange flower fell out of her hair. She cradled the lobster to her bosom and began to sing, 'I can can and you can can, I can can . . .' She kicked her legs up in the air and fell over. The

THE DANCE

feral cats were on her. She struggled to her feet, kicked a cat and fell again. She rolled on her back, still singing, rolled on to her side and went over the edge.

'Time to go home,' said Grandmama. They cleared the table into baskets. Jennifer threw Amicia's flower into the sea. It looked quite pretty bobbing there. 'Remember me,' she thought. She would not. But she would remember the dance. She split a lobster pincer with one crack of her teeth and made her pledge.

PACKING FOR INDIA

It wasn't snowing, but it might have been. So great a stillness surrounded the house, the air chilled with presentiment, the blank sky tinged mauve, the hills guarding their own. I had come from a long way into that cold afternoon; already my life in another country was cut off, and the people who crowded it had moved into memory; they were people I used to know. This house held the present, the unforgiving minute, the fleeting untenable last of a life; our mother's deathbed. We wanted time to stop so that her life might not end. We wanted it all to be over, too. Arm in arm, fear and boredom stalked the bedroom, and guilt followed at their heels. A terrier perhaps, with sharp little snappity jaws. The real dogs, two huge mastiffs, leaned against the bed, one on each side; damp muzzles probed the counterpane, eyes rolled in anxious devotion. The Marie Curie nurses hated to see these enormous beasts, constantly in their way, and banished them to the garden, closing the curtains against their reproachful stares. Our mother ignored the presence of the nurses; if obliged to acknowledge them she would treat them as slightly unwelcome friends of my sisters. For she was not ill at all, just resting after a nasty cold, and enjoying a little holiday away from her cats. Her morphine was dropped into tiny glasses of peach juice, secretly, for she certainly would have refused to take it. She drifted in and out of consciousness, sometimes feigning sleep, sometimes alert, sometimes both.

I saw her stroke a nurse's cashmere sleeve (the nurses all wore plain clothes and in the Scottish borders that means cashmere and tweed). 'Nice fluffy dog,' said Mother. The nurse gazed bleakly at the wall; two thick lucent strands of slobber, witness to the expelled mastiffs, were wincing slowly down the paintwork. 'Filthy great brutes,' she muttered, not quite under her breath. 'Will you be off soon?' Mother enquired, her eyes iceberg blue. 'I'll be right away as soon as I've got my coat and boots.' Where do you live?' 'Hawick.' 'What a bore for you.' Grim in her coat and boots, Nurse hurried through the hall and kitchen and disappeared into the capacious darkness of the walk-in drinks cupboard, briskly closing the door on our cries of good night and thank you and not that way. Silently she emerged and was gone out into the squalling sleet. She shouted something like 'See you tomorrow,' but in the event she did not return.

We took turns, the sisters and I, to sit with our mother so that she was never alone by night or day. Her window looked out to the high bare hills and the shifting clouds. In the morning the mist would lift in swathes and leave drops of water on the sword-shaped crocosmia leaves beneath the sill. The hens scratched about the flower bed and sipped the shining beads. She couldn't see them from her pillows, but when I told her, her face lit. 'Yes, that's what they do.' There were no mirrors in the room. I wondered whether this was deliberate, for her face was slightly distorted by cancer, only very slightly. She could not have moved from her bed to look in the mirror. Perhaps a mirror would have prompted recollection and sorrow. No one will know.

She was one of those women who even in old age retain a certain girlishness. The illness had reduced her, made her doll-like, but she was a faded and ravaged girl-doll, not an old-woman-doll, and evanescent glamour clung about her. On the end of the bed were propped, with difficulty, postcards, cuttings and photographs as demanded. Miss Anastasia Noble and two of her deerhounds, a seaside village where once we lived – 'Let's go there tomorrow!' – a holy cow in India. There were no pictures of any of us; just as well, I reflected, as I would not have appeared in them. Never once in childhood did any photograph of me stand among the others on her bedroom mantelpiece. But this was no time for ancient grievances. I thought that every minute, however fraught or tedious or just plain awkward, should be cherished for her. The intense pleasure she drew from the hens and their raindrops, the colour and texture of a grape, the cloud shadows on the hills, a cat's mask watchful at the curtain's edge, should be remarked, captured and contained. Perhaps most of all she enjoyed the gathering in her room in early morning. We would be elated that she had got through the night. Inconsequential talk, giggling, tea and toast for us, morphine and peach juice for her, while something of the dormitory obtained and something of what she called 'shoe-kicking time' – an hour for the exchange of secrets and intimacies, which unlike my sisters, I had avoided always. What confidences could I ever have shared? I, a spinster and a treacherous exile. I thought about the rows and distances there had been between us, and how they didn't at all matter now, at least to me. This was how we knew each other, and it was all right. My sisters had happier times with her, and that was all right too.

In these early mornings, when she is strongest, she is talking about her own childhood, in Scotland, but mostly in India. Why did she never tell us all this before? She is a small child, sitting on the warm red earth, watching the potter and his wheel. The red mud is shining and a white cow walks slowly down the hill path towards them. The potter slaps the clay. Her ayah smiles. A slow bird passes beside them through the sky; they are so high on the hill that birds are flying beneath them too. The cow calls out and now it is the sound of the great ship, moving down the Clyde into evening and starlight with a thousand little boats all round it. The people she doesn't know are waving and she is waving back. So much waving, so many faces glimpsed and gone into night or sea mist, so many journeys. A dark face now, coming from the shadows of the big white house, onto the verandah. The dark person brings a tray across the lawn. The child is sitting far away with her mother at a wobbly table under a spreading tree. Men are draped about the tree's wide branches; they swing their legs and laugh. Her ayah is there too; she never laughs but she is always smiling. Oh, then something bad happened. She will tell us about that another morning. Now she will sleep.

In sleep she cried out sometimes for our father; he had died two years before. Sometimes she was so deeply still that I thought she had gone and I was almost downcast when she stirred, and then I was shocked at myself and ashamed to find the long time of her passing unbearable. She grew smaller through those long October afternoons. In such profound sleep, her head tilted sideways and down towards her chest, she seemed perfectly closed and withdrawn, setting forth herself down a wide river towards the sea, over the rolling waters, not drowning but going very privately adrift. For a moment, just before it dipped behind the hills, the sun would send ripples of riverine light up and down the bedroom walls and over her quiet face. Then it was gone and the sky had blanched; jackdaws flocked across it, jostling their way to their roost in the tower. Until darkness fell the air was raucous with their squabbles. You become used to this quiet life, sequestered in the hills, the wind and the wail of the kettle, the dogs outside barking when the doctor comes, and the downstairs rooms all shadow and closed curtains so the dogs cannot see the doctor. Our mother thinks or claims to think that the doctor's visits are entirely social. Perhaps they are, for he is supposedly on holiday, like her, and he walks with his labrador up the two mile track to the house. The mastiffs don't mind the labrador, only the doctor. It is another world where small incidents stand in sharp relief against a muted, dreamy background. You don't want to look too much into this background; you know what is there; it could come out at any moment.

She tells us, one morning, about her ayah, who was being brought with them all back to Scotland. She died on the boat. She was wrapped in a Union Jack and the ship's officers dropped her slowly, on a long chain, into the sea. Everyone stood in church clothes on the deck and they sang Abide With Me. But the ayah didn't abide; away she went, whirling and brightly coloured, into the grey waves. I imagine dim shrouded forms enfolded gently in the brown shining Ganges. Rivers of death, rivers of forgetting, the clay dissolving. The sea seems very cold, too cold for the ayah.

This afternoon Mother says quite suddenly, straight out of sleep, 'There's a hare on the ceiling.' And there is. The shadows cast upwards by a huge vase of flowers, brilliant gold and scarlet gerbera are compounded into a perfect semblance of a hare, angular, dark and graceful, stilled in mid-leap. I am half asleep myself, and I am alarmed now to see her sitting up with astonishing ease. 'I used to be able to pack for India in twenty minutes!' she says. 'I must find my things. I need my white slacks. And my red shoes. I think they're over there.' She points to a corner full of dust. She starts to move her legs towards the side of the bed. She intends to get up. She must not do this. She cannot do this. She is a stick-woman. She is an old girl-doll. She will break in pieces. Oh no, she is a girl who is packing for India.

'Stay there, sit still, I'll find everything,' I say. 'No you won't. Just don't. You'll be in the way. You don't know what I want. And you never were the helpful sort.' Her voice has been strong but it is ebbing now. She whispers. 'I must have my red shoes. I want to wear them.' I hear the kettle begin its moaning in the kitchen. Someone is there. I rush out, find a sister and rush back. Our mother is muttering about missing the boat. Together after a protracted slow motion struggle, we restrain her, flatten her, tuck her in tight and try to make her listen to Radio 4. This doesn't work well. 'Too English.' She is still anxious that she will miss the boat. She still wants her red shoes. A flurry of snow patters against the window, the evening nurse arrives, the jackdaws float by. Another day gone forever.

So there we are one late autumn afternoon, my sisters, their daughters, and me. We are decorating the church for the funeral, bronze bracken and rose hips, berries red and black, leafy branches from the hollows where the deer sleep. A huge wind is rising and beating about the valley, about the ancient kirk. As the light wanes, the waters of the burn rise; we can hear them roaring now, but we think little of it. Next day dawns, cheerless and wild. The birds are blown horizontally across the white sky. The steep terraced garden is filled with flood water; tree tops poke up into the drenching rain. The great rivers have burst their banks and every valley is flooded. The funeral cannot take place. All the roads from England are closed. Like further straggles of storm-tossed birds, the black-clad mourners hover uncertainly about the house. By nightfall they are planning departure. No-one can wait around for a burial of undecided date. Bloody Marys take over the evening. Sleepers sag from chairs, the mastiffs slumber against knees, their heads propped on the dining room table. The wind drops, but not much.

Days pass and the waters recede. We gather in depleted numbers at the church, where the bracken and rowan and hips are still bright. The minister reads Tennyson's last poem, Crossing the Bar.

But such a tide as moving seems asleep,
Too full for sound and foam,
When that which drew from out the boundless deep
Turns again home.

Her grandsons carry her coffin to the grave. We stand about it and the minister speaks of sure and certain knowledge. The hills seem to have moved forward. They rise huge above us and the grave is brimful of water. The water reflects the hills. They are suspended there upside down and in the very depths of the grave there is a flash of sunlit sky. The minister swathes the coffin, which is very small, in the blue and white flag of Saint Andrew, the Saltire. The oldest great-granddaughter begins to howl; she clutches her mother's skirts. Her five siblings follow suit. They form a broad-based pyramid of lamentation. The wet flowers which lie about the grave's edge like a bridal quilt are shining after the rain. Every holy word has been spoken and she has been consigned to the earth and life everlasting, but she is not in the earth. Nor is she on the water which might have borne her gracefully downwards as it subsided. We have to leave her there unburied. We move off in little groups, all turning back to her. A small ship stranded among flowers, beside the water, beneath the trees, below the hills.

As we go down the track to the narrow road, a woman touches my arm and murmurs words of condolence. It is the nurse who walked into the drinks cupboard. 'If I could just call in one day', she is saying, 'I don't know if you'll have seen them. I left them that last night and I never got back. I think they were in your mum's bedroom, in the corner. My red shoes.'

IN THE CAGE

It was April, but it might have been midwinter, so wan and chill the sky. The few green leaves were dank and sullen; the new season was suspended, confounded in ancient cold, cold in your bones, cold, cold, my girl. On such a day there is nothing to lift the spirits, earth and air and sea spellbound and hushed in this cruel aftermath, the blackthorn winter.

As she drove down the narrow track through the heath she was utterly consumed by the bleak world, its only brightness shed by the snow light of the blackthorn blossom and the lurid yellow gorse. Beneath, the church and its tower, moored on their ridge above the marshes, were a discordant note, a looming lonely statement of human will and aspiration. She believed she had no time for such things today, or ever, come to that, locked in her carapace of misery, her face a wilfully downturned mask, her heart a stone. So now she was surprised to find herself seated stiff and upright in a pew, her hands knotted together, not in prayer but in a desperate unfocused anxiety which she wanted God to resolve. Inside her head black shapes and words collided and reformed and repeated themselves. While she yearned for some sort of absolution, she did not believe she could find it.

She had thought the church empty, but a woman was moving down the aisle towards her, also wringing her hands. 'There's a bird in here,' she said, and a tear rolled down her cheek. 'Poor thing, just look at it.' It was hurling itself over and over at the high window, its wings pattering on the glass; then it dipped out of sight, then it was back. Now it flew lower, resting for moments on the deep sill. So small a bird, a drab little brown thing. 'It's a nightingale,' the woman said. 'All the way from Africa, to be trapped in here. It should be up on the heath, singing.' 'It's not trapped really,' she told the woman. 'Look, the doors are wide open; it will find its way out.' How she wanted the woman gone, and the bird too; she had a great longing for sleep and she closed her eyes. In her own darkness and against her will she kept thinking about the bird. A nightingale. She had never heard one, let alone seen one. She imagined its journey over deserts, over seas, a mere speck of a creature flung about in winds, drenched with rain, baffled by sudden sunlight, its wings beating resolutely onward, until, perhaps using the tower as a landmark, it floated inland high above the church to its breeding ground in the dense thickets of the heath. If freedom is the knowledge of necessity, there in those twisted branches of gorse and blackthorn the bird was free and its song was a song of triumph. It had achieved its necessary purpose, and its eye was bright with it.

Not so this poor lost creature, bewildered, perhaps even stunned, for now the church was silent. The woman must have gone. And maybe the bird was gone too.

Gradually the familiar peace enfolded her, drifting down like early dusk among the pillars which reared like trees, beneath the windows whose glass was the colour of seawater. She might have slept, lulled by that sense of sanctuary, but then she was thinking again of the bird and how her sanctuary was its prison. She opened her eyes. The bird was there, motionless, perched on the end of the pew. She could not breathe. In a moment she had it clasped in her cupped hands. Through her fingers she could see it, quite passive; she felt the pulsing of its tiny heart and its warm folded wings. She remembered the childhood rhyme for hands so clasped: This is the church and there is the steeple; open the doors and out come the people. Solemn and purposeful, she stepped over the threshold bearing before her the delicate burden, now become a sacred trust.

She was happy here, free and light. Her world held nothing but herself and the bird. They were out in the churchyard, under the eye of heaven, and she flung her arms high in the exultant gesture she had seen in statues of the Virgin, declaring her baby to God and man and the universe. The nightingale would leap from her spread palms into the wide air, falter for a moment and then be speeding to its destiny. And life would go on and there would be a time for song. But although her hands lay flat and open as an altar under the sky the bird did not move; it was on its side, its eye glazed; its beak had opened in a soundless cry.

She found a stick. With cold stiff fingers she scraped a shallow grave among the other graves. She was not sad yet: perhaps later she would be. She had an odd sense that she had done what she had come to do, and now she could turn homewards. It started to rain and just as suddenly stopped. Wet leaves glistened in pale sunlight. At the top of the hill three hooded figures emerged from the scrubland and waved her down. 'It's the nightingales,' they said. 'Turn off your engine, just for a moment.' All the air was filled with a whirling confusion of whistles and chirrups but then she distinguished the long notes of piercing sweetness, the cadences, trills, and occasional weird gutturals. She glanced for confirmation at the hooded ones and they nodded. For a little while yet purged of self, she listened and she thought of the dead and the small bird with them down in the graveyard between the sound of nightingales and the sigh of the sea, and the world revolving slowly on its axis into hope. The beauty of sound issuing from invisible creatures in impenetrable undergrowth, thorns and twisted branches, reminded her of Leonardo's remark that art breathes in containment and is suffocated by freedom. She wondered if Leonardo ever knew a nightingale.